HARVEST AMERICAN
Writing

Silk Hope, NC

Other books by Lawrence Naumoff:

Taller Women

Rootie Kazootie

The Night of the Weeping Women

Lawrence Naumoff

Silk Hope, NC

A Harvest Book
Harcourt Brace & Company
San Diego New York London

Library of Congress Cataloging-in-Publication Data
Naumoff, Lawrence
Silk Hope, NC/Lawrence Naumoff.—1st ed.
(A Harvest Book)
p. cm.
1. Farm life—North Carolina—Fiction. 2. Sisters—North Carolina—Fiction. 3. Women—North Carolina—Fiction.
I. Title. II. Title: Silk Hope, NC.
ISBN: 0-15-188900-7
ISBN: 0-15-600207-8 (pbk.)
PS3564.A8754S54 1994
813'.54—dc20 94-42947

Printed in the United States of America

Designed by Lori J. McThomas

First Harvest edition 1995

A B C D E

This book is dedicated, with my love,
to Marianne Buie Gingher
and to my son, Michael Naumoff.

For various kinds of help, inspiration or support on this book, or in the past, my thanks to Alane Salierno Mason, Amy Peck, the *Wisconsin Death Trip* by Michael Lesy, Irene Reichbach, and Celia Wren.

Silk Hope is a farming community twenty-five miles west of Chapel Hill, North Carolina.

In the mid-1800s, an American sailor who had spent time in China planted mulberry trees in the area, hoping to establish a silk industry. When the trees matured enough to harvest their leaves, he discovered that the silkworms he'd hatched would not eat the leaves. He'd planted the wrong variety of mulberry tree.

Silk Hope, NC

Chapter 1

I can't say as ever I was lost, but I was bewildered once for three days.

DANIEL BOONE

FRANNIE RAN THROUGH a flock of pigeons.

"There she is," Natalie said.

The pigeons scattered into the air. Feathers floated down in the sunlight.

"I hate this," Natalie said.

Frannie was barefoot. Her shirt was sweaty and her loose hair had a pigeon feather caught in it. She was easily outrunning the man who was chasing her.

"I'm so tired," Natalie said. "I'm just so tired of this. Pull over and let's get her."

Jake looked for a place to stop.

"I never thought we'd find her," he said.

Frannie saw their car and with almost no break in speed she leaped in the open door.

"GO!" she yelled. "Go quick."

Natalie's face was pale. Though she was Frannie's older sister, at this moment she appeared to be unrelated to this wild-eyed young woman in the backseat.

"YOU FOOL!" Frannie screamed to the man and then looked at Jake and Natalie. "I guess you've been worried about me."

"Yes, we have," Jake said.

"I guess you're not going to talk to me. At least let me tell you what happened, okay? The guy started out all right. He had a soft voice and talked nice and asked me about myself and he seemed reasonable. Of course, then he snapped—but what's new? They all turn out bad. I'm so sick of crazy men. One minute everything's good and the next you find out you've gone off with the man from *The Texas Chain Saw Massacre*. More or less."

"Did he hurt you?" Jake asked.

"No. He wasn't quite that bad. I wonder if everyone nowadays is crazy and there's nobody normal anymore."

"Stop, Frannie," her sister said. "Please."

"No, I won't stop until I tell you what happened. This morning I woke up in a chair where I must have fallen asleep and I found him on the front porch watching TV. I thought the TV was in the room with me, but he must have took it out—"

"Taken," Natalie said, and then put her face in her hands and shook her head back and forth as if trying to avoid a bad thought.

"—taken it out while I was asleep and I sat down beside him and then I made coffee and we kind of vegged there watching a show about bass fishing and I got to feeling real good sitting there beside him in the morning sun and being close and all and so I kissed him and the next thing I knew he'd dragged me off the couch and into the house and started screaming about something.

"I couldn't even understand what he was talking about. He dragged me around by the arm all over the floor and knocked me into tables and chairs and then all of a sudden he shoved me into the bathroom and slammed the door and stood in the hall and yelled at me as loud as he could to BRUSH MY TEETH BEFORE I TRIED ANYTHING LIKE THAT AGAIN. I was shaking all over and I thought, Well, damn, my breath can't be that bad."

"Please, Jake," Natalie said, "get us home."

The car was stopped in a long line of traffic. When they began to move again, Frannie could see that a truck pulling a hog trailer had wrecked. The hogs were still in the trailer and one of them had broken through a cracked railing and was leaning out, watching everything.

"I love hogs," Frannie said.

Natalie was slumped down in the seat sobbing.

"We'll be home in five minutes," Jake told Natalie.

"Sorry about getting you involved," Frannie said. "Are you going to tell Mom? Don't, okay? She doesn't need this now."

Natalie was still crying and neither she nor Jake said another word until they turned into their driveway. Instead of going back to where Jake usually parked his car, he stopped under the shade of one of the old trees that lined the drive in front of the house and turned off the engine.

"Lecture time," Frannie said. "I guess you have to. Having a big sister is like having two mothers. Go ahead and let me have it. I'm going to get it sooner or later, so go ahead."

Strangely, for Frannie, instead of letting her have it, Natalie took her sister's hand and put it to her cheek and kissed it and stroked it and looked sadly at her and then, through her tears, said, "Mom died."

"Mom died?" Frannie asked back in a whisper.

"Yes," Jake said.

"She died?" Frannie asked again.

"SHE DIED THREE DAYS AGO!" Natalie screamed.

"We couldn't find you," Jake said. "Nobody could."

"OH, GOD, FRANNIE. HOW COULD YOU?"

Frannie looked at her sister. It couldn't be true. It was impossible that her mother could have died and she didn't know it and that no one could find her.

"You couldn't find me?"

It couldn't be true that her mother was dead and that her death had occurred while Frannie was out with three different men she didn't even know. Frannie looked from

Natalie, who still held her hand, to the old farmhouse and scanned the rooms and the windows as if her mother might appear in one.

"Why didn't I call?" Frannie asked herself, out loud. "Why?"

She looked at the parlor that faced the road. It was five sided and above it was a single gable with an ornately cut window and a metal spire like a lightning rod on the peak of the roof above the gable. All the finer homes that had been built a hundred years ago in this community had this same parlor and simple detail.

It was fitting that they had parked in front of this room under the shade of the trees that sheltered this house, because it was in this formal parlor, Frannie knew, that her father had been allowed to court her mother, and her grandfather had been allowed to court her grandmother, and it was in this parlor, not formal by then, that Natalie had been caught kissing her first boyfriend at the age of fourteen while playing Monopoly on the floor, while Frannie, out of unprovoked and simple sibling meanness, had run to tell on her.

It was in this parlor that Frannie knew her grandmother had lain in an open casket, and it was in this parlor that her mother, who knew she was dying, had asked to be laid out and received.

Because of this, Frannie stared at the parlor windows. The windows were dark, and though it was daylight, the room appeared terrifying, full of the ghosts she had feared as a child, the ghosts of the family members who had departed for heaven out those windows, and who, she had thought then, could just as easily come back through those windows anytime they wanted.

The glass in the windows in that room were the original panes, wavy and imperfect, rippled and unclear and milky, like the eyes of the dead.

"Is she in there?" Frannie asked, barely able to speak.

The eyes of the dead have seen more than the eyes of the living. Because of this, they do not have to be swept closed by the brush of a warm hand. Unlike in the movies, where the doctor or the wife or the husband or the daughter or the friend gently closes the eyelids and allows the dead the dignity of darkness, in truth, the eyes of the dead fall shut by themselves, having seen all they can bear.

"Are her eyes open?" Frannie asked.

Hearing is the last sense to go, the doctors now tell us. But it's not true. Hearing is the first sense to go. It often fails us while we are still alive, having heard more than we could bear, having heard words we wish we'd never heard, having heard sounds from our own mouths we didn't know we could make. After hearing those sounds we fall deaf, and the people around us have to speak twice, or more, to get our attention, and eventually give up. Once they give up the sounds remain like distant chimes, like the call of children far away, like the song of our own name coming back to us from someone lost long ago, so that we begin, finally, just before death, to only hear what we want to hear.

"Does Daddy know?" Frannie asked.

The doctors don't know what we know when they know

we know we're finally dead. It's a complicated proposition. How do others know you're dead if no one knows who should know but doesn't know?

"I didn't know," Frannie said and moved her other hand toward Natalie's. Now she held her sister's hand in both of hers. Just recently she had held the hands of strange and cold men in the night. It had been the wrong thing to do. At first it seemed right, and then it wasn't.

Most people do not know that the hands of the dead can clasp your own as if they were struggling to hold on to you. If you insert your hand in theirs and lace your fingers among theirs, their fingers will suddenly close around yours and in some cases you cannot get away, as if, now in death, having failed in life, they can pull you to them. This would not have been the case with Frannie and her mother, but it has happened and would again.

"Is she inside?" Frannie asked.

In 1888, when this house had recently been built, a visiting cousin died while there. Because four feet of snow covered the ground at the time—the deepest snow of the century—with drifts even higher, it was weeks before the body could be taken away to be buried. The body had remained in the unheated parlor all that time. On the mantel now in that room was a picture of the dead woman. She looked fine. She looked like she was resting in bed. Until today, it had been one of Frannie's favorite pictures.

"Is she in there?" she asked again, nodding toward the parlor.

"No," Jake said.

"She's buried, Frannie."

"Buried?" she asked as if she did not understand what the word meant. "Already buried?" she whispered.

In the melodrama of a composed and crafted life, now was the time for something to happen. Now was the time for the wind to rise up, for a storm to blow in, for a cloud dark as the inside of evil itself to appear over this car and suck Frannie away. Nothing happened.

"We've had the funeral."

"We couldn't find you."

"Everybody said to go ahead and put her to rest."

"It seemed like the right thing to do."

"The right thing to do?" Frannie repeated, still lost in this dream and wondering when she'd wake up.

"We called Millie."

"Even she didn't know where you were."

"We didn't call the police."

"That seemed like too much."

"Everyone felt terrible about it."

"Why, Frannie? Why?" Natalie asked. "You knew she was going to die soon. You knew it."

"But the doctor told us she had six months to live. I was there when he said it."

"As *much* as six months. He said she had as much as, not for sure."

"Oh."

"You just made it all the worse, Frannie. But what else is new?" her sister said.

"God help me, Nat, I'm sorry. I'm so sorry. I am. I didn't

know. I don't know what to say. What do you want me to say?"

It was the end of the twentieth century. Death had been around a long time. At first, no one knew what to say. There weren't any words. Only God knew why people died, and what to say. Then the people themselves decided they knew. They began to know how to use words to explain it. The words changed over time. The new words, though, after centuries of learning and scholarship and prayer, were crude in sound, abrupt and guttural and chopped like sticks spit into the air. The incantations of primeval hearts were mostly lost.

The sound of one word, though, remained. The sound of no remained and was passed on. Spoken at a time like this, from a soul as lost as Frannie's, it became a prayer that combined all words into one.

"No," she said.

Frannie, along with other people, had often had trouble with the words yes and no, as if they, the simplest of all words, were actually too complex to understand. She'd gotten into trouble all her life by using them in the wrong order, by substituting one for the other, by saying one of them when she knew it should have been the other, by refusing to think about what they meant and by simply hoping, at times, that someone—her father, maybe, or her mother, or her sister, or whoever was there—would figure it out for her and use the words in the right way.

Now seemed the right time to use one of these words, clearly the right time, and so she said it again, and then again.

"No," she said. "No, no, no."

In the backseat along with the half-empty grocery bags was a pile of unopened mail. Jake started the car and drove down the long private road to park behind the old farmhouse.

Frannie slid her finger along the seal of an envelope. She did this distractedly, opening, as one would, the unopened mail. It was something anyone might have done. There was the mail. It had to be opened. She did it as if this was a normal day and she had just come home and it was the next logical thing to do. She did not know what else to do.

Chapter 2

THE OLD FARMHOUSE in the community of Silk Hope was so large it had never been added on to since it was built. Of course rooms had been changed. The canning room was now the downstairs bathroom. Later, upstairs, another bath was made from part of another room and the half remaining became an upstairs laundry room. There had been no indoor bathrooms when the house was built. Closets had been added within rooms. In years past, not many rural people, not even well-off people, had many clothes. The earliest closets in that part of the South were merely rods hung across the diagonal in the corner of the room.

Even with all the partitioning, each person had always had his or her own bedroom, except, at various times, when the children shared a room because one or more of the grandparents or great-grandparents were still alive. In modern times

Natalie had always had her room and Frannie hers, and their parents their own, and during the early part of this latest family's life, their grandmother had had her own room, and that left one more as a guest bedroom, rarely used.

"So," Frannie asked, trying to move forward with her life and ask the questions she now wanted answered, "does Dad know? You never answered me."

She was sitting on her sister's bed and Natalie was there with her, leaning against the headboard on two pillows.

"How could he know, Frannie? How?"

The bedspread on which they sat was a quilt that matched the one on Frannie's bed. They had both been sewn by their grandmother, their mother's mother. They had never known their father's mother, but of course, because of the history of their mother's family, of the women in this family in particular, their maternal grandmother had lived on with them until her own death. Every bed in this house had a quilt that this woman had made and the old stretcher boards and frames for supporting them were in the attic.

"How could he know? Because you told him?" Frannie said.

The interior walls of this house were beaded pine boards. It was thought that this was a premium way to finish a house, and a couple today finding such a house rejoiced. Actually, in times past, the boards were considered second to plaster, but plaster houses in the country were rare and expensive, and wood could be cut and milled off your own property. The boards in this house were painted white except for the kitchen, which was a pale green. The floors were carpeted or covered with vinyl and under this was a layer of finished narrow pine flooring, and under it white oak subflooring, itself nailed into the white oak joists, and they, in turn, supported by six-by-ten white oak sills and girders. It was a well-built house.

"Think about it, Frannie. How could I tell him? How?"

"I guess you couldn't," she said and turned her face to the pillow.

"Would he even care? Would he?"

"Yes."

The house was originally built on stone piers. Later, when her father married her mother and moved in, Frannie's grandparents put in central heat and added the second bathroom and jacked up the house to accommodate the ductwork and set it back down on a brick foundation.

"You don't know that. You say it, but you don't know any more than me."

"But I do. And he would."

"Okay. Whatever you say."

"Didn't Mom have his address?"

"No."

"I thought she did."

"She didn't."

"I feel so strange," Frannie said and rested her head against Natalie's shoulder. "I feel so scared."

"Of course you do. Just talk to me. Ask me anything you want."

"Tell me what she looked like."

"When she died?" Natalie asked.

"Yes."

"She looked like she was asleep."

"She did?"

"Yes."

"I don't believe you."

"Well," Natalie said, "more or less."

Downstairs in the grand old farmhouse was the parlor, of course, and the kitchen and a pantry and a dining room and a room that began to be known, years after houses like these were built, as the den. Strangely, while a den long ago would have been associated with the lair of a wild animal, it became used to denote the most comfortable and most relaxed room in a house where people gathered.

The den had been a wonderful room in Frannie's house, and many of her best memories of her father and mother together and of all of them together were from this room.

"If she hemorrhaged in her lungs, she wouldn't have looked like she was asleep."

"Don't ask, Frannie. Just don't."

"I need to know."

"You don't."

"Was there a lot of blood?"

"No."

"I hate myself," Frannie said.

In the den of the modern house everyone became the same. The difference between being a child and being an adult was altered. Often, in the movies, or in certain books, there was that scene before the fire in the enormous hearth with mother reading to the children and father looking through the farm implements catalog.

Usually this was not true. It was nice to believe it and it felt good, but it was not true. What was true was that Mother probably could not read. Father had an arm missing. It had been caught in the thresher. It had not been cut off, but pulled off. A man never forgot what it felt like to have his arm pulled off. Having an arm pulled off changed you forever.

Even if Mom could read, she was often slightly deranged from childbirth and overwork, broken-down from the demands of daily life, from the fear of hunger, from dead children and a husband she did not understand, and, lacking the words to describe her condition even to herself, and never allowed to use the word no, once she'd used the word yes, she retreated into herself.

In Frannie's family, after Great-Great-Grandma Delia's mistake, the women were better looked after and were taught to be careful. It was handed down that they would be.

"I wish you'd taken a picture," Frannie said.

"Of what?"

"Of Mom."

"Of her dead?"

"Yes."

"Of her dead body?"

"Of her face."

"Why would you want such a thing?"

"I don't know."

"You're not making sense."

"Well, we have all these pictures of us alive, but nothing of the end."

She knew she was saying anything that came to her, but she didn't care. It didn't matter what she was saying or what her sister was saying, she needed to talk and fill up the empty eerie rooms of this house.

"You know what you're doing, don't you?" Natalie asked.

"Talking crazy?"

"Yes."

"I can't cry."

"You will," her sister said, holding her hand and leaning back on the pillows half asleep. She was exhausted.

"I want to now."

"Well, then, cry."

"Don't be mean to me, Nat. I know you hate me for what I did, but don't be mean to me now."

"I'm sorry."

"You are mad, aren't you? Really, really mad."

"In a way I am."

"I deserve it."

She began to walk around the room. She traveled aimlessly in circles at first and then began to trace and retrace a definite circle within the room.

"Can I sleep with you tonight?" she asked.

"Yes."

"Are you going to visit the grave?"

"Sure. When Jake gets back."

"Is he staying here now?"

"Some."

"Is he going to tonight?"

"I don't know. He's at his mom's."

Frannie kept walking.

"Who carried the casket?"

"I don't remember all of them. Uncle Silas's stepson and Dave Webster and Cary Broughton and I don't know who all else."

"Was it heavy?"

"I don't know, Frannie. It's on a little table most of the time, on wheels."

"Oh."

She was going in a tighter circle now and was about to make herself dizzy.

"Do you remember musical chairs?"

Natalie had really had all she could take of Frannie's nervous talking, so when she was asked that, she pulled the quilt up from the bed and wrapped herself in it and watched Frannie walking and talking and said nothing herself.

"I was thinking about musical chairs the other day. I don't know why but I remembered that time when I would have been about four, which means you would have been about twelve. Me and you and Mom and Dad and Granny all played musical chairs one time in the kitchen. It was raining that night and something had happened. Maybe it was when Daddy bought the Cadillac and used up all the money, but we were in the kitchen and suddenly he got up from his chair and put it in the corner and said, Let's play musical chairs, and he started making the music himself, singing something, and pretty soon everyone was scooting around those chairs until we ended up with one chair for me and you to go for.

"He kept on singing forever, watching us go around and around and all the grown-ups were laughing about it because he wouldn't stop and we had to keep circling and the longer it went on the more serious we got about it and I got so intent on it that when he stopped I was concentrating so hard you plopped down in the chair and I just stood there, having forgotten what I was supposed to do when the music did stop, and then everyone laughed at me and I started crying.

"It's awful to cry when everyone's laughing at you. It happens to children all the time. Something's always happening to children to make them cry that the grown-ups think is funny. I felt so awful that night because we were all having fun and then out of nowhere I was the one being laughed at."

She stopped walking in circles for the first time since she'd begun and looked at Natalie, who had fallen asleep. When Frannie became still, Natalie opened her eyes.

"I'm listening," she said.

"You weren't, but it doesn't matter."

"Go on and finish."

"It's just that you get humiliated so many times when you're little and then you grow up and you think it's over, but it's not. Nothing's over. Everything's the same. There are different people, but everything else is the same."

"I don't think anything stays the same."

"Can we go to the cemetery soon?"

"Sure."

"After a nap?"

"Sure."

"And you really aren't mad at me anymore?"

"No."

She got under the quilt with her sister and was quiet and thoughtful a few minutes and then said, "You know what?"

"What?"

"Now that Mom's dead, Daddy's going to come back."

Natalie turned Frannie toward her.

"He doesn't even know she's dead so what difference will it make?"

"Well, then, I'll have to tell him," Frannie said. "I'll just have to do that."

Chapter 3

FRANNIE WAS SITTING in the loft of the old barn. Though the barn had not been used for animals or storing feed for years, since before she was born, even, there was still the smell of feed in it, and in the corners of the loft and along the slick wooden floor sprigs of hay lay scattered about, now shiny and brittle as straw.

The old wood stanchions, where the dairy cows had been tied and given sweet feed when they were milked, remained in the room below. The wood of the stanchions was smooth, and Frannie loved to run her hand along the edges where the animals had rubbed and scratched themselves, again and again, over so many years until the rough sawn wood itself had become rounded and slick and polished as the arm of an old chair where you might sit and distractedly and dreamily feel the shape and finish of the wood.

That's the way Frannie felt when she ran her hand along the wood, dreamy and distracted and changed, for that moment, as if she were in her father's lap.

The old barn almost as much as the house made her feel that way and so she spent a lot of time in it and always had, at first as a child, not knowing why except that it was fun to be in it and that it made her feel good, and then later as a young woman, realizing there was more to it than she had ever understood.

Hay, rubbed against wood long enough, would polish it better than sandpaper. The rough hair of a cow or horse or hog was even better, and after the splinters popped loose and the grain settled what was left was the heart of the wood, the soul of the wood. It was this polished and smooth heart that transformed Frannie in much the same way that the heart of anyone, once reached, once discovered, soothed and comforted and invited the reverie of dreams, or the vision of what might have been, or would be.

The barn, then, was special to her, not only because of the wood and the smells and the cool darkness it offered on a summer day, but because it was where she and her father used to sit and talk. It was where she would find him when he left the house suddenly. It was here that he talked to her in a way he did not in the house, in a way he did not in the company of others.

The barn meant so much to her. In times past she had thought she might discover her father there. That he might be there that very minute. When she ran from the house and into the barn, he would, of course, not be there. At the same time she thought he might be waiting for her, she knew he wouldn't be. Both thoughts were equal, though she wished they weren't. But she had to imagine it and she had to see him sitting on the edge of the loft dangling his feet into the space below where the hay wagons used to be driven and where the huge fork, perched in from the rafters like a predatory and dangerous bird, would swoop down into the stack and lift it into the loft.

It would be to there he would return. He would not want to come in the house right away. He would wait for her to know he was there.

The barn was his in a way the house was not. Though it was a part of the same farm, of the land of her mother's family, he, like the other men in the family, knew the house did not belong to him. He knew that it would never be his even if he had remained with the family. The house, this house, the house where her mother had just died, and her mother before her, and hers before her, was the domain and legal property of the women in the family and would always be so.

This had come to be because of what happened to Frannie's great-great-grandma Delia, a woman from the mountains, who Frannie had been told she resembled.

Long ago, Grandma Delia had married a good man. This was many, many years ago when there were more good men than there were now. Corruption, of course, and evil lived nearby and found poor young innocent Delia and courted her and wooed her and confused her and seduced her away from her husband and promised her many things.

Delia fell for this other man, falling from where she had set herself, from what she had promised herself and her family, and in her confusion ran off with him. To make good on one of his promises, he had to take her away, far from the mountains of North Carolina to a farm he owned in Kentucky where she would not have to work as hard or live as crudely or do without, and Delia wanted this at the time, and she fled with him in the night, as they began their long journey by wagon to Kentucky.

They rode for weeks. They rode around the mountain trails. It was thrilling and her heart beat fast. They wound their way above or below this mountain or that with vistas of pristine valleys and homes and farms and people living beautiful lives alongside of rivers and creeks and rich, green fields. This, then, would be their life, as well. They were traveling to it and at the same time they could see it in the distance as they journeyed. It was more exciting than imagining a life. They could actually see it. Soon it would be theirs.

Delia had run away. It was best not to look back. The Bible had a story of a woman who looked back. It was best, as well, not to think about what might be said where she used to live or what the faces of the people she had known now looked like. She would never return.

Passion, often thought to be a modern phenomenon by women who now understood it better and had the words to describe it and the sense of what it meant in their lives, was just as strong long ago, only it was contained in a different word, not separated out as something distinct. It was thought of by women in times past as love. They called it love. In modern times the word has been split in half, and passion and love do not always mean the same thing.

To Delia, the love was strong. It was strong enough to persuade her to leave forever the faces she would see again and again in her mind, strong enough to bring her to journey these many weeks around the mountains beyond which she had never seen, until now. It was strong enough to make her leave her only child. At this point, because the love was so strong, she could not understand the consequences.

I love you. I will leave my husband for you. I will leave my child for you.

These words are still being said today. It is usually a mistake when you say these words. The women in Frannie's family were supposed to know never to say these words again. They were supposed to understand things better because of Grandma Delia.

After weeks, Delia and the new man finally came to the farm in Kentucky. This, he told her, is where we shall be. She began to live the life he wanted her to live, and it was good. There were things she could not forget, but still it was good and the passion, which was called love, was strong.

One day, when Delia was in the woods gathering ginseng, which was something the mountain people had always done and still do to this day, gathering it and selling it to the agents who used to arrive twice a year and who would in turn sell it to the Chinese, one day, out in the woods, Delia saw a man she used to know when she lived in the other life, in the other community, in the other state, in the other world, which she had left for love.

She talked to this man, surprised to see him, and discovered she was not in Kentucky.

She was nowhere near Kentucky.

She was, after all, only sixteen miles from her home. She was just a day's ride from her husband and her young son. Having been in this place only three months and having never been to the nearby town, she had no way of knowing where she was except by the word of the man she had followed.

This man had, of course, tricked her. He had driven her around in circles and up and down the mountain roads for weeks until he arrived, not at the fabled Kentucky plantation, but at his poor little farm just beyond her own. She had trusted in her love and she had been deceived.

Then Delia, so went the family lore, did the only thing she could think to do at the time. She returned from the woods back to the man who had tricked her. She did not even tell him that she knew. She did not, as women today think they would do, leave that moment and walk off from this man and never look back, because how could she? Where, really, could she go? Back to her own town and to her true husband and family? It did not seem to her at that time she could, but she slowly talked herself into taking action.

Three weeks later she confronted the man she had once loved more than anything else on this earth and when he struck her and refused to discuss it, then she did leave. She walked off the next day while he was away from the house. As she neared her community, people began to recognize her and she began to recognize them, even though she had been right in thinking their faces would look different and would forever be changed at least in the way they looked at her.

Her husband took her back. Many people advised him against this. She lived in shame and her own disgrace. People shunned her. Her husband did his best to treat her in the kindly way he always had. Her son did his best. Soon after that she had a daughter. She was the daughter of the real husband and not the other man. As the daughter grew, Delia was thankful that God had spared her the ignominious burden and penance of bearing the evil man's child.

It was in this daughter that Delia invested all that remained in her. She taught her about life and what it was she now knew, both the good and the bad of it. It was to this daughter that honor and strength and clear thinking and a true and virtuous life were taught.

Then, a sad thing happened.

Delia's husband died. Because his family and her own as well as the people in the town still shunned her and because there was no one now to provide for her and for her children and because, back then, a woman alone had no way to care for herself or make a living, Delia was eventually forced to return to the man who had tricked her. She had no one else to go to.

This was the sad end of Delia's life, except for what remained of her in her daughter, and it was this daughter who set forth in life with her special vision.

This daughter moved to Silk Hope where Natalie and Frannie now lived. She built the farmhouse for herself, along with her husband, with money that was left to her by the estate of the man who had tricked her mother, money that no one knew he had, money that he had never spent on a soul, not even on himself.

It was written into the deed and into all the wills that followed that the women in the family—the oldest daughter, or all the daughters, or if there were no daughters, the next closest female relative—that only the women would inherit this house and this land and therefore would always have a home no matter what else happened in their lives, no matter what occurred between them and the men in their lives. They would always have a home: this land, this ancestral sanctuary.

And now, by deed and by will, this house had been passed to Frannie and to Natalie so that no matter what would happen between Frannie and her men, or between Natalie and her men, the house would be theirs and only theirs and always theirs.

It seemed that Frannie would need this inheritance in her life. Most of the women did not need it. It seemed, though she was young, that Frannie would.

Chapter 4

FRANNIE DID NOT like Jake. She tolerated him because she loved her sister. Frannie's mother had liked Jake, and he had spent much of the last year in their home.

The two sisters had been waiting for Jake to come back so they could visit the grave site, but they decided to go on without him.

"I feel better now," Frannie said.

"Me, too."

"You never said if you remembered that time we all played musical chairs."

"We never did that, Frannie. Never."

"We did, too."

"We never did. It's not the kind of thing our father would have done."

They were in Natalie's car. It was a new car. She had a

good job in the front office of the textile mill that employed hundreds of the local people.

"Do you still have that letter?"

"Which one?"

"The last letter we got from Dad?"

"I don't know. Mom had it. She probably threw it away. It was years ago."

The cemetery where their mother was buried was behind the church. The church had been a country church until the town enveloped it in the same way it was enveloping the farm. The church still had land with it, even though it was now within the town limits. The cemetery was full and no new individual or family plots could be sold, though there was still more land that could have been used. It had been decided by the deacons that the remaining land should be left open in case the church needed to raise money. It could sell the land at high city prices its founders never dreamed about.

"I haven't been here in a long time," Frannie said as they drove up to the church. "I bet it's been two years."

"We wish you'd start coming again."

"Maybe I will."

The grave had been dug into the hard red clay soil that lay under this region. In times past two black men had dug all the graves in the area. They were brothers. It was difficult to dig a six-foot hole in red clay. It took a lot more than a shovel. Driving a pick into hard red clay with the force of a full swing often turned up only a wedge of dirt the size of the point of the pick. The old brothers no longer dug these graves. They were dug by a backhoe.

There was no headstone. Frannie wondered why. Natalie explained it took time to get them made. The grave looked raw to Frannie without the headstone. The clay was mounded up on the grave. It was red, not the red color of blood, but rather the thinner red of a slapped face, a kind of scarlet red with fleshly orange tones to it, but not the deep viscous red of blood.

Frannie and Natalie were quiet when they left the car and walked hand-in-hand to the mound. The leaves in the trees were still. It was blinding hot. Both of the women wore sunglasses. Often at funerals, even on a cloudy winter day, people wore sunglasses so tears would not be noticed, along with swollen eyes and the face of obvious grief. This was not necessary because people expected you to cry. It was even all right for men to cry. It was actually a bonus point if they did. Children often tried harder than the adults not to cry, or, sometimes, tried hard to cry, because the loss sometimes took longer for children to understand. Sometimes they cried because they saw their parents cry for the first time. It was frightening to see your father cry when you never had before. At the same time, it made you love him more.

Frannie did not cry. Natalie began again. Frannie was as quiet as she could be as she first stood, then knelt, at the foot of her mother's grave. The lovely old custom of reaching for a handful of dirt and then letting it sift softly from your hand onto the grave didn't work here because when Frannie scooped up a handful of red clay it came up in lumps and when she let it fall it dropped clumsily, and left her hand stained.

Nothing was working out as she had imagined. No headstone, no tears, no softly sifting dirt, no heartfelt eulogies, no lovely music. She had missed it all. She was too late.

"Maybe he was at the funeral and no one saw him."

Natalie stood above her and stroked her hair and let her talk.

"He once told me how much he loved us. He told me lots of things and he told me he loved Mom. I'm the one he talked to. I'm the only one who ever knew him it seems. And now it's strange, isn't it, it's odd, that both of us will have found out she's dead after it's too late. We both missed it."

Natalie held her sister's hand and began to worry about the affairs of the estate, and what next to do, and how to do it, and what she would have to do with the will and the money and the lawyers and the real world of paper and ink and legal words.

"I'm not messing with men anymore," Frannie said.

Natalie and Frannie both knew about the provisions from long ago for the house and land. They would also get $25,000 apiece in cash, plus the little bit of money in the checking and savings account. But that would be it. Even this small estate was difficult to think about and Natalie would let Jake handle most of it.

A family drove up. They carried flowers to an older site. The mother set flowers against the headstone, and then the father and then all three of the children did the same. They looked like a nice family. They were well behaved. There was something going on that seemed right. Frannie watched the man. You could never be sure with men. Frannie's father had walked out without saying a word.

The family stood for a moment of silence at the grave. They held hands all around. It was sweet to see.

"That must be her mother. Or her father," Natalie said.

They turned to go. First the father and mother walked on and then the oldest daughter started away. The younger daughter accidentally stepped on the back of the shoe of the older daughter and the shoe came off as she walked forward, and as the parents continued to the car unaware of what had occurred, the older girl spun around and shoved her sister so hard she fell on her back.

"Me and you," Frannie said.

"Yep."

They were almost to their car. The car with the family in it was backing out. On the front of their car was a decorative plate that said FIGURE EIGHT ISLAND. It was a fancy plate in a heavy gold-colored metal frame. Frannie had a plate on her car, on the front, as well. She had bought it at the mall one Saturday. It said, simply, in capital letters, YES.

"Can we swing by and get my car?" she asked.

Frannie's car was parked facing an empty building. Other cars were nearby. The lot was used by people who worked in the area during the day and by anyone at night who couldn't find a spot in the spaces up and down the street. Natalie let her out and then drove home.

Frannie took an old toolbox from her trunk. The toolbox was green and metal and inside it were all the tools she owned in the world. Most of them had been her father's. She had a claw hammer and a ball peen hammer. The ball peen hammer was a machinist's hammer and had a finely rounded end where the claw on a carpenter's hammer would be. Frannie knew how to use this ball peen hammer because she had helped her father flatten out and then round off heads of rivets with this hammer.

She removed a screwdriver and a pair of pliers as well as the size wrench she guessed she would need and began to loosen the screws that held the plate to the bumper. While she was doing this, a little girl walked up from behind the empty building.

"Where'd you come from?" Frannie asked.

"Back there."

The girl looked like a street kid from a movie about the problems of the proletariat in the thirties. It was rare in North Carolina in modern times to see a white child who looked that uncared for.

"Do you want this?" Frannie asked her after she had removed the plate.

"Uh-huh," the girl said.

"Where do you live?"

"Over there."

Frannie saw a small travel trailer set up off the ground on cinder blocks. The trailer was battered and misshapen as if it had come loose while being towed, and then wrecked and had been repaired as best as it could.

"Do you live in there?"

"Yes."

"Who do you live with?"

"My mother."

"Is she home?"

"No. She's at work."

Frannie put her tools back in the truck and picked up the girl and put her on the hood of her car and sat beside her.

"Where's your daddy?"

"He's gone."

"Have you always lived in that trailer?"

"Yes."

Frannie could see herself at some low point in her life, at the end of some horrible times that she could imagine could happen to her, living like this with a child, and it made her feel bad. Besides making her feel bad, it made her feel uneasy, and she wanted to be away from what she saw and from what she was thinking.

"Are you hungry?"

"I don't know."

"Would you like a hamburger?"

"Yes, I would."

"Here's ten dollars. Walk over there and get one and get something to drink and anything else you want. Okay? If your momma asks where you got the money, tell her a nice lady who has lots of money gave it to you, and then you won't get in trouble if she thinks you stole it."

"Okay."

She set her back on the ground, but held her longer than that act by itself would have taken, then she hugged her and kissed her face and talked to her while she knelt in front of her and rebuttoned the girl's blouse, which had been buttoned improperly, misaligned.

"You're going to be okay," Frannie told her, feeling herself about to lose it. "You are. You're going to have a great life," she told her and patted her on her back and sent her toward the restaurant. Frannie got in her car and began to cry, finally, like she'd needed to since she'd found out about her mother.

Chapter 5

Days later a lone man moved into a duplex across the road from the farmhouse.

The duplex had been hastily divided years ago by the alcoholic owner of the small house. Nothing inside made sense. When you entered the front door, you entered the kitchen. The only door out the back was through a closet. If you wanted to go out the back, you had to push aside the clothes and duck beneath the rod. The tiny bedroom was not much bigger than the closet and it shared a window with the living room.

It shared this window literally because the partition wall dividing the rooms had been abutted directly into the center of the window. If you raised the window from the bedroom it also raised in the living room, or vice-versa.

The rent was cheap, though, and the man who moved

into this place did not mind as much as someone else might have. His name was Ted Keller and he had just spent the last six years of his life in prison.

He was forty-eight years old. Prison had been a living hell for him, and he never wanted to go back. His job opportunity counselor had helped him get a position in a building supply warehouse. Ted was determined to make things work this time.

Ted Keller had three children from his first wife but he never saw them, and was, in fact, legally prohibited from doing so. His second wife, with whom he had no children, and from whom he was divorced, lived nearby, but he had not yet told her he was free.

Outside, as Ted stood at his bedroom window and dried himself from his shower, a cautious rabbit peered from beneath a bush and hopped silently into the yard. This rabbit was a lovely animal, and his fur was brown and soft and delicate as the tender insides of his alert ears, which stood above his head and twisted this way and that, always listening for whatever it would be that would end his life.

It had been a long time since Ted had seen a rabbit in the wild. He would never look upon a caged animal in the same way again.

The rabbit hopped and nibbled all around the edges of the yard. He was chewing on the young leafy growth of plants when a shotgun blast blew him six feet into the air and across the yard. At the report of the twenty-gauge load of birdshot, Ted hit the floor as if he had been the target. When he looked out the window again he saw the old man who lived next door and who owned this dilapidated duplex walk out with the shotgun in his hand and go to the rabbit and smash its head with the butt of his gun.

The old man went back to his house and returned with a hatchet and cut off the rabbit's two back feet and then tossed what remained of the animal toward the woods at the back of the yard. The rabbit sailed smoothly for a while but then struck a tree and fell back into the yard. The old man looked at the rabbit lying in the grass. He picked it up by its ears and slung it again. This time the rabbit impaled itself on the sharp point of a broken branch and hung six feet above the ground. The old man blasted it again with his shotgun, and the rabbit, in bits and pieces this time, fell to the earth. A piece of its shoulder and part of its head still hung on the branch. Ted could still see it as the old man went back to his side of the unit. As he stared at it, something red and moist and dripping fell. It appeared to be its heart. Ted sat on the floor of his bedroom and closed his eyes.

It was evening. He was free. He could do anything he wanted. All he had to do was walk out the door and do it.

Chapter 6

THE HOUSE FRANNIE inherited along with Natalie had 12 acres remaining of the original 160. Long ago when land was plentiful and first surveyed and divided, it was cut into sections. A section was 640 acres. As time passed, the sections themselves were quartered. That's why many old farms are 160 acres or multiples of it.

After the family stopped farming and the city grew around the land, Frannie's ancestors sold off parts of the farm to help pay the taxes that were assessed on the land for its value as a housing or commercial development, creating a situation where the land actually had to be sold for development because the amount of the taxes precluded making enough money from small-scale farming to pay them and certainly eliminated any possibility of living simply and cheaply and holding on to the land.

Now only the twelve acres remained. On the twelve acres was the fine old house; the big dairy barn, where Frannie and her father talked when she was young and he still lived with them; two corncribs shaped like narrow wooden slatted cages; a small sweet-potato house made of logs; a smokehouse for curing meat; and the sheds built around the big barn for machinery that was gone except for the pieces in the weeds and vines not sold for scrap.

There was also a tobacco curing barn and a packhouse, both of which had fallen in on themselves. There was a chicken house with wire mesh on the windows, built up off the ground on stilts to discourage visits by weasels, raccoons, possums, foxes, black snakes, and stray dogs, and there was one rotted hog house in the lowland beneath the spring.

The land directly above the spring was terraced and flat. Above it was another terrace. All the terraces and most of the rest of the land could be seen from the house, which stood on the highest plateau. The terraces were natural except for some grading done when the pond was built. They fell gently, as is the way of land that hasn't been disturbed, from one to the other.

The pond had been built after the war. The local agricultural agents at that time were promoting ponds as a way of controlling wet land and as water sources for cattle. There was federal help to lay off the pond and to build it.

Frannie's grandfather had built this pond. It had been the showpiece of the community. It was surrounded by an acre of dry land that formed a wide grassy apron around it. The pond itself was shaped irregularly, which was odd, as most ponds were round or oval. There was also an island in the middle of this pond.

When the pond was built, the land was bulldozed out, and the dirt from all the digging went to build the dam. Essentially, for most ponds, you were digging a big hole. To make an island in the middle simply means you left part of the land as it was and dug around it. For whatever reason, this was rarely done. Frannie's grandfather had done it, and this island held mysteries of infinite dimensions to all the children who had grown up nearby.

This island, then, by symbol and by its actuality, said something about the life around it, and created in Frannie, in her heart, a space to dream and made possible, where it might not have been before, desire and longing.

The total pond area itself was two acres including the island of a half of an acre. This half of an acre was like a dot or a speck in the midst of the once abundant land around it, but in a city, for instance, a half of an acre is considered a very large lot for a house and side and back and front yards. It was, then, a nice-size island.

The trees had been left on this island when the rest were cut for the pond site and therefore the island must have been in her grandfather's mind from the start. These trees flourished from the rich soil and water around them. The banks of this island were abundant in fish, and Frannie's dad had taught her how to cast her fly or lure directly onto the bank and then jump it from the bank into the water, creating the illusion for the fish that something on land had just plopped itself onto the supper table.

This trick nearly always produced a bite, if not a catch, and Frannie had spent many hours with her dad in their rowboat casting and talking and drifting and becoming close in a way that was accidental and true.

Natalie, of course, fished at times, both alone with her dad and with Frannie and him, but it was not the same. Whatever was passing between Frannie and her father was just for them and no one else.

Natalie was not Frannie and didn't need to be, and Frannie didn't want to be her. They were different from the moment they entered this world in every way, and, at the same time, alike in every other way.

Natalie hated to kill the fish, once caught. She hated to stun them and she could not do it. Frannie did not mind at all, and when she struck the fish sharply and quickly on the top of its head with a club and its body quivered and convulsed as its life departed while she held it and Natalie looked away, Frannie thought nothing of it.

Death, then, had meant something different to the two girls, and still did. Frannie did not mind, and even preferred, to look it in its eye, while Natalie would rather look away. Strange then that Natalie had been the one to have to witness her mother's while Frannie played, having missed it so that now she had an empty spot in front of her that she would fall into, a hole into which she would disappear at times, later returning but not the same.

Land, so solid, could be rendered empty and liquid, and once this was known, it was easy to understand why an island could mean so much.

It was to this island, that was, after all, only a chunk of red clay, only a tree-covered spot in the middle of the clear reflected beauty of the water around it, that Frannie and Natalie and Jake now paddled in the flat-bottomed rowboat, and the ripples of the oars and the slow wake from the ribs of this boat as it silently skimmed across the surface of this cool brown water were as lazy and sleepy and tender as the women above.

"It's so nice here," Natalie said.

"It's so quiet."

"It's such a special place."

"And it always will be," Frannie said and laid her head against her sister's shoulder.

"I hope so," Natalie said.

"Shhhh," Frannie whispered. "Let's just be still for a while."

They glided toward the island. The boat nudged into the mud against the bank and stopped.

There was a bench in front of them. The bench was crudely made from framing lumber and it was sunk into the ground oddly out of place, as if it were a bus stop in the middle of nowhere, as if a person sitting on it should be waiting for something to happen, for someone to arrive. The bench didn't make sense just to look at it. Sitting on it, though, was different, and hours could pass unaccounted for as if time were not the same there.

Frannie had built the bench six years ago when she was fifteen.

It was evening. Some wild ducks were at the far end of

the pond. They were paddling about near the overflow. Dragonflies dipped from the air toward the water and darted against its surface. A turtle with only its head visible floated in the middle while two red-winged blackbirds called to each other from opposite shores. An unknown number of bream and bass swam about while a lone catfish, huge and ominous and looking like a prehistoric remnant, dug itself into the mud below the bench where Frannie and Jake and Natalie sat.

"I haven't fished here in a long time," Frannie said. "I wonder why?"

No one answered her.

The sun was setting. The sky around it was red. It was not the red of blood drained from the dead and not the red of earth piled upon the dead and not the red of eyes bleary and tired from weeping and not the red of passion, or love, as it was once called, and not the red of sorrow or of anger, but the setting sun was the illusory red of things far away and of things unknown.

"I don't know what to do," Frannie said.

The sky itself was red and there were clouds and they were dark, but it could not mean it would rain because late one evening Frannie's father had taught her the red sky at night, sailor's delight, and red sky in morning, sailors take warning saying, and she knew it to be true.

"Do you think I ought to go back to school on the money?"

"It'd be a good idea," Natalie said.

"It would," Jake said.

"I kind of hate school," Frannie said.

"Jake could invest your money like he's going to do mine," Natalie said.

"I could set it up for you to get enough to go to school on, and let the rest earn for you while you do it," he said.

"Yeah, maybe."

"You ought to let him."

"I don't know. I'll see. I do know going back to school would be the right thing. I guess if it's the right thing, I ought to do it."

"That's a good way to think," Jake said.

"But I hate school."

"It would be wise use of the money."

"I need to start doing the right thing," she said.

The catfish, buried in the murky mud below them, shot forward after a minnow. The water churned and the thrashing startled everyone.

Above them turkey vultures and black buzzards drifted in the sky, heading east to the dead trees they returned to at the end of each day. They, like the catfish, were prehistoric-looking creatures, unchanged, for the most part, over time.

It was not a smart thing ever to tangle with a vulture or a buzzard. They were large birds, nearly the size of eagles, and when frightened or cornered on the ground they vomited on their enemies. The expression you make me want to puke may have originated with the vulture, and a man or a woman or a child would never forget what it was like to be vomited on by a vulture.

"Then again, I could take a trip," Frannie said. "That's something I've never done. Go a long way off."

The pond was spring fed. The farm itself had been fortunate to have had three springs on it, and two of them had been incorporated into the pond. If you went swimming in this pond, you would unexpectedly find yourself over a rush of cold water. This was startling at first. Then it felt good.

"But maybe I shouldn't," Frannie said, still thinking about the trip. "Maybe I ought to stay around here, especially now that Mom's gone."

The idea of the family, of a family, was something that haunted women to this day. The longing that they felt even in these modern times when knowledge had replaced religion and women felt they could make decisions based on what was right for them, for instance, instead of what they were told was merely right and had always been—even today, this longing for a family remained.

The longing was for the family they once had, or for the one they never had, for one that had failed, for one that couldn't be made right, for the one that they had seen or read about or simply knew had to be, and this dream would always be there and even smart-talking, wisecracking free spirits like Frannie Vaughan could not outrun what her mother had been, her grandmother before her, and on and on to Delia and beyond.

"Probably I'll just stay around here and not go anywhere," she said.

The longing was there. A part of it lost or betrayed rattled around in her like a pebble in her shoe, like a word she might have once heard that then replayed itself every night in her sleep.

"But then again, if I don't take a trip now, I might never," Frannie said, still on the subject while Jake and Natalie held hands and watched the waters for the catfish.

"I think I know where Dad might be. Maybe I'll go find out," Frannie said. "I might be wrong, though."

It was quiet again. The catfish was nowhere in sight. It might have missed the minnow. It might have caught it, too. A catfish has a big mouth. From not too far away, a diesel engine fired up. Someone called to someone else. Who these people were and what they wanted was another unknown. They weren't too far away, though, because there wasn't much between you and them when you only had twelve acres left. It should be enough, though, if you were careful and everything—positively, absolutely all the things you did—was right. Knowing what was right and what was wrong was still the trick.

"He ought to know what's happened to us," Frannie said.

Natalie was trying not to say anything. She felt sorry for Frannie and wanted only to protect her from herself as well as from all the things she knew that Frannie did not yet know.

Though Natalie tried not to speak, the more Frannie said, the more difficult it became for her not to at least say something and just before she did, Jake realized she was about to and put his arm around her and walked her off toward the other side of the island.

"Because if he knew," Frannie said, "he might come back."

She watched her sister and the fiancé disappear around the curve of the island until they were out of sight. Then it was even quieter than before. She stared into the water. The catfish slowly rose from below until it floated on the surface.

It opened its obscenely large mouth so wide that it looked like it could have swallowed Frannie's bare foot. When its mouth was open all the way, the catfish screamed, and the scream was so loud and so humanlike that Natalie and Jake came running from the other side of the island.

"Are you okay?"

Frannie now had her knees drawn up to her and she was calm.

"Of course I'm all right," she said. "But let's go back home. I don't feel like sitting here anymore."

Chapter 7

THE NEXT EVENING Frannie went for a walk on the land. There were old tractor and mule roads leading into the woods that had been used to get to the various hayfields, tobacco fields, wheat and cornfields. The roads went nowhere now, but were still there as lovely clearings with pine needles for pavement, but they were as empty as the main street of any town on the last day of the earth. That's the way she felt when she came upon one of these roads, as if she'd stepped into another world and she was the only person in it.

It was a trick to feel that way as the farm was sold off and the land developed. Now most of the roads ended abruptly against the backyards of new developments that surrounded the old farm.

On one side about eight hundred feet from the grand old house and across a small field and a few hundred feet of woods was a shopping center. At night the lights from the parking lot around it lit up almost everything nearby and the construction of this shopping center had all but eliminated the actual dark of night and the relative quiet of those nights that Frannie's ancestors and even she, herself, had once enjoyed.

Frannie's family had only sold six of the eighty or so acres needed to build the shopping center. The rest had come from other owners. Still, it had been necessary to sell. The offer had come only a few months after her father had left.

On another side of the land was the paved road and on a third side was the housing development that had been completed two years ago. People from this development wandered onto Frannie's land. She had many times watched as they walked up to her outbuildings and peered in the windows or poked around the outside as if they had come upon an historic site. The only time she ever said anything to them was if they actually went in the buildings, at which point she would step onto the porch and call, "Excuse me. Please don't go in there. You're on private property."

On the fourth side of the land remained an undeveloped stretch of woods and overgrown fields that had been bought by a developer years ago but never altered. If she followed the roads through that part she eventually came to another old farm site.

This farm site had no house on it. The house had fallen in and then what remained had been burned one night by vandals or drunks. It truly was like an abandoned city with outbuildings and sheds and toppled over grain bins with vines and blackberry briars and honeysuckle and morning glory and stout, foul-smelling prickly pigweed plants.

Her father, who used to call her Frankie instead of Frannie, had taken her there and told her about the life of the families who once lived here and what they had endured. To visit the old site and not know was like being deaf and sitting in a movie house watching a film. You could only get part of what occurred by looking at these buildings and imagining their decline.

This family, which was actually related to Frannie's in some distant way, had bad luck through the years. Diphtheria and yellow fever, diseases that only seem like words to people today, had wiped out families in times past, and this one had lost many children to both. On top of that, the patriarch of the family, an uneducated and simple man, though dignified and virtuous, Frannie had been told, had once traveled to a distant town to transact some business and once there, not knowing where to go, had asked a young man with an honest face if he knew a hotel where he could stay the night. The young man with the honest face showed him one and asked if he could sleep on some blankets on the floor that night, which the old man allowed, as one would back then, believing in the goodness and honor of people, and when the old man awakened the next morning not only were his wallet and all his money gone, but his clothes, as well.

Not knowing what to do, and being in his underwear, and frantic, the old man put on the boy's pants, which were ragged and came only to his knees, and put on the boy's coat, which barely got over his shoulders and reached only halfway to his waist, and ran out into the street to find the boy.

Wild-eyed and terrified and desperate and with no identification, the old man was carted away as a madman to an insane asylum, and he remained there for seven nightmarish weeks until his family discovered where he was and brought him home.

He was never the same again and would never leave the farm again and would never have anything to do with strangers, not even to have a casual conversation, and because of this, the farm declined around him while he mourned the loss of his dignity.

Frannie had loved this story when her father had told it, a private gift, like the nickname Frankie he used for her, something just between them. They sat at the edge of what remained of the clearing to this old site and talked for hours. She loved this story in the way one loves the poignant tragedy of someone else, in the way one feels it and is changed by the story, loved it not only because of the tragedy of the family's life, but because it was her father who told it to her, and with him, as his child, as his daughter, it was easy to believe that nothing bad would ever happen to her, nothing like what she'd just heard, easy to believe in the sanctuary of a wondrous childhood that would never end.

Things do end. Things do change. Now she knew.

If things would change and if there was no way to be sure that what you did would be the right thing and if lives had always been visited by betrayal and dishonor and greed, then what was Frannie to do with no father and now with no mother, and with a face that until recently had laughed at life, eaten it whole, looked it in its eyes and stared it down, licked it down its middle like a cherry popsicle until the sweet syrup of its pleasure had made her smile? What was a young woman to do now that she had been forced to consider that she did not know what she thought she knew, that like the old farmer who trusted the boy with the honest face, she had trusted that she would always be able to do what she wanted, that she would escape anything that came out wrong and that she would not have to wake up one morning and put on the clothes of someone else and run insane and screaming through the streets, because, as in childhood, there would always be a way out?

If you have to wear the clothes of someone else, your spirit suffocates. The pure blue of your eye fades. The broom-straw yellow of your hair grays. The parted line of your lips draws tight while your teeth grind new grooves into one another, and the ropes buried in the back of your neck tighten like a noose.

The noose comes later. In the beginning there is the unease of imbalance, the vague sense of possessory intrusion, that someone other than yourself has become you.

This change was, after all, only someone's death. Not your own. It was, after all, only the adamantine clot in your own heart you felt, and nothing more. It wasn't as if anyone had purposely done anything to you. She died. He left. You're still here. You have this home. Thank Delia for this. On your knees at the edge of the desolation of diphtheria and yellow fever and melancholia from another century when no one could see beyond the watery fatigue of sickness, now give thanks for what you have.

On the edge of all of this, then, Frannie rested on her side with her legs crossed loosely at the ankle and her head in her hand propped up to see into the distance, and all of her in the green moss beneath the cedar tree, moss so tender that to lie against it was like love itself, like being a child again, like having a mother and a father and a home.

Maybe, she thought, it was time, really, and not just in the talking of it but in the truth of it to find her dad, a man she had not seen or heard from since she was eight, a man who in the years he had been gone must have longed for her and for Natalie and for the woman he had loved so much as to have left her rather than hurt her anymore, loved them all so much he had departed rather than live on in shame, loved them all so terribly much, Frannie remembered, that he, her father, a mountain of flesh and heart and anger and despair, loved them all so desperately much that he had cried against her the night before he left, sitting on the banks of the island overlooking the pond beyond the house, out of sight, cried, but only for a moment, against the cotton shirt she wore that cool December day as he talked to her and pressed his face to her shoulders and her back as she sat, eight years old, on his lap and together they looked out at the dark surface where nothing moved and where the night slipped in until it was time for Frannie to change for bed and discover the damp back of her shirt and not understand what had caused it. She would never have known that man could have so many tears that he drenched her shirt with the grief of his conscience, something Frannie had inherited from him so that she, too, as she got older, suffered for mistakes that began to pursue her like a pack of mute dogs, always there, always coming, right behind her.

It is said by learned people in the glossy confident educated world that it's best to face your problems and mistakes, that it's best to confront them, to deal with them, as is said, to empower yourself with the strength to confront.

This is certainly not true. Had Frannie faced the rangy pack of mute dogs she had created out of the stupidity of her young life, she would have been chewed up until she looked like a cat run over by a car and dragged for miles. She tried never to look back as if in not looking back, she would not fail herself; as if in not thinking about certain men she'd known, certain ugly men, drunken men, cold and greedy men, she would not despair; as if in not remembering mistakes, she would not make any more of them.

When Frannie returned from the old site, Jake and Natalie were waiting on the porch, looking in her direction with worry on their faces.

I'm probably going to have to be like them, she thought. I'll have to be like them or be in trouble for the rest of my life.

She was thinking that because to her they looked like old people in rocking chairs at the end of their life and it seemed to her that as you got older you got in less trouble and maybe that was the trick, to be old before your time, sedated and well-considered.

She thought as she walked up to the porch, I don't think I can do it, though. You'd have to have a brain that worked, and mine doesn't. My heart, she thought, is in total control of my life and always has been.

"You look like you're thinking mighty hard," Jake said.

"Probably not too hard," Frannie said, "because I can't walk and think at the same time, you know."

"Jake needs to talk with us about some things," Natalie said.

"Oh, yeah? About what?"

"Money. And other things."

"Okay. I was going to ask you when we got it."

"We have it now," Natalie said, "but there are some papers to be drawn up and signed, but we can tap into some of it now if we need to. It's ours."

"It's uncontested," Jake said.

"Good. Maybe I'll buy a horse."

"That might not be a good idea."

"Why?"

"It just might not."

"Well, it's my money. It's my land. Our land. Why not?"

"Because things might change," Natalie said and looked to Jake to see if he concurred.

"Frannie," he said, "Natalie and I have been looking at the finances of our life, and yours, and of this place, and at the goals we have for our life, and what's best for us, and for you, and we think it would be smart if we put the place up for sale."

"Put what up for sale?" Frannie casually asked, so unaware that they could mean this house and the remaining land that she didn't even consider it.

"This house," Natalie said.

"And the land."

"WHAT!" Frannie screamed. "ARE YOU CRAZY!"

"We think it's the best thing," Natalie said. "I'm sorry, Frannie. I knew you'd be upset. Please try to understand. Listen to why, at least, before you blow up."

"Oh, no," she said and walked off the porch and into the yard. "You're not selling this place. We can't, anyway. It's in the deed to always be ours. No way. You can't sell it. And Jake can't make you. Or me. That's why it's been left to us. You can't do it. And I won't let you. I will never let you. Never. If you don't want to live here, if it's not fancy enough for you and your fiancé to live in you can move out. I don't care. But you can't sell it."

"I don't want to sell it, Frannie," Natalie said. "But it's the right time to do it and we have to."

"No way. No way. You can forget that."

She started to walk off and then turned to Natalie and Jake and looked at them long and hard.

"Don't do it, Nat."

"It won't be right away."

"But it can't be ever."

"Let's all go inside and relax and talk about it. I think you'll see why we have to and why it's the smart thing to do."

"This is Jake talking, not you," she said and glared at him as they went in.

Jake was quiet.

"It's both of us," Natalie said.

"No it's not. You've changed since you started going with him," she said and then shoved him with both her hands, hard, so that he tipped off balance and into the wall.

"YOU GO TO HELL," she screamed at him.

Chapter 8

FRANNIE WAS IN the mall where Millie worked. Millie was her best friend. They had been in school together since junior high. After graduation, Millie took a job in a music store. The store was in this mall, and Millie was always trying to persuade Frannie to come to work with her.

"I don't want to work there," she said.

"It's a lot of fun. It's almost never busy except when something big comes out."

"I don't like jobs."

"Well, who does?"

"I don't know. Natalie, probably. And Jake."

"It's a mind-set, Frannie. You just do it."

"I know. I've been thinking the same thing. You just do it because you need to just do it for some other reason."

"Yeah, like money."

"Right. And you just do it for the money because you got some reason to need the money."

"Well, do you need money now?"

"Sort of. Jake, in the voice of Natalie, won't release all my money to me. But I got some of it."

"I thought you told me the other day you wanted to get a job as soon as possible. That's the only reason I brought it up."

"I do, but not here. I want something more physical. I'm thinking of getting Nat to see about putting me on at the mill."

"Can she do that?"

"Sure."

"But why there?"

"Because it's more money than here. And also," Frannie said, "because she wants me to."

"Oh."

"I'm so messed up, I'm just doing whatever they tell me these days. I can't think for myself anymore."

"You need to cheer up. You are so down on yourself these days."

"Yeah."

"It's not like you."

"I got a lot to figure out."

Millie had to return to work. She had only stepped out the door to chat with Frannie and agree where to meet for lunch. It was eleven-fifteen and they wouldn't meet until noon.

Two teenage girls were walking together and chewing

gum. They looked like they were having a lot of fun with the gum, chewing it so actively and openly. Frannie's mother had disapproved of her daughters chewing gum. She had disapproved of the chewing of gum in general but particularly disliked seeing her own daughters doing it.

When Frannie's mother was growing up, chewing gum had been considered a low-class habit. It was thought that girls or women who chewed gum were cheap.

In Frannie's mother's time, and even more so in her grandmother's time, not looking cheap was ever in one's mind, unlike in Frannie's time where women were encouraged, her grandmother often said, to dress and act like twenty-five-cent whores.

"There's no such thing as a twenty-five-cent whore, Granny," Frannie would say.

"Don't be so sure, young lady," Granny would tell her. "Anytime I see a gal in skintight jeans and a T-shirt so snug she looks naked, I'm looking at one."

"That's just the way we dress now, Granny."

To kill time and because she was tired of sitting, Frannie went shopping. She wanted to do the thing she had always wished people would do for her, which was to show up out of the blue with presents the way a parent often did for a child after an absence.

She bought two blouses for Natalie and paid $170 and then went in six stores looking for something for Jake.

"This guy's kind of straight," she told a man helping her. "But nice."

She bought him a pocket-size computerized date book

that was also a calculator and a clock and could be programmed to beep out certain tones and print messages on its tiny screen for reminders. It cost $216.

"This is great," she said. "He's real big on being on time."

After she sat on the wall near the fountains, the two teenage girls who she had earlier seen chewing the gum were looking toward her as if to get her attention.

"Where'd you get those boots?" one of them asked.

"I think I ordered them from a catalog."

"I love them. I was hoping you'd got them here so I could get me some."

"She couldn't buy them even if you had," her friend said. "She spent all her money on a gold necklace for her boyfriend."

"Well, he said he wanted it."

"She buys him everything," her friend said. "She puts gas in his car. She bought him a set of tires."

"She's just jealous," the girl said. "Do you know what catalog it was?"

"I'm not sure."

"She wants everything she sees," her friend said.

"I do not."

While the girls were talking, Frannie took off the boots and handed them to the girl.

"Here," she said. "Take them."

"What?"

"I want you to have them," she said. "I don't want them anymore."

Frannie walked halfway across the mall in her socks, and

then leaned against a wall to take her socks off. When she met Millie for lunch, she was barefoot and strangely silent and blue.

At six-thirty that evening Jake and Natalie were holding supper for Frannie. She had left a note telling them she would be at the mall with Millie and would be home by six. She left notes now whenever she went out.

"I know I'm late," she said when she got home. "The movie was longer than I thought it would be."

"You went to a movie?"

"Yes."

Natalie served the plates while Jake got the iced tea from the refrigerator. Frannie plopped down in a chair.

"What'd you see?"

"This thing called *Seven Men*. It was really stupid."

"Why'd you see it then?" Jake asked.

"I just did. I didn't have anything else to do."

"You need a job."

"I've talked to some people at the bank," Jake said. "I could arrange an interview."

"Thanks," Frannie said.

"Do you want to work at the bank?" Natalie asked.

"No. Not really."

"Then why go through the interview?"

"I don't know."

"Would you rather work at the mill?"

"I guess."

"It's up to you, Frannie."

"Yeah, well, I'm thinking on it."

"How is Millie?"

"Fine."

"Why are you barefoot?"

"Can't a girl be barefoot on a hot summer day?"

Natalie let it drop and waited until bedtime to talk to her again.

"We're going to bed now," she said through Frannie's door. "Thanks for the gifts. You shouldn't have spent so much."

"I wanted to."

"We're going to read awhile and then go to sleep."

"You don't have to tell me what you do in bed."

"Can I come in?"

"Sure."

Frannie was in an upholstered chair with her legs over one arm and her back against the other. She was still barefoot and her feet were dirty.

"I want you to come to work with me."

"Okay."

"Tomorrow."

"All right."

"You'll do it?"

"I said I would."

Later that night while her sister and Jake whispered in their room, she slipped out the door and sat on the grass in front of the house. She heard a screech owl's mournful call and at the same time heard sirens and traffic and voices in the other direction. Dogs barked. Lights from cars appeared on the road in the distance.

Then it was quiet again, but only for a moment.

The idea of quiet, the sense of it, is something people who've lost it long for. Quiet, though—absolute quiet—is not something one would really want. In the absolute quiet of the absence of sound and in the absolute darkness of a night without light, you lose the sense of who you are and where you are and what you are.

You are lost then, from what you thought you were and where you thought you were. All that remains is what you are at that very moment and often what you are in the absence of what you thought you were when there was sight and sound might not be something you would care to know, or could easily understand.

This idea of silence and of absolute senselessness except the sense of you and only you is another one of those things that seemed like a good idea at first, and then it wasn't.

It was good for Frannie, then, that it was not purely quiet and completely dark because at that time Frannie did not know who she was anymore. Probably, she thought, it was time to be what everyone else thought you ought to be. Probably it was.

Chapter 9

FRANNIE PREPARED FOR the interview at the mill while she and Natalie had breakfast.

"I hope I do well," Frannie said.

"You will."

"I usually don't."

"You will this time."

"Thanks, Nat. I have to remember to keep my mouth shut. I usually say too much. You know how I am when I get nervous."

"You'll do fine. They'll hire anybody."

"That doesn't make me feel any better."

"I mean you will get the job, so relax."

Frannie arrived early and sat in her car in the parking lot looking at the blank walls of the building. There were no windows anymore in the lower floor walls. At one time, she could see by the bricked-up arches, there had been, but none now. Some time in the past, for what reason she did not know, maybe because the people inside spent too much time looking out the windows and dreaming of another life, the windows had been bricked up. But maybe there'd been another reason.

The mill was as old as the town itself, and had been a real cotton mill at first, turning raw cotton into cloth, but now was a packaging mill, receiving bulk goods and repackaging and shipping them out again.

The personnel director's name was Claude Osteen, and Frannie had been wondering what he would be like. She saw him going into his office before it was her time to be interviewed. He had a round face and thin lips and a shirt that seemed too tight for him around his neck and a tie that fit him like a choker. She felt sorry for him.

"He looks like he's real busy," she said to his secretary, trying to make small talk.

"We're all busy."

"I never have minded being busy if I liked what I'm doing," she said, but the woman didn't answer her so Frannie looked through some magazines and felt the buttons on her blouse to be sure they were fastened and arranged herself on the chair the way she'd seen other people do when they tried to look proper and alert.

She sat this same way when she was in his office, trying to look him in the eye and concentrate on what he was saying instead of thinking what a pitiful nervous wreck he seemed to be.

"So, you want to become a part of this family, is that right?"

"Yes, sir, I do," she said.

"Your sister certainly is a wonderful employee."

"I know. She's wonderful at everything she does."

"If I recall," he said, nervously flipping through her application and looking at the pages as if he couldn't find what it was he was looking for, "she went to college, but you didn't, is that right?"

"Yes, sir. She went to Piedmont Community College for two years. I really didn't like school all that much if you want to know the truth."

"And," he said, still looking through the papers but not at her, "you don't have any experience in the type of production we do here. Is that right?"

"Yes, sir, you're right, but I learn fast."

"You learn fast."

He was making her nervous now, and she felt herself starting to go into one of her talking jags.

"Well, I do. I learned to ride a horse in one day. I learned to ride a bicycle the first time I tried it. I can water-ski really good and I learned that in one day. That's the way I am."

"Do you know what we do here?"

"Sort of."

"We package and sew and fold and warehouse certain products."

"Oh."

"Do you know what we package here?"

"Underwear?"

"That's right. Men's briefs, boxer shorts, and things like that, both silk and cotton. We give the market what it wants."

"Yes, sir."

"Tell me about your past jobs," he said, coming back to why she was there.

"Which ones?"

"I see you worked in a photocopy center, two restaurants, an old-age home for two days."

"Well, I had to get out of there. The smell got to me. I'm sorry about that. It's true I only lasted two days, but I'm not going to do that here."

"And you worked at a courier service. Tell me about that."

"I drove all over town. I delivered stuff from one business to another, letters, packages, and things like that. I don't even know what was in them. I might have been delivering dope for all I know," she said and laughed and looked up from her lap to see that he hadn't heard what she'd said and that he had put his head in his hands and covered his face and was rubbing his forehead and temples with his fingertips.

"Are you okay?"

"I'm sorry, Frances. I have a bad headache. Certainly you can have a job here if you want it. Let me call Ethel to help you decide what it is you want to do."

"Maybe you ought to take the day off."

"I can't," he said, suddenly punching in some numbers on his phone line. "Ethel will be here shortly," he said. "It was nice to meet you, Frances. I hope you'll be happy here."

Ethel was a black woman about twenty years older than

Frannie and she wore a scarf around her head and she looked to be about six feet four. They sat across from each other at a table with a wall of snack machines behind them.

"So you're Natalie's sister, huh?"

"Yes, I am."

"Well, how come you want to work here? Didn't she tell you any better than that?"

Frannie saw she had a friend here, and so she said, "Well, I don't want to work anywhere, but I have to. I've got to get some money together and fast. So, here I am."

"Girl, you and me both," Ethel said and then laughed. "You and me and everyone else on this green earth."

"Listen," Frannie said, "do you have to take a drug test here?"

"Not unless you want to."

"How about a lie detector?"

"No, ma'am," Ethel said and laughed. "I've never seen a lie detector machine before. Why?"

"I always wanted to take a lie detector test. I always thought it would be fun."

"You're crazy, girl," Ethel said. "I believe you're going to be fine here. I believe you are."

They walked toward the back. When Ethel opened the door to the work area the noise was so loud Frannie had to lean closer to hear her.

"See those women at that table. That's what you'll be doing if you want the job."

The women were standing at a long table. There were

dividers between each of their spaces. Behind each woman was a large box and in this box were hundreds of briefs or T-shirts. Some of the boxes were men's and some were boys'. The women took an armload to their table and then sewed labels, one by one, to the garments.

After that the garments went into a bin and every few hours someone counted them and each woman received credit for the number sewn. The bins were replaced, and the count began again.

The full bins were dragged to a flat dolly and pulled by one man to another set of women who packed the garments into plastic bags, either three or six to a bag. These went into another bin and they were counted and emptied and these women got credit for their production. It was pay by the piece.

"Do you want to pack or sew labels?"

"Who makes the most?"

"It depends on who goes the fastest without mistakes."

"I'd better pack."

"All right. You can start now as far as I'm concerned. You can take Belle's place. She's on maternity leave."

"You get that here?"

"Are you pregnant?" Ethel asked.

"No, and I don't plan to be."

"Well, then, do you want to start now?"

Frannie looked at the walls and the bricked-up windows and the dusty beams high above on the ceiling. She looked at the fluorescent lights hung by chains from those beams and the dirty wooden floor beneath her that had the tables and the machinery, all painted green, bolted to it so that nothing could move and nothing could tip over and nothing could slide or vibrate out of position, and she took a breath and said "Sure" and with that, she went to work.

Chapter 10

"I'M WORRIED ABOUT her," Natalie said.

She and Jake were out to dinner. They splurged on an expensive meal each week. Jake paid for it one week, and Natalie treated him the next.

"She surely has changed," Jake said.

It was a modern arrangement, of course. In times past the only money most women had was what they got from men. Sometimes there would be a price to pay for this money.

"She hasn't been out at night in I don't know how long."

Whether or not there was a price to pay and whether this price was terrible was a matter of opinion. In the past, the price of poverty and shame was greater than the price most often asked.

"It's been since your mother died."

In times past, land was better than money, and a woman

who had land and the strength to hold on to it was a fortunate woman. Often fathers loved their daughters in a way they were never able to love their wives and left them land and houses. Sometimes even these women lost the land, having become confused about when to use certain words and how to understand strange feelings for which there were, in those times, no words.

"You know I almost started to say she acts like Mom's death was her fault," Natalie said. "But that's not it."

Because women now knew all the words they needed to know and because Natalie knew these words and because she also knew she loved Jake and because Frannie now knew all the words and what they meant except, according to Natalie, what she now knew with Jake, Frannie didn't understand that it was no longer necessary to cling to the house and to the ancestral mandate as if there might be trouble that could not be understood or predicted or overcome.

"I don't know what it is," Jake said. "Is it something to do with your father?"

There were new laws and there were books and there was the testimony of those who had been there before to provide an opening into those moments of clarity and wisdom and caution necessary to prevent the mistakes that followed using certain words at the wrong time.

"I don't think it's even that. She hasn't spoken about him or about finding him since that first week."

Because there now existed in popular thinking a sensible lawful order of how to live and what to say, the importance of caution and history had diminished because the present now held all there was necessary to know.

"Maybe she needs to get out more," Jake said. "You know, get out of the house, get out of herself, get out of her blue mood."

Blue was a color from the past. Modern colors were blended and blurred and they all had new names that never existed before. The new colors seemed to be in motion, while the color blue was still and deep.

"She's doing okay at work," Natalie said. "She's quieter than her usual self but with Frannie that could be a blessing in disguise."

The main course was served. They had driven thirty miles from Silk Hope to eat at a restaurant in Greensboro they had read about. The meal would cost $135 for both of them, including wine and the tip.

Natalie was eating pork chops and rice and asparagus. The chops were dressed up with hats on the ends of the ribs with collars of parsley. The chops were so tiny they must have come from a very young pig. Because farming had ceased on their land by the time she was born, Natalie would never have known how much fun a little pig could be.

"We ought to fix Frannie up with somebody. It might make moving out of the house less traumatic," Jake said.

"I hate we have to sell it."

"I do, too. But it's a fact. And the market is right. Everything says to do it. But I know what you mean, and I don't like having to have been the one to tell you."

"I'd rather it have been you than anyone else. I wouldn't have believed anyone else and then we would have probably lost the place."

Jake was eating a steak with a scoop of mashed potatoes beside it. Surrounding the mashed potatoes were florets of broccoli arranged like a fence. A cow or a steer, in its entire life, never had as much fun as any pig had in any randomly chosen hour of its life.

It was best not to think about these kinds of things while you were eating. It was best, often, not to think at all. Thinking had always been one of Frannie's problems, whereas Natalie accepted what was there and moved on. It had always been this way and it still was, which may have been why, while her sister and Jake masticated politely over conversations of not why things were but what to do about them, Frannie herself sat at home in the dark on the porch in her blue mood and wondered why.

Chapter 11

BY THE LIGHT of a dim moon shining through the branches of the trees, in the shadows, Ted Keller could see a woman sitting alone on the edge of her porch.

Beside him, in the unit of the duplex next door, the old man who had shot the rabbit had his television on loud and when Ted turned off the sound on his own set, he realized he was watching the same show as the man next door.

The woman across the road was singing or talking to herself. When Ted got away from the old man's TV he could hear her better. He could not understand the words and did not know the song. While she sang, she lazily kicked her legs as if she were in a swing above the ground.

The old man coughed and then coughed again. The second time he coughed, he gagged, and Ted could hear him working something up from his throat. It took a long time, and for a few moments it seemed as if the old man would choke.

The woman across the street stopped singing and walked toward the duplex. When she was a few hundred feet from the road, the old man walked out the front door and spit something from his mouth.

Ted saw the woman turn around and start back. She walked a few feet in one direction, and then stopped again and walked off in another. Soon he couldn't see her anymore.

Back inside, he turned off the lights in his own unit and watched out the window. He thought the woman he'd been watching was the younger of the two women who lived there. She seemed like a nice young woman, and he wanted to talk to her, but it had been a long time since he'd talked to a woman except a guard, and his history with women was not good.

It might be best, he had told himself many times, to just forget about them once he got out. The women in his life had caused him a lot of trouble.

From the darkened house he saw the young woman come out into the road from the edge of a field and pick something up from the road and then disappear back into the field.

He watched TV awhile and then went to the bathroom and brushed his teeth and combed his hair and went to his car and started it and then turned it off and went back inside.

He picked up his telephone and put it to his ear. It had only recently been installed and he wasn't sure it was working. He looked through the phone book he'd been sent in the mail but his name wasn't yet in it.

He turned on the yellow porch light and sat in the cool night air, and just as he settled down, the woman appeared in the road.

"Hi," he said, startled that she was suddenly in front of his house.

She continued on without speaking, and he watched her turn into her driveway and go to her house. Soon the lights came on in the rooms and soon after that a car with two people in it turned into the same driveway and drove up.

It was ten-thirty and he could do anything he wanted.

Chapter 12

JUST BEFORE SUNSET Frannie went outside. The house was so empty it made her uneasy. Her mother's room was closed up and neither she nor Natalie had done anything with it since the death. In years past on days like this and all alone in the house or on the land, Frannie had her dog Flash with her, but Flash had died three years ago and she hadn't gotten another dog because she was too busy at the time with being Frannie and being wild and having fun and drinking and running around and driving Nat and her mother crazy with her irreverence, all just like her father, her mother would tell her, meaning it to shame her, though it hadn't.

She went to the barn and closed the door behind her. In a corner near the old milk room was a broom. In the milk room and along one side of the barn was a concrete floor. Her grandfather had a twelve-cow dairy at one time, and state laws after the war mandated concrete floors. The floor was now cracked and covered with straw and dirt.

The straw was dry and the dirt was fine as cake flour. She began to sweep it off the floor and as she did a lazy plume of dust rose in the last light of day coming through the west window. The way it came through the window in the sharply angled rays of the setting sun made Frannie think of pictures of Jesus or the saints or of Mary from Sunday school and how there was always a halo of heavenly light illuminating them.

She stood in the shaft of light with her broom in her hand and looked out the window and closed her eyes and waited for something to happen, for something to come to her, for something to tell her what to do, what to think, how to be, now that everything had changed.

She stood as still as she had in church with her family when she was eight years old and her mother and father were fighting and Christmas was coming and she wanted everything to be peaceful and she wanted them to give her a horse and she believed that morning in church, completely and absolutely, that if she closed her eyes and was devout and pure and went deep enough in her heart and reached God, that everything she was asking for that morning—and they were only things that were right for a child to ask—that everything would come true.

By the first week in December her father had left and there was no horse and Christmas was never the same again.

She must have stood in the old barn longer than she realized because when she opened her eyes, the sun had gone down, and outside there was only the moon to illuminate her path as she returned to the porch and sat on the edge and hung her feet off and swung her legs.

She began to talk to herself and then she began to sing anything that came to her and then she stopped singing because someone across the road had begun to cough so loudly she could hear it all the way to where she was, four or five hundred feet away. As she listened she realized it was the old man who lived alone. Less than a year ago she had seen the old man fall at the mailbox, and as she watched him, he had rolled out of sight into the drainage ditch beside the road. She had run down and helped him and he had shuffled back to his house, the kind of neighbor everyone knew wanted to be left alone.

He was gagging so acutely now that she went to help him, and as she did, he got control of himself while leaning against the outside wall with both hands. After she was sure he was okay, she went across the field to look for the tree she had seen lightning strike the other night.

Lightning struck trees all the time and it was not unusual for a tree to die from it. Fires rarely started from lightning in that part of the state because it was so green and wet most of the time, but she had seen flames this time flicker up from this tree while she watched out her window.

She picked her way around the vines and saplings and fallen limbs until she was where she thought the tree was and found it easily because of the charred splinters on the ground and the dead limbs and dried leaves on the entire half of the tree where the bolt had hit. This tree would soon die and there was nothing she or anyone else could do to save it. She had seen this before. It was not a great loss. It was part of the noble cycle of natural life and death.

It was a sad night for Frannie. She was not sure she was going to like her job. She was bored but did not feel like doing anything or having fun. The party girl was missed in town, and though the people who knew her also knew her mother had died and this explained her absence, they didn't know that all the other sadnesses of her life had caught up with her.

As she came even with the duplex, the porch light on one side of it came on, and the new man who had moved in stepped out and looked at her.

"Hi," she said, but he said nothing and appeared startled by her presence. He had a nice face. His hair was neat and short and he seemed about forty but also, she noticed, as she had noticed on so many other people lately, he seemed sad and worried and afraid of something.

This was what she had begun to see in people's faces when they stopped talking or when they thought no one was looking. The animation and sparkle that she had once thought was there would go out quickly. It is part of everything else going on right now in my life, she thought. The trees are dying, people are sad, and now I am, too, and I don't want to be this way.

Chapter 13

FRANNIE WORKED AT her table. Her legs were tired and her feet were sore from standing on the concrete floor. There were three women to a table and the other two were Linda and Grace. The table was divided into three sections and in front of it were hundreds more and behind it, the same. Everyone was packing, sewing, or checking. One of the tables off to the side was for the two inspectors.

"You're catching on fast," Linda said.

There was a wide aisle between the tables and the conveyor belt. It was up and down this aisle that the men pulled the wagons with the bins as they transported them to the conveyor.

"I never saw anybody catch on so fast," Grace said with a wink at Linda. Earlier they had discussed trying to cheer Frannie up.

"Thanks."

It would have seemed reasonable to have the conveyor closer to the worktables so there would not have to be the extra step of loading the bins onto the wagons and then pulling them to the belt and unloading them, but at this mill, like most small mills in the South, the operations were carried on as if the place might shut down any day, and nothing would change because no money was being invested in the building or the equipment.

"I believe you'll break the record someday," Linda said.

All around her the men were dragging the wagons back and forth and unloading them and the women were sewing and stuffing and talking at the same time.

"Your momma would have been proud of you," Grace said. They had heard about her mother's recent death.

"Thanks," Frannie said.

"What is the record, anyway?" Linda asked.

"About twenty-five hundred," someone behind them said.

"I did eighteen hundred one day," Grace said.

"You did?"

They were all joining in now to help Frannie.

"I did. My wrists and elbows hurt all night when I got home. I won't try that again."

"What's a good count for an average day?" Frannie asked.

"About a thousand."

"How much do you make for a thousand?"

"About sixty dollars."

Suddenly Frannie noticed a change in the sound of the room, as if something had stopped. She looked behind her and saw Mr. Osteen walking down the center aisle. He was looking to his right and to his left as he walked, inspecting each table. As he got to Frannie's table he picked up a canned drink and a pack of crackers and put them on the shelf below with her purse.

"No snacks allowed except at break," he said. "And only in the snack room."

"I'm sorry," she said.

He walked off.

"We should have told you," Grace said.

"I didn't think he'd be coming through today. Ethel doesn't care."

"What's wrong with him?" Frannie asked.

"How wrong? What do you mean?"

"He seems so sad."

"He's not sad," Linda said. "I never thought of him like that."

"Mean, maybe, but not sad."

At lunchtime Frannie wandered off in the opposite direction from everyone else. The women working with her shook their heads and commented on it to one another. She kept going until she was outside on the loading dock and she could see no one else nearby. She ate her sandwich and then rested her head on her drawn-up knees and closed her eyes. After a few minutes she lifted her head and saw a man twenty feet in front of her slowly eating his lunch.

"Don't mind me," he said. "You go ahead and take a nap if you want one."

"How long have you been there?"

"Since before you sat down."

"I never saw you."

"I was right here."

He had only one arm, and when he wanted to use his thermos, he put his sandwich down and slowly drank. Everything he did seemed to be in almost slow motion.

"My name's Reuben, by the way."

"I'm Frannie."

"I know. I've heard about you."

She put her head back down and closed her eyes and saw white lines and red dots all over her lids, and she rubbed her forearms where they were sore from packing. She needed to make much more money than she would ever make here so she could buy her sister's half of the farm, but this would have to do for now.

Across town inside the bank Jake opened the door to a small and narrow hallway, carpeted and quiet. A customer followed him. The door closed behind them by itself. Jake unlocked a door made entirely out of glass except for its handle and hinges.

"Will you be needing the inner room?" he asked politely.

"Yes, I will."

"May I have your key now?"

He used both keys to open the customer's safety deposit

box and then quickly left without glancing toward the customer or trying to see what was in the box.

"Ring the bell when you want out," he said, making sure, as he'd been trained, to meet the customer's eyes and not let his gaze wander toward what was in his or her hands.

Soon the bell on the safety-deposit-room door dinged lightly and briefly. If you had not been trained to listen for it and if you did not know what it meant, you would think it was a telephone that stopped before completing its first ring.

The lid on the box was closed but not thoroughly enough to slide into the slot in the wall.

"Shall I secure this lid, or would you like to do so?"

He asked this rather than merely taking the two seconds to do it himself. In training he'd been taught that his hands were to touch only the bottom and sides of the box, never the lid, except at the customer's request.

"You can do it."

He snapped it into place.

"All right?"

"Sure. Go on and lock it in."

"I'll need your key again."

They went out the glass door. Jake locked it. They continued down the hall.

"Thanks," the customer said.

"Of course. Have a nice day."

The customer started away from him and then stopped. She looked back at him and he very formally and very alertly stood before her waiting to see what she wanted. She took a business card from the holder on his desk and wrote something on the back of it. She gave it to him and walked out. After she was gone he turned the card over and read what she'd written. It said:

Lighten Up

and under it a face was drawn with a big smile. The dot over the *i* had the same smiling face above it.

Frannie looked at her watch and saw she had ten minutes before lunch was over. The man with one arm was watching her, but she said no more to him before going up a steep set of iron stairs to a heavy metal door and opening it into an enormous and empty and dark room.

The room was exactly the same size as the one below where she worked, only it was nearly empty and dimly lit by the few high windows along the sides and the red exit lights at each end. It was a room big enough to have played football in if the ceiling had been higher.

She peered down the vast space and suddenly took off running. She ran so hard and so fast it would have looked to anyone that she was fleeing from something that was out to kill her. She ran so hard she almost fell over from getting ahead of her legs and she slammed into the wall at the other end and rested a minute before she calmly walked back toward the door she had entered. She ran down the stairs where Reuben, the one-armed man who worked in the warehouse, was sitting on a box as if he'd been waiting.

"Come here," he said.

She stopped at the last step.

"Come here."

"Why?"

"See that door over there?" he asked.

"Yeah."

"That's where you're supposed to be. The women from up front aren't supposed to come back here."

"Oh."

"There's a lot of dangerous equipment and it's not safe for you to be back here."

"Oh."

"You're not late yet, you know. You still got two minutes."

"I know."

"Why were you running so hard, then?"

She left without answering. She returned to her table. If she could pack two thousand a day she'd make a hundred and twenty dollars a day or six hundred dollars a week. That would be more like it. She needed to make as much as she could because it was up to her to do what had to be done and there was no one but her to do it.

Chapter 14

JAKE AND HIS mother were in the parlor of their house. His mother had been a schoolteacher until she married his father late in her life and they'd had Jake.

"So you don't need anything at all?" he asked.

His mother stood up. She didn't want to remain seated. It was too hard to get up after sitting a long time.

"I could use my health and good bones and ears that could hear like they used to."

She'd been spry until a few years ago. She'd outlived her husband, and their simple life in their modest home had been well ordered.

"I wish you could have all that."

Jake was their only child.

"Why didn't you bring Natalie?"

"I will, next time."

"And how about her sister?"

"Maybe."

"Why is it that I've never met her?"

"Because you probably wouldn't want to."

"Of course I would."

"She's unpredictable. At least, she has been in the past. Right now I'd just say she's weird."

"How?"

"Depressed. Confused."

"I'd still like to meet her."

"She's wasting her life. She's made a mess of things, and I don't know if she's serious now about growing up."

"She's too young," his mother said, "to declare she's wasting her life. You almost sound like your father with that preachiness."

"I do?"

"You used to hate his lectures. Now you're beginning to sound like him."

"So it goes. Maybe he was right."

"No, he wasn't right. He made a lot of mistakes and that's one of the reasons we have no money. If it weren't for my teacher's pension, I'd be in trouble."

"I hated being poor," Jake said. "That's one thing I always did hate."

"No one likes it."

"I won't ever live like we did, ever again."

"Don't go too far with that," she said.

"I'll be fine. I know what I'm doing."

"Okay, Pop," she said and Jake stared at her to see what she had meant but she merely winked and left the room.

It was Saturday morning. In less than an hour he had to be at Natalie's to go to Hillsborough with her and Frannie. He had a lot to do before then.

While Natalie showered that morning, Frannie went in her mother's room and began to go through old letters and photographs. She came across two pictures of women from the nineteenth century. In one, a woman grimly faced the camera, dressed in a simple black garment with a white scarf wrapped neatly around her neck and tied in a bow at her throat.

In the other, a woman was dressed in a light-colored blouse with puffed sleeves and an ornate collar. She had a happy look on her face, bright eyed and smiling, and she seemed to be revealing something in her wide-eyed delight. Her hair was long and loose and slightly mussed and looked teased by the way it stood out from her head and had such body and fullness.

The woman's hair in the other picture was parted down the middle, pulled tightly, and braided in the back and the braid was wound and pinned off her neck and against the back of her head.

In that picture the woman looked like all the other pictures of women from those times—reserved, hard working, practical, dutiful, and composed—while the woman in the other picture looked free and in possession of some knowledge the first woman had missed. The strange thing about the second woman was that she looked thoroughly modern with her loosely falling, casually combed hair and her delighted and exuberant face.

This struck Frannie as so strange—she had never seen a woman from that far back in a picture who looked the same as pictures today of free-spirited and high-as-a-kite models in magazines—that she turned the pictures over to see who they were and when they were taken. She was shocked to read that the pictures were of the same woman, taken only two years apart, one in 1882 and one in 1884.

She was even further flabbergasted to read the locations of where the pictures were taken. The first, with the somber face, was taken in New Bern, North Carolina, an old city near the coast, while the second, with the happy face, was labeled on its back:

Morehead Asylum for the Female Insane

and then under that was the notation "1884, our beloved Daphne has passed away in the hands of strangers."

Frannie was so in a state of disbelief that she read and reread the names. They were the same. She looked at the faces again and again, and only by careful study could she believe that it was the same person.

The amazing thing was that the woman who had been declared insane and locked away looked like everyone tried to look today. She had the same wide-eyed, exhilarated, and delighted-with-life look that women today often put on when photographed. Her hair could have even passed as trendily fashionable out on the streets today. She appeared expectant, as if something wonderful was about to happen to her, as if she had known the most divine pleasure and was soon to know it again. She looked alert and intelligent and fearlessly open to whatever it was that she would next discover.

And then there she was two years earlier, and it was impossible to guess what this meant, how it came to be, and who it was, and why she had died, and Frannie was so curious she sprang off the floor and ran wild-eyed and looking like this woman to find Natalie to ask her what she knew.

"I do know about it," Natalie said, taking the picture from her and looking at it and nodding. "I do."

"Who is it? Tell me. I'm absolutely crazy to know about this woman."

"Well, wait," Natalie said, "and let me try to say exactly who it is. The relationship, I mean. It's our father's mother's . . . no . . . it's our father's grandmother's aunt."

"What?" Frannie asked. "Who?"

"It's like Dad's great-grandmother's sister. Daphne was her name. Aunt Daphne."

"How do you know this?"

"I know it because Mother and I looked through the pictures once and she told me. Anyway, it says Daphne on the back."

"How come I never knew about this? How come nobody ever told me about her?"

"Well, Frannie," her sister said, brushing out her wet

hair and getting ready to blow dry it, "there are probably dozens or more pictures in all the stacks of Mother's stuff neither you nor I know anything about."

"But not like this. This is extraordinary."

"Why?" Natalie asked and turned the blower on low so she could still talk above it.

"Why? Because look at her. Look at her face. She looks like people look today, not like they looked back then. This is the only picture I've ever seen of a woman from back then who looked like women do today."

"Women don't look like that today."

"They do. We do. We all do."

"You mean the hair?"

"I mean everything. Can't you see it?"

"No, I can't. She was insane, Frannie. She certainly wasn't going to take a regular picture if she was out of her mind."

"But look how happy she is. And how full of life compared to those other pictures."

"Well, you could interpret it that way, I guess, if you wanted to."

"Don't you see, Nat. Don't you get it? There was probably nothing wrong with her except she just didn't fit in. I bet there was nothing wrong with her at all."

"We'll never know, Frannie. We'll just never know."

"Isn't there someone I could ask? Isn't there anyone left who might know?"

"Dad's Aunt Iris might, but she might be dead by now and the last we heard of her she lived in St. Louis."

"Do we have her number?"

"Frannie," Natalie said and turned off the blow dryer so they could speak in a normal tone, "think about this a minute. You're going to call this ninety-something-year-old woman, if she's still alive—"

"Well I'm not going to call her up if she's dead."

"—and after all these years of hearing nothing about us and us only having met her one time that I can remember, you're going to ask her to remember back to this woman and tell you about her."

"She might be able to. She might."

Frannie was so excited she was walking around in a circle like the day she found out her mother had already been buried, going around and around the room while Natalie combed out her hair in front of the mirror, not feeling at all what Frannie was going through.

"I'll try to find the number if you want, but don't get yourself all worked up over something that might go nowhere, though I must say it's great to see some color in your face again, and kind of nice to have the old hyperactive sister back again."

Suddenly Frannie stopped going around and around and sat in a chair and crossed her arms.

"I'm not hyperactive," she said.

"I meant it as a compliment."

"It didn't feel like one."

"I'm sorry. I didn't realize this meant so much to you. I'll look in Mom's address book when we get back. Or you can now. But I can't now because Jake'll be here soon and we've got to leave and I'm not ready yet."

"Where is it?"

"It should be in the drawer beside the bed."

She started out the door and then looked at Natalie a moment and then spoke.

"I love this woman. I love her face. This is what they thought was crazy?"

"But she was, Frannie, or they wouldn't have put her away. It's just a picture. Everything else is what you're reading into it."

"Except it's all there."

"Maybe," Natalie said and turned the blow dryer back on.

Chapter 15

FRANNIE HAD BEEN unable to find the number, and she had gone to the barn when she saw Jake drive up. She watched Natalie come tearing out the door the way she herself had flown from her mother's room after discovering the pictures, and now she watched her leap into his arms. After a few moments of kissing, they gazed toward the barn as if they were trying to discover where she was. Then they went in the house.

From the loft she could see the old hogpens at the corner of the barn. They led outside to an area fenced with wire mesh that her grandfather had built after he stopped dairying. When he was running the dairy, cows were all he had time for, but when he stopped, her grandma had told her, he began to raise his own meat and eggs and sell off the young pigs he didn't want.

Now, Frannie thought, all that remains of their life is about over. Unless I figure out a way to stop the sale by getting the money, somewhere, somehow, and buying it myself.

She heard the door slam. Natalie called. Frannie climbed down the ladder built flush to the side of the wall and got her purse and met them at her car. They were going to Hillsborough for the annual Hog Day, which, though it was a celebration of the hog, was actually a celebration of the dead hog, the hog as meat, the hog as barbecue.

"Let's take my car," Frannie said. "You guys are always taking me everywhere in yours."

"Sure," Jake said.

"Are you okay?" Natalie asked.

"Of course I am. Why wouldn't I be? You think because I had some momentary wild idea about those pictures that I wouldn't be? Is that what you think?"

"I wasn't sure," she said and looked at Jake.

Obviously, they'd been talking, but Frannie didn't feel like giving them the opportunity to question her.

"I can't wait to get there. I loved it last year. I hope they have the pig races. And the biggest hog contest. Isn't that great? And the food'll be great and I've skipped breakfast and I'm starving. Do you want to stay the whole day? I mean, how long are we going for?" she asked.

As she drove, she watched Jake's face to see what he was thinking about what Natalie must have told him and wondered, too, how she'd portrayed her wild-eyed enthusiasm.

Probably, she thought, like the woman in the picture, probably like that.

Well, she thought, I am like that.

Jake and Natalie, however, talked about houses they'd seen for sale in town. She tried not to listen, tried even harder not to say anything about how she felt about them selling the farm and moving to town. Later, when she was ready, would be her time for talking.

They parked in the big dirt lot near the livestock area. There were live hogs in attendance and big hogs won prizes for being big though the big ones didn't make good barbecue at that size because they were too fatty and were sent off later, after winning the prizes, to be turned into sausage and lard.

There were pigs who won prizes for cutest or loudest but the biggest prize money went to the people who'd killed and cooked the best dead hog. The money went posthumously to the hog reincarnated as barbecue.

"Why don't we go our separate ways and meet back here at the car in three hours. Okay?" Frannie asked.

She went to the live hog exhibits. She studied a program and then studied the hogs. The hogs were not submissively hanging their heads and waiting to be told what to do like cows. They were trying to decide how to get away from where they were and they were digging in the dirt and talking to each other and pushing each other out of the way and lying in water troughs and standing in the middle of feed they'd spilled so no one else could get to eat it and pushing on gates to determine if they would open and darting away in short speedy sprints toward one another, generally having a good time, which was sad, because as intelligent as they were, they hadn't figured out that the smell in the air was their slaughtered cousins and aunts and uncles and nephews and nieces, which proved no matter how smart you were, no matter how happy you might be, you never knew just who it was and what it was and when it was that someone was planning to end your life.

"Hi, pigs," Frannie said to a group of them.

"Them pigs is mean."

Frannie didn't answer the woman who'd spoken.

"Them pigs'll bite your fingers off."

Frannie looked at her. Judging from her size and appearance, she thought, someone at some point in her family history must have crossbred with a hog.

"Are these your pigs?"

"All of them in that corral is mine."

"These little ones here?"

"All of them."

"Are they weaned?"

"Yep."

"How old are they?"

"Six weeks."

"You mean they wean off after six weeks?"

"You got to wean them off yourself. They'd keep suckling the rest of their lives if you didn't."

Frannie stuck her finger near one and let it bite her.

"They will bite you to kind of taste you," the woman

said, "but they won't generally bite your finger off. I was just teasing you."

"Do they really get mean?" Frannie asked.

"A big one'll get mean sometimes."

"Are they hungry?"

"I reckon."

"Can I feed them something?"

"Like what?"

"A hot dog or a biscuit. Something like that."

"If you want to. It seems like a waste, though."

Frannie bought some biscuits and threw them to the hogs. The huge old woman rushed the fence as if she was going to jump in with the hogs.

Frannie walked past the pens of various size hogs and watched the people nearby in chairs brought from their farms along with coolers and feed bags and scoops and shovels and radios. Some of them were listening to music, and some were just staring ahead or sleeping.

At one pen she watched a girl brushing a pig. She talked to this pig and the pig made a sound now and again that seemed like an answer.

Behind her on two fold-up lounge chairs were the girl's father and mother. While their daughter worked, they looked at each other and shook their heads in sweet affection and held hands and then closed their eyes and rested in the cool of the shady tent.

The scene of this family touched Frannie, and she thought, This is what I want. Of course it is. Why has it taken me so long to figure it out? Why? Why have I run around like a crazy person these last three years of my life when everything I wanted was right there?

She saw a man who would have been about her father's age standing by himself looking at the animals. He seemed sad, and Frannie wondered if that was how her father looked after he had run away. She felt drawn to the man, but she did not go to him. She did not want to be sad today.

Across the way, she could hear laughter and an insistent voice over a loudspeaker. She saw some large sows and one boar. The boar had testicles the size of cantaloupes, which was how she knew it was a boar. Otherwise, he looked the same as the big sows.

"Ride one of these here monster-size hogs and stay on a full minute and you win two hundred dollars," the man called to the people around the fence.

Some teenage boys were lined up to try. It cost five dollars a try and the sign said the money went to the county 4-H clubs. Each time one of the boys leaped on the back of the sow she would take off so fast he rolled over backward into the muck and manure and straw.

Frannie thought about the two hundred dollars. She needed all the money she could get. She got in line. Then she thought, a mouth full of manure would not be too great.

There were only three things you could hold on to. Two ears and a tail. The hair was too short. The neck didn't exist. The bellies were too fat to lock your legs around. It seemed to Frannie she would have to straddle the shoulders and hold on to the ears.

"Next."

It was her turn. She was wearing a skirt, but so what, she thought. Let them have a good show if that's what they want. She removed her shoes but left on her socks.

"This little gal's got something in mind," the announcer said. "I sure do hope she don't go over backward with that little short skirt on," he said, causing the crowd to cheer and hoot.

She approached the hog and stopped in front of it.

"Hi there, old buddy. Old girl," she said.

The sow, which weighed about 600 pounds to Frannie's 120, bobbed its head at her and sniffed the air and circled away.

"I'm not going to hurt you."

"Folks," the announcer said, "this little lady's going to have a woman-to-woman talk with that old sow."

She slowly kept after the animal and followed it around the pen while talking quietly until she was able to get close enough to pet it. She rubbed it behind its ears and scratched its bristly back and slapped the flies away from its eyes and then slowly leaned over it and put her weight partly against its back.

"I believe she's using horse-breaking tactics," the announcer said. "We ain't got all day, little lady. You got to make your move soon."

Frannie kept rubbing it and talking to it while she tried to decide how to get on.

"We ain't got time for you to develop a relationship with that old piece of lard," he said.

People began to clap and hoot and chant at Frannie, so she thought she'd climb on and hope for the best.

"Uh-oh," the announcer said as the hog stood still for the first ten of the sixty seconds she had to stay on. "She's about done done it."

Then the sow took off and reached full speed faster than a sprinter in an Olympic race. Frannie leaned forward and locked her arms around what passed for a neck and began to be thrown around like a rag. The sow was going so fast Frannie seemed to rise in the air off her back as if she were a scarf trailing in the wind behind a thoroughbred at full gallop.

"Look out, there, gal," the announcer called out.

The sow made a sudden turn and Frannie somehow made the turn along with her but her skirt kept going straight and ended up around her waist and just as she made the decision to drop off when she could find a safe way to do it to keep from being humiliated any more than she'd already been, the announcer rang a bell and two men rushed out on foot and drove the sow into a corner and helped her off.

"By golly, she did it," the announcer said, "and gave us old men some sweet dreams, to boot."

After she received her money and brushed the bristles off her skirt and threw her socks in the trash and put her shoes back on, she saw Jake and Natalie coming toward her.

"Oh, Frannie, it was awful."

"You made a fool of yourself," Jake said.

"You make a fool of yourself every time you open your mouth," Frannie told him.

"I'm glad your mother isn't here to see this," he said.

"You leave her out of this."

"You could have been hurt. Really hurt," Natalie said.

"You just keep him away from me or he's going to be hurt," she told her, all the while halfway wishing she hadn't done it, but certainly not going to admit that to them.

"I'm sorry," Jake said after Natalie gave him an imploring look. "I was just worried about you."

"I can take care of myself."

"Do you want to go home now?"

"No. I want to stay the whole day."

"Well, we don't," Jake said.

"Murray and Cindy'll take us home later," Natalie said. "We'll just go with them. They're right over there."

After they left, Frannie noticed a strange-acting man following her. He hung back but stayed with her no matter where she stopped or what she did. Finally she looked him in the eye until he backed off and went away.

I swear, she thought, I attract them. Like flies to honey. I always have.

Back at the judging tent, she noticed a different woman had taken the enormous woman's place.

"Are you with these pigs?"

"Yep."

"I was talking to your mother or grandmother about them a while ago."

"They're good pigs."

"Are they healthy? I mean, do pigs get sick?"

"Sometimes they do, but not like horses or sheep or anything."

"What are they doing here? Why'd you bring them?"

"They give a prize for the best litter under fifty pounds. We entered, but we didn't win. But that doesn't make them worth any less."

"What's going to happen to them when you take them back?"

"Daddy'll raise them up to top hog size and sell them."

"For what?"

"I don't know how much he'll get for them. The prices at the market change. Two or three times a day sometimes."

"Oh."

"We just take them over and get what we're handed. That's the way it is on a farm. You can't set your own price."

"I see."

"How come you're so curious?"

"I was thinking of going into farming someday. Soon."

"Do you have land?"

"A little."

"Farming's pretty much of a hobby these days, my daddy says. He works at the furniture plant full-time just to be able to farm."

"I was thinking about doing it for fun."

"Uh-huh."

"That's why I've been asking about pigs."

"I see."

"You could just raise them up for yourself, right?"

"Sure. The meat tastes better if you raise your own. They

put some kind of preservative in them at the grocery stores that makes the meat taste like formaldehyde."

"How much would one of those pigs cost?"

"About seventy-five dollars. Feeder pigs are high now."

"Would you sell me three of them for two hundred?"

"I don't know if I could. Daddy said I could sell them if anyone offered, but I don't know if I could cut the price."

"It's all I've got."

"I just don't know."

Frannie pulled out the two one-hundred-dollar bills and held them out to her. "It really is all I've got," she said.

"Oh. Cash. Well, that's different. We love cash. Pick out any three you want and back your truck up and you'll be in business."

"I want the friendliest."

"The friendliest?"

"I want them to like each other."

"Well, I suppose they do. That black-and-white one's a good one."

"Okay. Do you have anything to put them in?"

"Like what?"

"A box."

"A box? Listen, they'd eat up a cardboard box in ten seconds if we stuffed them inside it."

"A wooden one?"

"I don't have anything like that. We haul them in that trailer."

"Can you haul them for me?"

"I suppose Daddy would, but he'd charge you for it.

He'd have to. And he won't be back until late this evening."

"How much would he charge?"

"How far away are you?"

"About an hour's drive."

"I don't think he'd go that far unless you'd be willing to pay him pretty well."

"Is there anyone else who might do it? Cheap?"

"Probably."

"Do they take a nap this time of day?"

"They sleep off and on all the time."

"Maybe we could get them while they're asleep and ride them home in my car and get there before they wake up."

The woman looked at Frannie as if she was crazy.

"I don't think that would work," she said.

"Well, I've got to do something."

"What kind of car do you drive?"

"A Chevrolet."

"That won't do."

"Could we put them in the trunk?"

"I guess."

"What about air?"

"You'll have to leave the lid halfway open."

"How long would I have?"

"Before what?"

"They suffocate."

"Just keep some air circulating and you'll be fine."

"Would you help me load them?"

"Sure."

Two men from nearby helped. They herded the pigs toward the women and Frannie caught one by the back leg and cradled it against her. The woman caught another by the back leg and carried it to the trunk of the car.

"I think we better get the other one caught and ready," she told the men, "and put them in all at once. If we open it back up to shove the third one in, they'll all get out."

"You're hauling them in that?"

"I sure am, unless you want to haul them for me," Frannie said.

"I wish I could, but I can't."

They caught the last one and Frannie closed the lid against a rag doubled up over the latch to allow air to enter. She squeezed the rag between the lid and the latch, and then tied the lid to the bumper.

"Just don't put your good luggage in there anytime too soon," one of the men said, and he and his friend laughed and shook their heads.

"Yeah, I don't think those pigs is toilet trained yet," his friend said.

"You better get going. The sooner you get there, the better."

"Okay. I forgot to ask you, though, are they boys or girls?"

"I didn't look, but the most they'd be would be girls and ex-boys."

"Ex-boys? Oh. I get it."

Frannie had a nice drive on a two-lane country road through two small towns. When she came to the second town she realized she hadn't eaten lunch and went to a fast-food restaurant and bought four hamburgers and a bag of fries. She ate one of the hamburgers and then unwrapped the other three. As she did, she noticed two women looking from her to her car.

Curious, huh? she said to herself.

The women were at an outdoor concrete table under a molded plastic umbrella near the back of her parked car.

"Hi," Frannie said.

The women leaned toward each other and looked at her car.

"Nice day," Frannie said and began to slip the hamburgers one by one, into the trunk.

"I got my sister's children back there," she told the women. "I told them if they didn't shut up and quit fighting I was going to make them ride the whole way back in the trunk."

The women looked at her sternly.

"You know how children are. You have to get firm with them now and again."

Frannie spoke into the trunk.

"That's all you're going to get until we get home. And don't make a mess."

The two women stood up.

"Hell, don't worry yourself about it," Frannie said. "Them kids are just a bunch of pigs anyway. Those hamburgers'll keep them until we get home."

They looked around to see if anyone else had heard and would do something about it.

"I'm going to wear their little bottoms out when I get

them back," Frannie said, leaning out the window as she drove off. "I didn't want to baby-sit for them in the first place. They all act like that pig of a man my sister married."

Then she cackled loudly, like a wicked witch, and as she bumped onto the road the pigs began to fight over the food and squealed and shrieked loud enough for everyone to hear.

She had just begun to think about what Jake and Natalie would say when she heard a siren and saw a police car closing in. She realized he wanted her to pull over. He stopped his car far back from hers and walked slowly toward her as she prepared to get out.

"Stay where you are, ma'am," he said. "Stay in your car."

She saw him leaning toward her trunk and listening to the sounds from within.

"I can explain this."

"Ma'am, we received a report that you had children in the trunk of your car."

Oh, Lord, she thought. They believed me.

"I don't."

"Would you open it up, please ma'am."

"I can't."

"Why is that?"

"Because I've got pigs in there, and if I open it, they'll jump out."

"I need you to open it up, ma'am. I have to see what's in there."

"But it's just pigs. I bought them at Hog Day. Can't you hear them?"

His backup arrived.

"She says it's pigs in there."

"Let's see what you got," she said. She had sergeant's stripes and assumed command.

"Okay, but wait. I'll untie the trunk lid and I'll raise it a bit, and you can see what's in there, but don't make me open it all the way up or they'll jump out."

The pigs backed toward the rear of the trunk as both officers shined their flashlights into the space and made the three pair of eyes inside glow.

"Ma'am, how come you're hauling pigs in the trunk of your car?"

"It's the only way I can get them home."

"Have you got a sales receipt?"

"No, I don't."

"May I see your driver's license, please."

She gave it to her and the woman radioed it in and then came back.

"There's nothing on her," she said.

"It's really a job for the animal-control officer," he said.

"Listen," Frannie said. "They're okay. They really are. Look at them. And I just live thirty minutes from here."

"Let her go," the first cop said. "She needs to get them where they're going before they turn to lard."

She'd gone less than a mile when without warning the snout of two pigs appeared under the bottom of the rear seat. Then the pigs lifted the back of the seat off its brackets and tossed it onto the floor. All three burst from the trunk into the car itself.

"OH, NO!" Frannie screamed as the pigs spilled into the car and began to leap around.

"NO, PIGS. GET DOWN!" she yelled as they repeatedly jumped at the glass, trying to get out.

One then leaped into the front. It lunged at the windshield and at the side windows. The ones in the back continued to crash about and then they all began to leap from the front to the back. One would leap into the front and then once there would leap to the back again and then two would tumble over the front and then at times all three would be in front with Frannie, crashing against her legs and tangling with the pedals and running over her lap.

It seemed to Frannie she had a thousand pigs inside the car with her.

She looked for a spot on the shoulder to pull over. Finally she drove into the shade and turned off the engine.

"DAMN!" she screamed.

She didn't know what to do. For a moment, when the car stopped the pigs stopped, too, but then they began to lunge back and forth, still trying to get out, which made Frannie realize she did not dare open the door for fear the pigs would follow her out.

"OH, HELP," she yelled to no one. The few cars passing by on the country road couldn't have seen what was going on in the car from where she had parked.

"STOP!" she yelled and shoved the pigs off as they tumbled against her.

"IN THE TRUNK," she screamed and began to fight

with them to throw them back through the opening they had made in the thin partition.

"GET IN THERE, DAMN YOU!" she yelled as she tried to catch them.

It seemed impossible. The more she cornered them the more frantic they became. She did shove one into the trunk but as soon as she let it go to get another, it raced back out.

"AHHHHH!"

The backseat was punctured and ripped. She peered into the front to see what it was like and what the pigs were doing and saw them on the floor, two on the passenger side and one in among the pedals, looking at her with explosive expectancy.

As she lowered herself into the front, the pig at the pedals leaped over the hump in the floor and landed on the others and they were off. They flew about the car like projectiles shot from rubber bands, and Frannie shut her eyes and held on.

Natalie saw the car before Jake or their friends saw it.

"Look," she said. "It's Frannie."

"Pull over."

"I think there's someone with her," Cindy said.

"My God," Jake said. "There're pigs in there."

"No."

"She's gone too far this time," Jake said. Murray pulled over. Natalie ran to Frannie, who had seen her coming.

"Help," she said. "Help me."

"What's going on?"

She rolled the window down an inch.

"I bought these pigs. I didn't have any way to get them home so I put them in the trunk, but they got out."

"You did what?" Jake asked.

"It's none of your business."

"We're selling the farm, Frannie. You do understand that?"

"I'm not talking to you," she said.

Unexpectedly, while they talked, the pigs settled down in the backseat and watched the humans as if they, themselves, were interested in what was being said.

"I don't understand," Natalie said.

"Just help me get them back into the trunk."

"How? I mean, what can we do?"

"Open the door carefully and help me get them pushed back in. Just don't let them rush out past you."

Jake pulled Natalie to one side and they had a talk.

"Hi," Frannie said and waved weakly and apologetically to Murray and Cindy.

"Jake and I don't think you ought to be allowed to take them home."

"I'm going to."

"You need to take them back where you got them."

"I can't. I bought them."

"You can't bring them home. Jake says there're zoning laws that forbid keeping livestock in the city limits."

"Look, we have a farm. There's plenty of room."

"It's against city regulations," Jake said. "I know it for a fact."

"Fuck your facts," Frannie said.

"Stop it, Frannie."

"I'm taking them home."

"You can't."

"I am."

She put the car in gear and drove off. The pigs began to jump about again.

"Let's follow her," Jake said.

"I don't want to," Natalie said. "I don't even want to see it. She's going to wreck."

"We could get home first and prevent her from releasing them."

"No."

"Okay. She's your sister," he said.

"She sure is, but I don't know what to do with her."

Frannie was chastened on the way home, and eventually the pigs became quiet. It was as if a terrible wrestling match had ended, or a screaming match that left everyone exhausted.

One pig had found a catalog and seemed to be looking at it, turning its pages with its snout.

Another had discovered a plastic Coke bottle with the cap on. It had the bottle between its hooves and was trying to eat the cap off. It tilted it up now and then while looking out the window at something that caught its eye.

The third pig had sniffed up an old pair of Frannie's jeans and had them around its neck like a shirt. It grunted and the other pigs looked at it and grunted back as if giving their opinions on how it looked.

Though Frannie was still embarrassed while talking to Jake and Natalie later that evening, she didn't feel weakened enough to let him run over her like he seemed to be doing to her sister, and after a few minutes of keeping herself under control, she let him have it.

"You don't tell me what to do," she said.

"You have no choice," he told her.

"What do you mean, no choice?"

"I mean you have no choice under the law, and in light of the fact that you and your sister are financially obligated, unless you ignore the facts, to sell this place now, rather than later, after you've lost all your money trying to keep it. The yearly taxes on it are now forty-six hundred dollars."

"Let me tell you something, Mr. Man," Frannie said. "First off, you—you understand who I'm talking about? You, standing there in front of me—don't have anything to say about this matter one way or the other. You're just a guy in pants who wears a tie and works in a bank and you don't have crap to say about what I do in my life. Or for that matter, Natalie's either."

"He does so."

"Just because she sleeps with you doesn't mean you can tell me or her what we can do and you'll find out after you marry her that neither one of us likes to be pushed around."

"You don't know what you're saying."

"Just because you're some little man clerk at some little bank in a mall doesn't mean you have the right to make decisions for me, got it?"

"He has whatever right I give him in this matter," Natalie said. "And he knows far more about this than we do."

"He doesn't know anything."

"Frannie, listen," he said, being as calm as he could be. "If you'll look at the figures, you will see. There's no need for anger or recrimination. I love both of you, and . . ."

"You keep that baloney for someone else," she said. "It's New Age business bullshit talk and it won't wash with me. This place is mine. It's ours. It's me and Nat's and that's the way it is supposed to be and that's the way it always will be."

"Frannie, listen," she said. "That will was drawn up in a time when things were different. When women didn't have laws to protect them like we do. It means nothing now. Nothing. It's not important now."

"You're not thinking clearly," Jake said. "You're thinking with your emotions rather than with your head, and that's going to have destructive and wasteful consequences."

"You get out of here. You get out of my house right now. I'm tired of listening to you. Get out!"

"I'm trying to help you," he said, refusing to be drawn into the fight.

"Get him out, Nat," she said.

"It might be best to leave. Let me and her talk awhile. Okay?"

"Sure, I'll leave. But remember the things we've discussed. We've got to stand together on this, sweetheart. It's important to our life."

"I know what you're saying. I understand. But let me talk with her."

"You don't have to ask his permission to talk with me," Frannie said. "Just tell him to clear out."

"And Natalie doesn't need you to tell her when to talk to me," Jake said. "You got that?"

"Both of you, stop it," Natalie said. "I'll talk to whoever I want to when I want to."

"See," Frannie said to Jake and made an ugly face at him. "I win. You lose."

After he left, the two women stared at each other a few moments and then Natalie took Frannie by the hand and they went into the den.

"Reason must prevail here. It really must," she said.

"That sounds like him," Frannie said.

"It's me and it's common sense and it's right."

"Nope. It's him. It's his words and he's wrong and I won't listen to it."

"Well, what or who will you listen to? Tell me that. If not me, then who?"

"I'll listen to you. I'll always listen to you, but not when you use his words."

"We're right, Frannie. We happen to be right."

"You happen to be wrong, and I won't let you sell it, and that's all I'll say about it."

"Don't walk out on me," Natalie said.

Frannie stormed into her room and took the picture of the woman who had died in the asylum and studied it and then looked at herself in the mirror and made her face resemble the expressions in the photographs, first as Daphne was in the world, grim and determined and dutiful, and then boundlessly happy and intimate with bliss.

"You don't look like her," Natalie said from the doorway. "Not at all."

After supper Frannie checked on her pigs. In the beam of her flashlight she saw them sleeping against one another. She noticed they had been in the water trough and that it was still half full. When she was satisfied they were all right, she climbed into the loft and peered down at them in the weak yellow light. In that light everything beneath her looked comforting and familiar.

Yellow is often meant to be the color of fear within, of being afraid. It is also the color of warmth, of fire, of the tips of flames as well as the color of wheat, the color of work and of thoughtfulness and of good sense played out in the pattern of the field, in the color of the grass, in the color of the grain in the bin.

That yellow that had resembled the color of virtuous labor was not the new yellow we saw today, the fluorescent yellow of slick excitement. The absence now of that true color was compelling and unavoidable in much the way the swollen belly of an unmarried woman with child would have been in the time of Frannie's ancestors.

The daughter of the old man, whose clothes had been stolen and along with them all that he'd chosen as belief, had lived on the farm next to Frannie's land and had become pregnant by her sister's husband. Rather than betray him to her sister, thus betraying herself as well, she left home and took up as a maid in a distant town.

A woman alone in the world in those days was without advocate and one who had shamed herself was even more so and was vulnerable to the whims and urgencies and proclamations of men and other women.

Once shamed and once scorned, a woman then had no choice but to accept whatever was offered, and this woman, the daughter of the man who went mad himself, accepted the offer of a man who would take her in, who would marry her, even with child.

The farm, then, next to Frannie's, was not a good-luck farm as hers had been, and it failed in much the same way that people themselves fail, through confusion and madness and mistakes, its fields sown with sorrow and despair.

The farm, then, lacked the strength of Frannie's farm, and it now lay undeveloped and fallow and barren as the scraped insides of a woman once shamed. At night, alone on that farm, at the old homesite, a young woman from modern times, a strong young woman, even, would not have to know the history of that place to feel afraid.

A woman like Frannie, having walked through the woods at night and stood in the middle of the clearing among the weeds and shadows of empty sheds and fallen houses, would not have to be ashamed of being afraid where she stood. It was all still there, and even though the laws were on the books and even though the words were now precise and dazzling, the mistakes and confusion were as bewilderingly common as ever.

Chapter 16

TED WALKED OUT the door of his duplex. It was swollen from the humidity and it wouldn't close without slamming but he did not want to make that much noise late at night.

Sudden sounds and unexpected movement disturbed Ted. Now that he was free, he wanted things peaceful and smooth. He was startled that night when the screen cracked like a whip as the door swung toward him. He thought for a moment he had stepped into a trap.

He looked at the moonless sky and up and down the road and then crossed to Frannie and Natalie's neatly mowed yard. He had watched Frannie mow it that afternoon. The grass was soft beneath his bare feet.

There were two lights on in the house, in Frannie's dead mother's house, in her ancestors' house, in the house where women would always have their own place regardless of what the men in their life did or didn't do, regardless of what the world was like or wasn't like, regardless of mistakes they themselves made or didn't make. This house would be there for them.

There was sanctuary in such a house, in such a home. There was the strength of history in it, of the history of these women, and of their strength as it survived.

The sanctity of a home was more than the latch on the double-hung windows, more than the cogs that held the storm sashes in place, more than the mortised locks, more than the dead bolts, more than the rifles in the glass case left by the men of these women, more than the ancestors' six shooters stored in the attic, more than the telephone beside the bed, more sanctified than even the quiet of the countryside and the steady breath of people sleeping, of women and children unprotected except by this house.

The sanctity of the house was more than all the secure elements of a cool night with conditioned air tumbling through ductwork braced against joists cut from trees that had known their own sanctity and had been cut by men who knew right from wrong when it had been easier to know it, knew it better than it was known now by far, better than it was known to Ted as he walked barefoot toward this sanctuary, and paused in the field to think.

Chapter 17

FRANNIE FED HER pigs early. She had to be at the mill a half hour before Natalie.

"How are they?" Natalie asked.

"They're doing okay. Jessie's kind of depressed. I think he's starting to fall in love and just realized he doesn't have the equipment any more to do anything about it."

"You call him Jessie?"

She'd had the pigs a month. Natalie had not talked with her about getting rid of them again, and she had made Jake promise to let it go and deal with it later.

"Yeah."

"I didn't know that. I saw Millie, by the way."

"You saw Millie? What'd she say?"

"She wondered why you never call her anymore. She said

she's called you, but you never seem to want to do anything."

"I need to get up with her."

Frannie parked her car. She was almost late. A man was sitting in a car in a reserved space and his door was open, but he was in the seat with his hands on the steering wheel, and as she got closer she could see his face was on the top of the steering wheel between his hands and he was biting it.

"Good morning, Mr. Osteen."

He lifted his head and closed his lips over his teeth and then rubbed them with his fingers before he spoke.

"Good morning, Frances."

"Is everything okay?"

"Yes, it is. And you?"

"Fine. Just fine."

From the warehouse door she could see Reuben. As she left Mr. Osteen to go in the side door where the production workers entered, she looked back and Reuben was still there.

"What are you looking at?"

"You," he said.

She went inside. Linda was waiting for her. She was agitated and seemed to have been there a long time, which was odd for her, as she was often late.

"I'm in trouble," she said.

Frannie put her lunch on the shelf below her table and looked around. The other women nearby weren't at their tables yet.

"What's wrong?"

"They've got me for something."

"Who? Who's got you for what?"

"Management. They've got me for taking home the product."

"What product? I don't understand."

"For taking home briefs and T-shirts."

"Have you been doing that?"

"I guess."

"For how long?"

"I don't know," Linda said. "I just take a few each day. To sell. A girl's got to do what she's got to do."

"It's okay with me. It's not what I'm into, but I understand."

"I was on my way out yesterday when they stopped me and found the stuff. I'm in big trouble."

"Can I do anything?"

"Yeah. I want you to come to the meeting and tell them you've never seen me do it before and you work right beside me all day. Tell them if I did happen to have some, it must have been just that one time."

"Sure."

"I'll make it up to you. Whatever you miss on your count. I'll load into your bin for however long you take off when you speak for me."

"Forget it. I'll do it for you for nothing."

The meeting was for late afternoon. Frannie worked hard all morning. At lunch she ignored the sign that said the abandoned second-floor warehouse space was off limits due to insurance regulations and went there to eat and be alone. She had not been up there in weeks and most days ate with the other women. Today she didn't feel like company and wanted to close her eyes and get away from the noise and clamor and constant talk that would not have stopped even at lunch if she'd stayed below.

She leaned against what looked like a large dormer constructed on the floor and against the inside of the wall, which had, where a window would have been, a double door. She ate slowly. She was trying not to add anything into the soup of thoughts she was already cooking all the time.

About the time she was finished with her lunch she heard the freight elevator stop and saw the accordion metal door pushed back and watched a man get off.

Great, she thought. Now what?

"Hi," he said.

"Hello."

"I saw you come up here. I was waiting until I thought you'd be finished eating."

"Uh-huh."

"Do you mind if I sit down?"

"I was planning on eating alone."

"Is that right?"

"Yeah. That's right."

"I always did kind of think it was strange to see a woman eating alone."

"Yeah?"

"You know, in a restaurant or something."

"This isn't a restaurant," she said, not able to come up

with anything else and unable to make any sense out of where he was heading.

"No, it sure isn't."

He stared at her and she thought, Why me? Why do they always choose me?

"I know you," he finally said. "You don't remember me, I guess."

She looked at him carefully.

"I don't know you."

"Sure you do."

"No, sir, I am afraid you're mistaken."

"Not a chance," he said. "I used to see you when you hung out at the Lone Pine."

Oh, Lord, she thought. Is it possible?

"Oh, yeah?"

"I sure did," he said. "You never did go out with me though."

Thank God.

"But you did with my good buddy Donnie."

"I am sure I don't remember."

"You did. You got to remember him."

"Listen, mister. I don't remember you and I don't remember him. Okay? I'm eating now. Can you see that?"

"I think you do remember. Him, for sure."

She didn't answer.

"And probably me. We've talked a long time before. A bunch of us sitting around together."

"You got me mixed up with someone else."

"Nope. I know all about you," he said, and the way he

said it caused Frannie to realize it was time to put her sandwich down and get off the floor and stand up level with him.

"Listen, whoever you are. I may have been there a few times, but I sure as hell don't remember you so why don't you just go back downstairs and do whatever it is you do."

"I thought you might want a little company."

"I don't."

"You know, Donnie sure did speak highly of you. Very highly."

She knew how to talk to men like this, but she also knew them well enough to be afraid of what could occur when a woman used the word no with them.

"That's nice," she said, "but whatever it is you're thinking is not what I'm thinking so why don't you just think yourself out of here."

"Sure. Okay. I just thought I'd come see if you remembered me. Maybe someday we can get together."

"I doubt it."

"Too good for me?"

"Forget it, buddy. Just forget it."

"Well, then, go to hell, bitch."

As he said that, Reuben stepped out from the stairway entrance.

"Go back downstairs, George," he said. "You know better than to be up here."

"What about her?"

"She doesn't work in my department."

"Hell. Why don't you mind your own business. This isn't none of your affair."

"Your business is my business as long as you work in my warehouse."

"Okay, boss man. Whatever you say. She sure ain't worth losing a job over."

He left and Frannie slowly sat back down.

"Kind of ruins a gal's lunch," she said.

"I'm sorry about that. Of course, you know you shouldn't be here."

"I'm not hurting anything."

"True."

"But thanks. Thanks for running him off. I appreciate it."

"He won't bother you."

"You look like you could tear him up even if you do have only one arm."

"My one arm serves me well."

"If you only have one arm I guess it about gets to be as strong as two."

"Maybe."

"Would you like to join me?"

"Downstairs I would. It's nice and cool out on the dock."

"You really don't want me up here?"

"No. It's not a good idea. If someone from management catches us, it wouldn't look good."

"You're not management?"

"A warehouse foreman is not management."

"Right."

"Do you want to go down now? I left my lunch out there when I saw George sneaking up."

"Nah. I'll just come down later."

"It's your life, Frannie."

"I've been told that before."

"I guess I should have said it's your job."

"Yeah. I guess I better think about that."

"I won't say anything. But you better not let Osteen or Bosco catch you up here. Unless you think your sister could help you out."

"I'll be careful."

He left and she settled back down to eat, leaning against the door and gradually becoming more relaxed. She ate slowly and then stretched her legs out in front of her and stretched her whole body as if she were just waking up and when she did, she pushed too hard against the door behind her and it opened inward.

As it fell open she tumbled back into the opening that led, like a covered and terrifying sliding board in a house of horrors, down to the warehouse below. She slowly rolled head over heels and then slid on her side until she shot out of a passage covered by a dusty curtain right onto the floor of the dock in front of Reuben.

"Forget it," she said when he came over to her. "Don't ask," she said and started walking off. "I'm fine—okay? Just fine."

She wasn't hurt but she was so embarrassed her face was as pink as if she'd slapped herself.

"I didn't do that on purpose," she said, still walking away. "Don't get that in your head, you durn fool."

Back at work Linda asked her what happened.

"I fell in a pile of dust in the warehouse."

"Is that where you were eating?"

"Yeah."

"You should have eaten with us."

"You're telling me."

"That stuff is in your hair, and your jeans are ripped."

"Oh, Lord."

"Go clean up."

"I will if I can find Ethel to get permission."

"Do it anyway."

"I don't want to get marked down for leaving my station at the wrong time."

"You better get cleaned up before we go to the meeting. And pin that hole shut if you can. You can see your butt right through it."

"I'll do something."

The other women returned.

"What happened to you?"

"I fell into something."

"You better watch out," one of them said, "going back in there with all those men."

"I wasn't with any men," Frannie said. "I was just eating and thinking."

"Thinking about Reuben, maybe?"

"Thinking about nothing," she said. "A man is the last thing I need in my life right now."

"Right," Linda said. "We've all said that at one time or another."

"Yeah. And it lasts about a week or two before you forget about how much trouble they are."

"Reuben would be a good catch."

"I'm not thinking of catching anyone."

"He lives with his mother."

"He's never been married."

"Almost, once," someone said, "but that was it. I think she broke his heart."

"He likes Frannie," another said. "Is that where he bit you?" she asked, looking at the tear in the back of her jeans.

Frannie shook her head and continued working as fast as she could, refusing to be drawn into the conversation.

When it was time for Linda's meeting, Ethel, the piece-work supervisor, came by their table and told them where it was being held.

"Can I go clean up a little?"

"Of course."

Frannie grabbed a pair of silk boxer shorts off the table and held them over the tear as she walked to the bathroom. Once inside, she removed her shirt and washed her face and arms and shoulders and neck and then shook her shirt out until most of the dust and grit was off. She turned her back to the mirror to view the tear in her pants and felt it with her hand. The rip was so big she could slip her hand inside to her bare skin.

It *would* be the day I wore the jeans too tight to wear my panties with, she thought.

She put on some lipstick and brushed her hair and then, shrugging her shoulders at herself in the mirror and laughing a little, as if to say, well, let's see what they think of this, she slipped the boxer shorts over her jeans and joined Linda, who'd been talking with Ethel outside the door.

"Oh, great. They'll love that," Linda said.

"It's all I can think of right now," Frannie said. "Let's go."

Ethel stared at her disapprovingly, but said nothing. In the room, Mr. Bosco, the owner; Mr. Osteen; and three randomly chosen production workers, who would act as Linda's peer review, looked at them as they entered.

"She's got a reason," Ethel said before anyone else had a chance to speak.

"Is this supposed to mean something?" Mr. Osteen asked. "I mean, is there some symbolism to this?"

"I just ripped my pants at lunch, okay? You don't want to see my ass, do you?"

That shut the men up, and Frannie walked past them to her chair.

"They fit real well, by the way."

The meeting began with a review of the charges, and Frannie was asked if she had ever witnessed anything concerning the charges.

"I've never seen her take anything before," Frannie said. "I don't know what she had with her or why she had it when you supposedly caught her with it, but I've never seen her do anything wrong."

While she talked, she looked at the faces of the people in the room. Mr. Bosco was silent and intent and bored and the rest of the people were doing their best to seem serious and attentive and a bit shocked, even though, according to Linda, everyone took a few things here and there.

While they talked, Mr. Osteen began to chew on a nail, and Frannie watched him work on it until it was hanging by one end and then saw him clench it between his teeth and tear it loose. When he did, he ended up with the loose nail between his teeth and without seeming to know he was doing it, he spat it over his shoulder and onto the rug.

Then she saw that his cuticle was bleeding but that he didn't know it was, and while he drummed his fingers on the table little smears of blood appeared on the surface all around his hand.

A secretary came in and told Mr. Osteen that his daughter was on the phone calling from school and needed to talk to him right away. He left the room and Frannie felt more confused than ever because she realized she had never considered that this man might have children, might have a daughter, and that he was, in addition to being someone about to have a nervous breakdown at work, a father, and one his daughter cared about enough and trusted enough to call him away from a meeting in the middle of the day with something she needed to talk about.

He couldn't be a good father, she thought. Could he? Could people be entirely one way in one place in their life and entirely another in another place in their life? She didn't know, and as everyone talked, she thought about it more.

Yes, she decided, because her own father had been one way with her and slightly different with Natalie and very different with his wife, their mother. So it was true. You were the way you could be with whomever you were with. If you couldn't be good, then you weren't. That's why, she thought, no one but her in the family ever longed for her dad's return, because not one of them knew the same man she'd known. That's why they didn't understand why he had to be told that the woman with whom he'd been an entirely different person, as far as Frannie knew, was now dead and gone.

After Linda had been given a written warning and after everyone left the room, Frannie saw Mr. Osteen through the open door of his office, still on the phone, and still talking to his daughter, she was sure, because his face was light and his eyes were misty and his lips were no longer pinched and even his voice was not the same.

Her heart began to break when she saw this. She thought about her own father and where he might be and what his life was and if people understood him and knew him and liked him in the way she had, in the way she knew he deserved to be, or if he was lost in what she presumed to be his own exile, desperate and misunderstood and haunted and lonely. Now more than ever, she knew she had to find him or at least let him know about her life and about the family, that whatever it was he'd done or thought he'd done was over and forgiven.

Beyond that, she now knew she must remember forever, for everyone, that the hearts of men may fail and the reasons could not be known from the face and because she knew this and because she could feel it so deeply and because she owed it to her father, she should not forget the hearts of men, no matter what.

"I got lucky," Linda said.

"You sure did," Frannie told her.

"Are you going to wear those the rest of the day?"

"I guess."

"You better not walk out the door in them."

"I got a jacket you can tie around you if you bring it back tomorrow," someone else said from behind Frannie. "I should have thought of it before."

"Okay. Thanks. I'll bring it back. I promise."

"Aren't you glad for me?" Linda asked. "You don't seem to be."

"Sure. I'm glad you didn't get in trouble. Of course I am."

"Your face doesn't show it. You look mad. Or upset."

"I'm sorry my face isn't the way you want it. Maybe I should cover it up," she said and slipped a pair of briefs over it.

"Come on, Frannie. I just wanted to thank you for helping me out."

"I'm sorry," she said, taking the briefs off her head. "I guess I'm thinking too much again."

"You walked out of there like you were in a dream," Linda said.

Frannie didn't answer her. Sometimes it was best to hold a vision within. Once spoken, it was lost in the way a gift presented to the wrong person was wasted, in the way that a night spent in the arms of someone wrong was wasted.

"Yes. You were lucky," Frannie finally said as if just now catching up with the conversation. They went back to work then, and though her hands were flying, her mind was going even faster. There was so much in her thoughts that some of it spilled out and she began to move her lips and talk to herself. The women around her pointed her out and quietly laughed and imitated her furrowed brow and her questioning look and her hushed whispering lips as Frannie had a conversation with herself for the rest of the day.

Because the production workers began before the front office employees, they also ended their day sooner, and Frannie got home before Natalie, always, and checked the mail at the end of the driveway and did whatever else needed to be done before her sister returned.

When she arrived that afternoon, the man from the duplex was standing at his mailbox.

"Hi, there," he said.

"Hello."

"I'm Ted Keller."

"I'm Frannie Vaughan."

"I saw you cutting the grass the other day. You folks need a riding mower with all that yard."

"It's good exercise," she said and returned to her car.

"Let me know if I can help you. Anytime."

"Thanks," she said. She parked in the shade. She heard the pigs calling her and she yelled, "I'll be there in a minute."

She set the mail on the kitchen table. There was nothing for her. There was no letter, no unexpected letter with strange handwriting from someplace she'd never heard of.

Before going to the barn to feed her once-little pets, she went back to the pile of pictures in her mother's room where she'd found the one of the woman who'd been put away for being too happy and took out an early picture of her father, and then one she thought was from the year he left them.

She took these with her along with the one of the woman who became too happy, and put them in her pocket while she fed the pigs and roughhoused with them until she'd had enough.

She climbed into the loft and leaned against the hewn post that ran from the foundation to the ridgeboard high above, and she set the pictures on her lap.

In the early picture, her father had on a hat, not a cowboy hat, or a cap, but the kind of hat she thought was called a fedora, at a jaunty angle, off to one side. In one hand he held a cigarette. His other hand was in the pocket of his sport coat and he looked a little, in the way some pictures of men from times past looked, like a gangster, but a happy gangster, with a sense of humor and a love of life and sparkling eyes and with a wry smile that would promise, she imagined, a good, lively, and never-boring life to a woman. Her mother, for instance.

In the second picture, it was the same man, and then again it wasn't. The promise was gone. Worry had replaced it. The cigarette was still there. The hat was gone. The hair was thin. The look was of submission, not to life, nor to anyone, but, at the very least, to the camera, submitting to having the way he looked and the way he felt and what had come about recorded, submitting to it defiantly but quietly, looking in the lens and saying, sure, take my picture if you have to, that's about all you'll get, so go ahead and take it.

She heard Natalie drive up. It had been quiet until then, except for the shuffling of the pigs. Even with the development and the traffic and the shopping centers, somehow, at times, it was still quiet on her remaining twelve acres, with the pond and the island and the roads that went nowhere, the fields empty, the corncribs empty, it was as if, at times, the old people were still there, and the world was unchanged.

"Are you in there?" Natalie called.

"I'm here."

"What's going on?"

"I'm up here recovering," she said and put the pictures away.

"I heard about Linda."

"Yeah?"

"Someone told me you fell down in the warehouse."

"Boy, news gets around that place."

"What were you doing there?"

"Eating lunch. I fell on my face in front of Reuben."

"That's what I thought."

"Huh?"

"I figured you were back there talking to him."

"Why'd you figure that?"

"Because I saw you talking in the parking lot with him

the other day and you both had pleasant looks on your faces."

"Really? Well, well, well," she said.

"I know about him."

"You do?"

"His father worked there before him, but died a long time ago. They're good people."

"That's nice."

"What is that in your pocket?"

"A picture."

"Can I see it?"

"Sure."

She sailed it carefully to her and then followed it by scooting down the ladder. Natalie looked at the picture and then put her arm around Frannie and walked her back to the house.

"So, how're the piggies?" Natalie asked.

"They're doing great."

"Good."

"How's Jake?"

"Great."

"Good," Frannie said and then they both laughed.

"I'm glad everything's good and great."

"Me, too," she said. "Meeeee, too."

"Jake's eating with his mom tonight. Do you want to go out?"

"Actually, I wouldn't. I'd rather stay here."

"Okay. Let's make something other than grilled cheese, though. Let's make something really nice."

"Oh, I want to. I do. I really do. Let's think of something

we used to love when we were kids and find Mom's recipe and make it."

"Okay, let's do," Natalie said and with her arm still around her younger sister, and with Frannie's arm around her waist, they walked back to the house.

Chapter 18

JUST BEFORE HE drove off, Ted saw the two women walking into their house. It was too far away to hear what they were saying and too far away to see the expressions on their faces, but he saw them walking together and it touched him.

Because he was lonely for the company of a woman and because he hadn't seen his second ex-wife, Dolores, since before he was sent to prison, he went to see her. It wasn't an easy thing to do, but then again because he'd changed and because he'd been taught in workshops to talk instead of letting things drive him crazy, he wanted to do it. They talked a few minutes before he got around to what he'd wanted to say to her for a long time.

"You know why I robbed that store?"

"Sure," she said, looking at him with disgust and annoyance as well as caution. "Because you thought it'd make you a big man."

"Nope."

"Oh, yeah. That would've been it. You always did want to look like a big man, when you never was."

"Nope. That wasn't it."

"Let me guess, then," she said sarcastically. She had no desire to talk to him.

"Go ahead."

"You did it because you wanted to, which is why you've did everything you've ever did since I met you."

"Nope," he said. He wasn't going to let her get him mad, though she certainly had a lot of practice at it and was good at it.

"You did it because you was drunk and running around with Lonnie and showing off for him like a schoolgirl."

"Nope."

"You did it because you didn't have no money because you couldn't hold a job because you were always getting in a fight with someone because of the size of that chip on your shoulder."

"Nope," he said and crossed his arms and leaned against the side of her trailer home and smiled.

"You did it because you got tired of beating up on me and wanted to find out how it felt to beat on some other woman."

"Nope. And I never did beat up on you."

"Like hell."

"I was defending myself."

"Right."

"Go on and guess."

"Guess? I could go on with reasons for the rest of my life, and all of them would be true."

"You're still way off."

"You did it because you and Lonnie were running around with those common trash girls and taking them down to the beach and living high all the time and telling me you were working construction down there."

"Not it."

"You did it because you thought you could get away with it and thought you were smarter than everyone else like you always thought."

"Keep going," he said. "When you run out of things to say, I'll tell you."

"I won't never run out of reasons to tell you why you caused me the six worst years of my life. Thank the Lord we never did have children."

"I wouldn't have minded having them."

"I would have. With you."

"You're just as mean as ever. I come over here to talk nice to you, and you're just as mean as ever. I've changed, Dolores."

"Oh, sure. You couldn't change short of having a complete brain transplant. Which is another reason you robbed that store and beat that woman, because your brain was fried like an egg from liquor and drugs."

"Mean, mean, mean," he said and shook his head. "But it don't do a thing to me. I'm past it."

"Good. I hope you are."

"You ready for me to tell you?"

"No. I don't want to hear anything you've got to say."

"Is that any way to talk to me after what I've been through and all that we had together, once?"

"We didn't have nothing together."

"You're cold, Dolores."

"You taught it to me, Ted. You taught me how to be mean, how to be hateful, how to be whatever I had to be to make it."

"See, I taught you something."

"Leave, would you? I don't want to see you again. Okay?"

"I want to tell you why I set out that night to do it."

"Tell me."

"I did it for you."

She laughed as hard and as sharply as if someone had slapped her on her back and knocked it out of her.

"I stole it for you. I wanted us to start over and have some way to pay off the mess we'd got ourselves into. I did it for us. I guess it don't sound too smart now, but I swear that's what I was thinking."

"Lord, man, how dumb do you think I am?"

"Not too dumb to know the truth when you hear it."

"I wish you'd never showed up. I was hoping to spend the rest of my life without ever seeing you again. You haven't changed a bit. You're still the biggest liar what ever lived and you're still just as good at it as ever. What do you want, really? Why did you come over here?"

"To see you. To clear things up. A lot of things can eat on a man when he's away like I was."

"Well, I am all cleared up and if you aren't, that's your problem."

"So you won't talk?"

"No."

"It'd be better if we did."

"What is it you want, really? Money? Is that it?"

"I don't need no money from you."

"Well, that'll be a first."

"You're a mean and hard woman, Dolores. Can't you forgive me?"

"I could forgive about anyone but you, Ted. Just about anyone."

"It kind of makes me mad for you to be so mean to me, Dolores, when I'm coming over here to be nice and tell you I'm sorry."

"Save it for someone else. I've heard it too often."

"Well don't you have nothing nice to say to me?"

"I can't think of anything."

"Well, I think you're looking real nice. I do."

"Uh-huh."

"You've lost weight, haven't you."

She stared at him without answering.

"You about done got your figure back like when we first met."

"Yep," she said. "I knew it. I figured you'd get there sooner or later."

"I don't know what you mean."

"The answer is no. No, you're not coming in. No, I ain't interested. No, you're not getting back in my bed if I live to be four hundred years old."

"Damn you, Dolores, you hold a grudge bad."

"I hold on to the truth, that's all I hold on to."

"You ought to give me a chance to prove how I've changed. I can be real nice now. I've learned how."

"The answer is still no."

"I ain't asking anything like that."

"Like hell. I can see from the way you're looking at me."

"Please give me a chance. I'm terrible lonely."

"That's not my problem anymore, thank God."

"I guess you've got a boyfriend."

"I guess that's none of your business."

"I signed that divorce agreement when I was in jail as a way of showing you I didn't hold no hard feelings."

"Thanks."

"Could I give you a hug? Just one?"

"Don't even think about it."

"Damn."

"You better go now."

"I come here to make it up to you and be nice about it, but I got to tell you you're making me mad."

"Go get mad at someone else. Your days of getting mad at me are over."

"I hope you go to hell," he said.

"I won't, but you will."

She went inside and locked the door. He heard it lock and then he heard another lock turn, after which he saw her look around the curtain to see if he was still there. He drove away slowly.

Chapter 19

FRANNIE HAD TROUBLE sleeping. Jake was asleep with Natalie in her room at the far end of the hall. In the other rooms the ghosts of her mother and all the women in her family all the way back to Delia were asleep. Only Frannie was up.

She searched through her desk where she had often sat but rarely done her homework all her student life, dreaming, instead, or doodling or reading magazines.

She found some thick paper like posterboard and began to compose.

She would do this, she thought, without telling anyone, without talking to anyone, without discussing it with Natalie, without giving anyone the chance to discourage her. She would do this because she had to do something to find her father even though she thought it would probably not work. She had to do something.

The composition would be simple. It would ask the questions Do you know this man? Do you know where this man is or was or might be? That's all it would ask. It would not ask if you knew what he was like, or why he'd left.

She would only ask if anyone knew where he was or had been or might be. She would only need to know that much.

She would not ask in the composition why he never called her or wrote or returned. She would not ask why he let her live with a broken heart all these years. She would not ask what kind of man would leave two children and a wife and never look back because she did not know that he had never looked back. She had been told he had done this. It seemed it might be true, but she did not know it for herself.

She would not ask why he began a life with them if he did not intend to see it through. She would not ask that, because she almost knew the answer from the pictures. They told her why it had begun. They did not tell her why he did not see it through. The pictures from the last of his life with them did not tell her either. Those pictures, unlike the early ones, said so very little it felt like falling in a hole and never hitting bottom.

She would not ask why it was that her mother and her sister had no longing for this man and if they had, what it was they had done with it. She would not ask that, because she had already and there seemed to be no answer that made sense, that seemed true, that could be believed.

She would ask, Does anyone know this man?

She would ask, Does anyone know where he is?

She would ask that if anyone did, they should call her or write her and let her know.

This is all she would say. She would not tell them how important it was. She would not tell them that it had taken her years to ask this simple question and that it had taken the death of her mother and her own absence from that death to make her understand that she had to know answers to these questions she now asked and also the ones she didn't ask, before he too died or before anything else in her life changed so fast and so completely that it, like death, like abandonment, left her awkward and different and as open and defenseless as a solitary desert rose in bloom, too tender, too sweet, too lovely, too vulnerable for anyone passing by not to pick, not to take for himself.

She wrote, then, on pieces of paper, these questions, and she cut them into neat shapes the size and style of cards, and she printed, as neatly as she could and as clearly as she could, what it was she had to know.

It was eerily quiet when she finished. For a few minutes there were no sounds at all. Nothing. No noise, no movement, as still as if the world were actually now waiting for something to happen.

It must have been like this for Delia when she awoke on the side of the road in the remote mountain valley after running away. It must have been like this for Frannie's father when he awoke early that first morning after he'd departed.

Now, no longer a child, Frannie began to understand the loneliness of adult confusion and its consequences.

From down the hall, she heard the radio beside Natalie's bed. Then she heard talking, and then it was time to start the day. It was time to go to work and time to be with people and time to make something occur, if only putting three T-shirts or three pairs of men's briefs into plastic bags. Somehow that was important enough to spend an entire day doing and get paid for it.

She went to feed her pigs. They were still asleep when she approached. They lay with their eyes open watching her even after they awoke. She petted Alice, her favorite, and then, on a whim and because she wanted to and needed to feel better than she did, she had the idea of putting Alice on a leash and running with her, like jogging with a dog. Somehow it seemed it would be fun.

They ran down the driveway and then back up, and then they ran around the barn a few times, and then into the enclosure.

"Look at her," Jake said.

"I am," Natalie said.

"Is she actually disturbed? I mean, clinically, in some way?"

"Of course not."

"Then why is she doing that?"

"I don't know. Really, I can't say. She's always been that way. She's been that way, and, at the same time, kind of sad and lost, both ways, at once. Maybe it is time she grew out of it. Maybe it is."

"It is time. Absolutely."

"If you knew her like I do, though, you'd realize that mostly this is a way she's figured out to be so she won't be as sad a person as she really is, I think. It seems that's what it is. I'm not sure. That's just something I've always thought."

"What's she got to be sad about? I mean, other than what we all have to be sad about."

"I just think she has a sad heart. Some people do. I don't. You don't. She does."

From the window they watched her vault over the enclosure by putting her hands on the top of a post and leaping over and then watched her running toward them. As she neared the house they saw her abruptly notice they were watching her and saw her stop and put her hands in the pockets of her jeans and laugh and shake her head in an embarrassed way, as if to say, yeah, I know, you think I'm nuts.

"Hi," she said as she went past them on the way to her room. "See anything interesting?"

"You," Natalie said.

"I know. I'm a one-woman show."

"Have you eaten?"

"I'm going to get something on the way. I want to get there early."

She left. Then Jake left. Then Natalie left. The house stayed. The pigs stayed. The land stayed. The memories stayed. It was home. For a while, it was still home.

Chapter 20

LINDA HAD TO use the rest room. Ethel was nowhere in sight. She raised one hand, which slowed her packing, but continued on with the other. Production workers had to sign out if they needed to be excused from their workstation at other than official break times.

"Where is she?"

On one side of the room, the conveyor had crushed a large box of T-shirts. Three men had stopped the belt and were attempting to remove the torn material from the sprockets.

"I'm dying," Linda said. "Dying."

The other day Grace had been packing so fast she inadvertently stuffed a part of a candy bar into the bag along with the shirts and dropped it into the bin. Frannie told her about it, and they all had a laugh.

"I'll wait," Linda said. "I'll just wait."

For about twenty minutes it was less noisy than usual because the belt's worn bearings were still. Frannie saw a bird's nest twenty feet up in the corner of a brick pillar. A bird flew from somewhere down the room to the nest.

"Mill birds," she said aloud but no one paid any attention to her or the bird since they were all working on their count. "Like jailbirds."

A new man was pulling a load of bins toward the shut-down conveyor. A load was three bins high. The bins were constructed to fit onto one another. Each bin weighed about a hundred pounds. By the time the man was stacking the third layer, he was having trouble lifting the bins above the second layer.

"He won't last," Linda said.

"I bet kids would love to play on that belt," Frannie said.

Linda raised her hand again.

"I can't wait. I really can't."

"Then go."

"I don't want to get in trouble."

"Go," Frannie said. "It's a stupid rule, anyway. It's probably illegal. Go."

"I can't. I'll get docked."

"By God," Frannie said, "If Ethel isn't here to okay it, then you have the right to go. I give you that right. Okay? I give it to you."

"Sure. You bet."

"If they say anything to you I'll be all over them like a white tornado."

Finally Ethel appeared and signed a slip for Linda to carry with her when she went to the rest room. While she was gone, Frannie took a few of the cards she'd written about her missing father and secretly slipped them, one by one, into the folds of T-shirts and sealed them up and sent them into the bin.

A few minutes later, she did some more.

"What'd you put in there?" Linda asked.

"Nothing."

"They have inspectors. They open a certain percentage of everything we do."

The lunch bell rang. Frannie went to the parking lot to her car. After she finished her sandwich, she walked to the lawn behind the mill and sat under a tree. Reuben watched her from the door of the warehouse.

She was nothing like the first woman in his life who had been the only woman in his life or, at least, the only woman he'd ever felt anything for and been serious with, and after she left, he'd never been interested again until now, until he'd seen Frannie.

She wasn't the best-looking woman at the mill or the sexiest—though she put on quite a show—or even the brashest, though she was brash enough. Because he was a careful man and because he was a thoughtful man and because he didn't want to make a mistake even though he had no idea at all that she ever knew he existed anymore than she was aware of any other man in the building, he watched her sitting in the shade and tried to understand why he was attracted to her.

If the reason was that he would be forty in a few years and that he was tired of imagining and only imagining what this other life that everyone else seemed to be a part of was all about, being in love, having a partner, having children, having a reason, finally, beyond that of yourself and only you, to proceed through life in an honorable and responsible way, if it was that, then why now, and why her, and why not before and someone else?

What was it in her that touched him to watch this young woman sitting under a tree and talking to herself and then realizing she'd been talking out loud and looking around to see if anyone had noticed? What was it about a woman who would tumble down a chute that hadn't been used in years and land at his feet and rise up red-faced and angry and embarrassed and mouthing off and yet still unable to hide what was in her, a tender heart, a spirited determination, a fierceness for life in the middle of a sadness he did not understand?

Of course, he thought, he could be wrong. He could be badly wrong. He had been wrong before, though it seemed to him that he should find out if he was right.

He put his hand in his pocket after he'd jumped off the dock and walked toward her and saw her look at him and then away, hoping, he assumed, he was not coming to talk to her.

"I don't mean to bother you," he said.

She looked up at him.

"If I'm interrupting anything, tell me."

She stared him in the eye as long as she could hold it until she had to blink and look away.

"Listen, if I'm out of line, I'm sorry, but I wonder if you would have dinner with me."

She looked back at him and waited to see if he would say anything else.

"I just thought maybe we could have dinner or go to a movie tonight."

It seemed to him as he finished the last word that he'd been badly mistaken, that he had fooled himself into thinking she'd be remotely interested. But he had to know. Now he did. He'd been wrong.

"I don't know," she suddenly said. "Let me think about it a minute."

She watched how he sat near her, but not right beside her, giving her room to think and not crowding her. She looked at his face, trying to read what was behind his invitation. She looked across the lawn toward the old mill building, which was red brick from one end to the other. The parking lot behind it and the lawn on which she now sat, according to an historic display in the lobby, had once been used for stables for the horses the men and women rode to work, and then later as a field for the company baseball team. There had even been a pond for fishing and swimming for the employees. The ball field was paved, and the pond was filled in, and cars covered the rest of it as far as she could see.

She glanced at Reuben and wondered how he'd lost his

arm. She looked at his face again and the hairs on his arm, which were golden in the sunlight, and she looked in his eyes as he patiently stared off into the distance, respectfully waiting for her to decide. She was not used to being with a man like this.

He was a quiet and reflective man, something she'd already noticed, and so, as she thought about it, it did seem in keeping that he would wait patiently and with dignity for her to decide. What she noticed this time, however, was that he was also a handsome man, unusually so, in an old-fashioned and completely natural way, and she was sure he did not know that he looked this good to her, or to any woman, for that matter. She was sure he had no idea at all.

"I don't think I can. Not tonight," she said. "But thanks for asking me."

Later that evening Frannie and her sister and Jake took a walk to see the pigs. Something was brewing if they suggested a look at the pigs. They were completely, Jake for sure, uninterested in them, so as they chatted, Frannie watched for whatever it would be.

"They certainly are growing," he said.

"Yes, they are."

"What exactly are they called?"

"Pigs."

"He means what breed are they?" Natalie said.

"Oh," Frannie answered, playing dumb.

"Are they purebred?"

"I'm not sure. I think they're Yorkshires or Hampshires or something like that."

"How much do they weigh at this point in their life?" he asked.

Frannie looked at him as if to say, come on, bud, just get to it.

"I haven't put them on the scale lately. Probably about one hundred and fifty pounds."

"I see," he said.

"Are you thinking of going into the hog business?" she asked.

"No, actually, I'm not, but I believe the more knowledge a man can have about everything, the better off he is."

"Uh-huh," she said, and then began to whistle. After a few moments, Natalie took Jake's hand and looked Frannie in the eye.

"We want to tell you something," she said.

"I thought so."

"We've set a date. For the wedding."

Although she knew it was coming in the near future, it made her stomach tighten up when she heard it.

"How wonderful," she said. "How terrific. Can I come?"

"Can you come? You'll be the maid of honor if you'll agree."

"Shucks," she said, "I might be the matron of honor by then, you never know."

"What do you mean?" Natalie asked, suddenly too serious for what Frannie had thought would be a joke.

"Oh, heck, I might just up and get married myself one of these days."

"To whom?"

"I'm kidding, Nat. I'm just kidding."

"Will you, then? Be the maid of honor?"

"Of course. It'll be great. I want to wear a miniskirt, though. A formal miniskirt."

"I don't think so," Natalie said. "That's not what I had in mind."

"With nothing on under it," she said, suddenly feeling mean and wanting to hurt her sister and Jake. "And topless, too. How about that?"

"There she goes again," he said to Natalie.

"There I go again? Huh? What? Me? There you go again. How about you?" she said to Jake. "You self-righteous asshole. Don't you know I hate you? Don't you know I always have? Don't you know you'll never be my friend?"

"Oh, no, Frannie. Don't," Natalie said.

"Everything about you is phony. I wouldn't trust you as far as I could throw you. I can't stand the thought of you being in my family. I can't stand the thought of you being my brother-in-law. It makes me sick. I'll never be your maid of honor because I don't honor this. Not at all.

"You're crazy to marry him, Nat. He's ruining everything. He's going to tear us apart and sell the house and destroy everything. Can't you see it? It's awful. Nothing will ever be the same again. Nothing. Once we lose all this and once you go off with him and live in town, we'll lose each other, too."

"We won't," Natalie said, feeling sorry for her rather than angry, feeling sad that she was so frightened and wrong and out of control. "We won't ever lose each other."

"But we will. And all for him? No. I won't be your maid of honor. I'll come to the damn wedding and I'll sit there and be nice and polite, but I won't be your maid of honor. I'll be your sister, that's all. Your sister who loves you and who you think is crazy. I'll be her. That's what I'll be because that's all I can be. Damn, I hate this world. I hate it."

"Don't say any more," Natalie said.

"Oh God, I feel awful. Everything's over, just like I knew it was. Things really are never going to be the same anymore. Everything's changing. Oh God," she said and then burst into tears and fell into her sister's arms and cried so hard for a minute that she couldn't talk.

"It's okay," Natalie said. "Everything's going to be all right."

"I'm sorry. I'm so sorry," she said to both of them. "I just can't stand anything else in my life. I can't. I'm a wreck. I thought I was getting better, but I'm not. I'm just a mess," she said and began to walk off into the night by herself.

"This is a bad day," they could hear her saying. "A real bad day. A terrible day. An awful day. A lost day. A lost sister day. A lost father day. A lost life day. Oh my. Oh me, oh my. Not a good day at all," they heard her say as she walked into the field.

"Don't go too far," Natalie called.

"I've already gone too far," she said.

Later that night Frannie walked past the duplex and saw Ted through the window, watching television. In the lighted windows of her own home, she saw no one.

What if I saw myself in there? she thought. That would have to mean I was dead.

She continued down the road. There was a creek farther on. There was land to the side of the duplex and no houses. The land was too low to build on. It was in the floodplain. No septic tank drain field would perk there. Anything you flushed out would rise to the top of the ground and come back after you.

Farther on was a series of nine cheap look-alike houses that had been built shortly after her father left. They were on land that had once belonged to her family, which her mother had been forced to sell when her father left.

Inside three of the houses, the lights were still on. Six were dark. Two dogs began to bark. First one barked and then the other. Beside the road a child's Big Wheel scooter was wrecked in a ditch. A dog ran at her. She turned around. The dog stopped.

There was a dirt road to her left where she used to ride her bike when she was younger. She used to hide from Natalie and her mother up this road. She once saw a man parked in a car on this road, and she hid far back in the woods and observed him. He looked toward the house and stayed a long time and then drove away. She had been thirteen years old and she later thought it might have been her father, but at the time she remembered only feeling afraid of the strange-acting man. Maybe she'd been smart to have been that afraid.

Had she been smarter and wiser as a child than now as a woman? It was thought that wisdom and clear thinking were the properties of adults. Often this was not true. Fearing something in the dark was reasonable. Being fearless and bold and chasing after what it was you thought was there was sometimes not a good idea. Once you were out there on a dare or in a rage or in the rush of ardent belief, whatever it was you eventually found was yours, and you then belonged to it as well.

She told you not to go. He told you not to go. We told you not to go. What do these words mean to a child? Why do they not mean the same years later?

"Hello."

Ted came out of nowhere and scared Frannie.

"Goddamnit!" she yelled. "You scared the hell out of me!"

"I'm sorry."

She could see who it was by the light of the moon once he emerged from the trees.

"I saw you walk by. Actually I was worried about you out here this time of night."

"I'm fine."

"Do you come out here a lot?"

"Sometimes," she said and started back to the paved road and toward her house.

"I really didn't mean to scare you," he said. "I was walking down here not knowing where you were and then all of a sudden you were right in front of me."

"That's all right. I'm over it."

"I won't hurt you. I just came to see if you were all right."

They passed under a streetlight. He smiled at her apologetically and shrugged his shoulders.

"We could sit on my porch and talk if you want to. If you don't need to be back home right away."

Frannie walked on without answering him.

"It's been a long time since I asked a woman to sit and talk with me," he said. "Maybe I'm not doing it right."

The streetlight above her hummed and at the same time made a sizzling sound as if something was frying or about to burst. Moths and strange long-bodied insects batted against the globe, and one of them fell from the light and into Frannie's hair.

"It's nothing," Ted said as she flinched and struck at it. "Let me pick it out. Hold still a minute," he said, but she knocked it out herself.

From the weeds alongside the road, a possum appeared with a half-eaten hamburger in its mouth. Trailing from its mouth along with the hamburger was the multicolored wrapper from the restaurant. The possum waddled across the road in no hurry and only glanced at them, casually.

"I'd like to talk," he said. "That's all I'm asking. Just to sit and talk."

Farther on in the middle of the lane a bird was in their path. Its neck was broken and its head lay against its back. It lay with such wide-eyed horror and open-beaked amazement it appeared to be alive and looking up at Frannie as if to tell her something, as if to say, "I broke my neck! Help! I broke my neck!"

"Is it too much to ask someone to talk?" he said. "Tell me if it is."

The lights in one of the houses went out. One second the house was lit up, inside and out, with lamps and spotlights and ceiling fixtures all glowing, and the next second it was completely dark. Then a door opened and someone hidden by the dark said, "Go away."

"Do you know who that was?" Ted asked. "Why won't you answer me?"

Frannie looked at him and saw he was sad and confused and lonely and afraid, and her sad heart connected with his like it had all her life with lonely and confused men, and she said, "I'm sorry. It's been a crazy night."

"That's all right."

They sat on the porch. He brought them both Cokes in glasses with ice. He was awkward. He didn't know what to talk about or whether he could look at her or not, or be able to look her in the eye when he did. This touched her, and she felt more sorry for him.

After about a half hour she saw Jake's car coming down the driveway and as it began to turn onto the road, its lights illuminated her and Ted on the edge of his little porch.

"Are you all okay?" he called to her.

"Absolutely fine."

"Natalie's worried about you."

"I'll go back in a minute."

A few minutes later as Frannie was leaving, Ted touched her arm lightly.

"Could I take you out some night? Tomorrow, maybe?"

She didn't answer right away. She didn't say, let me think about it, as she had with Reuben. She just thought about it without saying anything, and the silence made Ted uncomfortable again.

"Or the next?" he asked.

She looked at his hands. The one holding the cigarette was shaking. The smile on his face was uncertain and pained, as if this was a man who hadn't smiled much in his life.

"Sure," she said. "That might be nice. I'll leave a note in your mailbox telling you which night."

"Thank you," he said. "You just made my day. My week. My whole year."

"I'll let you know soon."

"Can I walk you partway back?" he asked.

"I'll be fine. I was born here. I know every inch of this land. I'll be just fine."

Chapter 21

BY LUNCHTIME THE next day, Frannie had apologized to Natalie countless times.

"I forgive you."

"You swear?"

"Yes. But one thing, please."

"What?"

"Apologize to Jake."

"Do I have to?"

"You don't have to do anything. But it'd be the right thing to do."

There it was again, the right thing to do. How did everyone know about this?

"If you say so."

"I do."

"I never want to hurt you, Nat. We've got to stick together. Forever."

"You won't lose me. You won't, no matter what you do or say or whatever changes there are."

"All right."

"Do you remember what I used to say when we were kids and you got mad at me?"

"What?"

"I'm rubber. You're glue. Everything you say bounces off me and sticks to you."

"Yeah. It would make me even madder."

"Well, that's kind of the way it is."

"I know."

"Jake is going to look out for us from now on. You'll be glad of it someday."

"Maybe."

"Will you apologize to him this evening?"

"I'll try."

"Good."

"But I might be going out."

"Where? You haven't been out in months."

"I'm not sure yet."

By the end of the day Frannie had inserted the remaining cards asking the whereabouts of her father.

"You going to get in so much trouble for that," Linda said.

"It's harmless."

"To you."

"To anyone. To them, to Bosco, to everybody."

"You should've asked first if you think they won't mind."

"Then they'd probably have said no."

"See."

"And then I'd have done it anyway."

"I wish you'd let me see one."

"It's a personal thing. It's nothing that'd interest you."

"Okay. I'm not going to ask. You stood up for me. I'll keep my mouth shut."

While Frannie packed underwear, Ted loaded trucks with lumber, nails, paneling, flooring, roofing, whatever it was that was needed on whatever order he was filling. It was relatively easy work and he was mostly on his own finding what was needed to fill the order. Once the order was complete, a driver took it to the job and Ted began on another list.

At lunch Ted and a man he'd made friends with were throwing a knife against a stack of black insulation board.

"You know what I like to do with a woman?" Eljert asked.

"What?"

"I like to get them drunk and then do whatever I feel like with them."

"It's been so long for me, I can't even remember what you do with them," Ted said.

"Have you ever had one pass out on you while you were doing it?"

"I can't say. Maybe. I don't know."

"I had one what did that and damn if I didn't think I'd killed her."

"Was she all right?" Ted asked.

"Eventually."

"You got to be careful with women."

"Some of them, maybe," Eljert said. "With this one I was doing her pretty good and all of a sudden I realized she wasn't saying nothing and wasn't moving and I thought, Damn, that's the first woman I ever screwed to death."

It made Ted uncomfortable to listen to Eljert talk this way. He was trying to think of women in a new way now that he was supposed to know better from all the counseling he'd had in prison.

"Maybe she didn't want to do it," Ted said. "Sometimes it's hard to tell if they do or don't."

Eljert threw the knife twenty feet to the stack of insulation board. It hit on its handle and bounced off the pack.

"I like a young girl the best," Eljert said. "They're so stupid you can tell them anything and they'll believe it."

"That woman counselor at the prison told us we didn't have the right to have sex with a woman if she didn't want to, even if it was your own wife."

"Hell, the Bible says you do."

"That's what I always thought."

"It don't matter now, though. Them modern ones want it all the time."

"I don't know anything about it," Ted said. "I haven't had any in so long I forgot how."

"I was married once," Eljert said. "She was a pretty good old gal for a while. Until she got the smart mouth."

"I've been married twice."

"That smart mouth is a disease they get once you sign on the dotted line."

"That's true. They all seem to get it."

"Do you reckon you could kill a bear with a knife?" Eljert asked out of nowhere.

"I don't know."

"I seen a movie once where a man had to do it. I mean, just the knife and nothing else."

"I'd hate to have to try."

"I've killed hogs before and goats and I've slit the throat on cows after we shot them, but I don't believe a man could kill a bear by hisself," Eljert said.

Ted threw the knife. It went in.

"I got to piss," Eljert said and picked up his knife and started to walk away. "Damn that counselor woman, anyway," he said, as if he'd just that moment heard what Ted said earlier. "A man, any man's, got a right to a woman if they ask for it, and all of them's asking for it these days."

At five-thirty that afternoon, just as Natalie got home, Jake called to say he had a meeting and would see her later.

"It's just going to be us tonight," she told Frannie.

"Oh."

"Are you going out?"

"I haven't decided."

"What were you doing when I got home?"

"When?"

"You were running somewhere."

"I was exercising the pigs. I can let them loose now and

run with them. All of them, even without a rope. They just run all over the place following me."

"You're getting awfully attached to them."

"I'm not really. Maybe to Alice. She's the only one with personality."

"Can I ask you something?"

"Sure."

They were in the yard under an old white oak. From one of the limbs a thick rope with a double knotted end on the bottom of it hung and it was from this rope, by standing on the knot, that Frannie swung back and forth while they talked.

"What do you see if you look into your future?"

"Absolutely nothing."

Natalie phoned Jake at the bank.

"It's been almost an hour and I haven't heard a word from her. Not even a sound from the room. I asked her to think about her future and she ran inside. You know, we may have to look after her. Always."

"That's what families are for."

"She may have to move in with us when we leave."

"If that's what you think is needed, then so be it," he said.

"You're so nice. You really are."

"Why wouldn't I be? I love you."

"But that doesn't mean you have to be nice to my sad sister."

"Sure it does. It's part of being with you."

"Most men wouldn't be that way."

"Most men don't have you."

"Frannie needs somebody like you. It would change her so."

"She'll have to change herself first."

"You take such good care of us. I wish my mother had had a man like you."

"He couldn't have been all that bad."

"He was and he wasn't. You know how things like that go."

"Yep."

Natalie paused in the conversation and listened to a noise in the house.

"Wait a second," she said and laid the phone on the table when she saw Frannie about to go out the door. "You're not even going to say good-bye?"

"I'm sorry. You were talking so I was just going to slip out."

"When will you be back?"

"I'll be back tonight. You don't have to get that look on your face. I'm not going to disappear anymore. I told you I wouldn't."

Natalie returned to the phone.

"I could hear the whole conversation," he said. "How did she look?"

"Fine. Really nice."

"Could you tell where she was going by how she was dressed?"

"I haven't a clue about it. It was almost like she was trying to sneak out."

"Poor thing," Jake said.

"I don't think she wanted me to ask her anything. I got that impression."

"Well, I for one am glad she's going out."

"Me, too."

"She's been down long enough now. It's time she got back into life and moved on."

"I know, as long as she doesn't start back where she left off."

"She won't," Jake said.

Frannie saw that Ted's car was gone. He must have left early, she thought.

They were meeting at the Lone Pine, which is what she had suggested to him in the note. It was her new resolve to meet a man at a certain place because she then had her car right there if things didn't work out. She could leave. Alone.

Getting in the car with an angry man or a drunk man or a quiet, scary man was something she hoped was in her past. Not that it always went wrong. It was merely that when it did, she wanted to be able to leave on her own terms.

In the parking lot, she tried to work up some enthusiasm.

Come on, Frannie. Don't be a drip. Show the man a little fun. From the looks of him, he needs it.

All around her, people were getting out of old and new cars and trucks and vans. They all looked like they were going to have fun. One would think it was easy to at least look like you were having fun.

Come on, she told herself. You know how. Just turn it on.

A pickup with Texas plates on the back bumper and four people in the cab and eight in the bed drove up. They were all Mexicans.

Uh-oh, she thought looking at the short dark-skinned stocky men getting out. Fight night.

The truck was old and ragged and when the driver turned off the engine it kept running and backfiring and wouldn't shut off until he put it back in gear and choked it out.

The timing's bad, she thought. When it won't shut off and the motor tries to run backward, it's mostly always the timing.

She looked at her watch. She was fifteen minutes late. It was seven forty-five. She hadn't eaten supper. It was time to go in.

Jake and three of his friends were finishing sandwiches in one of the men's apartment. They were members of a private investment club. They met once a month and either pooled their money or went their own way after discussing what they thought might be hot or on its way up.

Jake had made some money lately but hadn't told Natalie about it because he wanted to make a lot before he surprised her with it.

"If I had a million dollars right now, or even a hundred thousand I could risk, I'd buy this little gene group over here," someone said, looking through a stack of papers.

"It won't work."

"It's too late for them."

"Everybody thinks it's the plastic or computer stock of the future, but it's not," Jake said. "It's going to be too highly regulated and too insurance-driven to ever make any real money."

"Yeah, like pharmaceuticals don't make money?"

"Hmmm," Jake said. "That's true. You got something there."

"The real money's in informations systems," another said. "But they're all big players. There's no ground floor."

"Right," Jake said.

They talked some more. It was decided they would go their own way this month. That suited Jake because he wanted to invest in something special to give Natalie for a wedding present.

"Hi," Frannie said. "It's me."

"I'm glad you came," he said.

"You got my note, I guess."

"I did. I kind of didn't think you would do it."

"I told you I would."

There were no blacks in the Lone Pine except in the kitchen. The Mexicans were at one end of the huge room, which had a dance floor, and the locals were at the other.

Frannie made herself look up from the table directly at Ted. There was a small tattoo on his bicep.

"You're looking at my tattoo."

"I was trying to figure out what it said."

"I got it at Subic Bay, in the Philippines."

He rolled up his sleeve.

"It's a fish," she said.

"It's a shark. I was in a club once. We called each other the Sharks."

"Oh."

"You want a beer?"

She looked around while they waited to be served. She recognized some people in the room. She hadn't been there in months. She began to feel she didn't want to be there now.

"This is a nice place," Ted said.

Years ago this building had been a family restaurant called the China Grove Supper Club. Frannie's father had brought her family here more than once. She could remember a small orchestra off to one side. Her parents had danced together. It seemed they had. It was a long time ago. It seemed like being there made everyone in the family happy.

"It's been a while since I've been here," Ted said.

They had also gone out, as a family, to the first Oriental restaurant in town. On really special nights, when Frannie was four or five years old, she remembered, they would go out to a restaurant and then to the drive-in. Her parents would make her take her pajamas with her and change in the backseat while the movie was playing. Her parents knew she would fall asleep watching the movie. When she did, they could carry her to bed already in her pajamas.

"I lived about thirty miles from here a few years back," he said.

After she changed, she would get back in the front seat

and sit between them with Natalie. It was nice there between her parents in the dark out in the world with something extraordinary happening on a bright screen right in front of her eyes.

"I only got over here once or twice, now that I think about it. Maybe it wasn't this place. I can't remember," he said.

There were different ways she felt as a child. She felt one way with her mother, another way with her father. She felt one way at home, and another way out in the world. The ways she'd felt as a child were still with her.

"I was thinking about this place and then there it was on the note you left me. That was weird, like you'd been reading my mind."

On a certain night each week when this location was the China Grove Supper Club there was a talent contest for the children in the restaurant. Natalie wouldn't do anything, but Frannie remembered singing a song. She couldn't remember what it had been. It might have been "Here comes Peter Cottontail hopping down the bunny trail."

"You're kind of quiet," Ted said.

After the talent show she felt great. She walked back to her seat through a room of friendly faces. In the middle of all those faces were her own parents. They were happiest of all with their little girl.

"Of course, you were kind of quiet the other night in the road, too," he said.

Someone else won the prize. The prize was a free dinner for the family of the winner. It was a nice prize and worth real money back then, but she remembered that for her, at that time in her life, the best prize of all was making her parents happy.

"I don't mind you being quiet," he said. "I'm like that myself sometimes."

When Frannie was in the third grade one of her classmates' father died. This made everyone sad. No one knew what to say to the girl. They knew they had to be extra nice, but no one knew what to say. It was almost as if she was not the same person once her father died, that something had changed about her and that she would never be the same again. That's the way it seemed to all of Frannie's friends.

"Of course, maybe it's me," Ted said. "Maybe you'd rather not be here," he said, and Frannie heard him, but couldn't stop her thoughts to answer him, and, at that moment, didn't care to.

A father who died was different from a father who'd disappeared. When your father died, everyone was told to say they were sorry and to be nice to you and the hearts of all your friends would be with yours that day, or that week, or for however long it took to understand what had happened.

No one, though, had known that her father had disappeared, and when it was finally known it wasn't talked about. Anywhere. Not at home, not at school, not on the playground. The children who knew, and the grown-ups who knew, looked at her as if there was something wrong with her, actually with her. That's the way she remembered it.

"I was surprised when I found the note, because I figured you didn't really want to go out with me. I guess I was right."

It was a long time before Frannie's mother told her about her father leaving. It was at least weeks, and maybe months. Days are often the same for children, because every day they're told what to do and what to think and what not to do and what not to think, and it was only in the moments in between this steady instruction that a child would begin to get a vision of what was really true behind and beyond all the words.

"I reckon I ain't too good with women," he said. "I sure don't ever seem to know what to say."

In the fourth grade, when Frannie was nine years old, she said something funny but smart-mouthed on the very first day of class. All the children laughed and even the teacher laughed before she caught herself, but from that day forward she'd had to sit in the front of the room with the teacher with her desk facing the class, for the entire year. She thought it was to punish her, but as time passed, she realized the teacher loved her and that something in her had connected with Frannie that first day and she wanted to be closer to her than to anyone else. It was one of the best years of Frannie's life.

"Of course, most of the time," Ted said, "when you're out with a woman, they do all the talking. Most of the time, anyway."

After Frannie's father left, her mother never took the daughters out to supper anymore. It was so absolute that she never took them out that it was as if it wasn't allowed. Many things changed during those years, and the evidence of a family betrayed, of a family wounded, became another one of those ways a child learned to feel, like being with Mother, one way, like being with Father, one way, like being without Father, a new way.

"I reckon the food'll be here pretty soon. It sure is taking a long time."

Why would it make such a difference? Frannie often thought. There was food and there was shelter and there was money and there was the kindness of family, as it remained, and so why would it make such a difference? It was because of the moments in between the words of those around you, and the sparkling acts of vibrant, sweetly promised fun. It was because there was no answer given, no reason, no warning, no gift to spare her the driving madness of having to know why.

"You hardly touched your beer," Ted said. "If you don't want it, I'll drink it while we wait."

Knowing that he was out there, maybe even nearby, but not knowing where, and not knowing why he would not call or write or come by or let her know, let her, of all people, the best friend he'd ever had, the person of all the people in this world who used to sit with him in the barn or by the pond or in the rowboat or on their island and listen to him talk about his life, and how he came to be her father, her mother's husband, listen to his thoughts on all the things in this world they shared together, how could it be possible that this man was out there somewhere and never saw her again? How could it be?

"I'll just order another one when the food comes," Ted said.

And then the heartbreaking thought she had that he was hurting and lost and driven mad by the mistakes of his past or by the erroneous conclusion that she never wanted to see him again, and that now that she was a woman and capable and strong with the same heart and understanding and warmth of childhood still there for him if he needed it when there might be no one else in this world he could be with in the way he'd been with her, the idea that she could make it right was sometimes too much.

"I think that's our stuff coming now," Ted said, looking down the corridor at the waitress approaching.

If a person, a young woman, for instance, began to cry in public, what did it mean? How could a waitress or a passing couple know what the tears meant, or what they should do? Why would a young woman begin to cry in public in a strange place where laughter and dance and music and the gathered moments of bliss were meant to begin, why, then, would a young woman begin, instead, to cry?

"Are you all right?" Ted asked.

"I've," Frannie said, almost not recognizing her voice as her own as she suddenly answered him, "I've got a contact coming loose. I'll be right back. Go on and start without me. Don't let it get cold," she called back as she went toward the rest room. "Okay?"

Natalie didn't cry when Jake gave her roses. She put them in three separate narrow vases, two in each one, and set them in three different rooms.

"Now I can see them wherever I go," she said.

"I bet you forgot."

"I almost did. It was such a busy day. But I wrote a check and when I had to think of the date, it hit me."

"One of these days I'll get you on it."

"No you won't."

"I'll be the one that remembers our real anniversary and you'll be running some big corporation and you won't remember."

"That's nonsense. I don't even want to run a big corporation. Or a little one."

"I thought you wanted to keep working," he said.

"I do, as long as we need me to. For however long it takes to get where we want."

"The sale of this farm will be a gift from your ancestors to our life. And to Frannie's, of course."

"It's a shame, really, but their world is over now. Those days are gone, the same way this land's been changed by development."

"That's the secret to success," he said. "Go with the flow. Change with the times. Look ahead and see what's going to be, not what was."

"You're so smart," she said. "Stay the night."

"You know I will, sugar."

"Good. Let me put the light back on for Frannie. I cut it off without thinking when you came in."

As soon as Frannie walked off, Eljert, Ted's friend from work, came up to the table.

"Man, are you with her?"

"Yeah. I guess. What're you doing here?"

"I'm just here."

"With who?"

"Me, myself, and I. Me, myself, and I's the only person what can get along with me these days."

"Yeah, I know what you mean."

"You're in for some fun tonight. I know that little gal."

"You do?"

Eljert saw Frannie coming out of the ladies' room. He walked off and gave Ted the thumb's-up sign. Ted lit a cigarette and drank some of his beer while he watched her coming down the aisle.

"I'm sorry," she said. "I've been rotten company. I'm really sorry. I'm a dope sometimes. I looked in the mirror and thought, hey, who's that?"

"It's okay."

"The food looks great. I told you to start eating. You should have. Who was that standing here when I came out?"

"A friend from work."

"This is really going to be a good night. I can feel it now. It's like I've had amnesia and I just woke up. That's the way I feel. Go on and eat," she said.

"Yeah," he said, staring as if trying to understand the change. "I will."

"Can you dance?" she asked with a mouth full of food.

"A little."

"Heck, I've danced with men who couldn't dance a step and still had fun."

"I can do better than stand there."

"I like to dance. I like to do everything, for that matter."

It was working now. It was finally working. She had found a way to turn it on.

"Like what?"

"Like what what?" she asked.

"You said you liked to do everything."

"You name it. Water-ski, dance, go to concerts, the beach, the mountains, heck, I like everything."

"It's been a long time since I've been to the mountains. Or the beach."

"How come?"

"It just has."

"Well, man, you got a car. You got gas. Get in and go."

"It's not that simple."

"It ought to be. If you like to do something, you ought to be able to do it."

"Is that right?" he asked, suspicious of her manner. "Do you always do whatever it is you like?"

"Well, don't take it so hard. I just mean it in a roundabout way. I mean, a person ought to have the right to do what he wants to do."

"I don't get you, Frannie. Where're you coming from all of a sudden?"

"From Mars, I guess," she said and ate for a few minutes without talking, figuring she must have gone too far in the other direction. Not knowing how far to go had always been her problem.

After a few minutes Ted said, "I didn't mean for you to get quiet on me again."

"Yeah, well, I was just eating. I was starved. I'm glad we came here. They give you plenty of food. I'm always hungry. Have you ever noticed how some women don't seem to ever be hungry?"

"I suppose."

"It's a lie," she said. "They eat in secret. I just go ahead and let it all hang out. I love to eat. I'm blessed I don't get fat but that's because my metabolism runs so fast. Like my mouth," she said and they both laughed. "That's more like it," she said. "That's the first real smile I've ever seen on you."

"Sometimes there isn't much to smile about."

"Sometimes you just have to make it up for yourself. You know what I mean? More talk, less thought is my new motto."

"Sometimes I wish I didn't have no memory. No memory at all."

"You are getting down," she said. "I must have given you my disease. I'll get you back up. I can make you laugh. I can make anyone laugh."

"Yeah," he said, contemplating her. "I think you could."

"Did you hear the one about the man who had a pet duck?"

"Nope."

"He took the pet duck into the feed store and bought a bunch of stuff for it and the feed-store owner asked him if it was charge or cash and the man who owned the duck said, put it on his bill."

Ted smiled out of the side of his mouth and shook his head but didn't actually laugh.

"Okay," she said. "How about this one. There was this woman once who was driving down the road and she saw a pig. She stopped and put the pig in her car and she didn't know what to do with it but she kept on driving, thinking to take it home— Have you heard this one?"

"No."

"After a few miles a highway patrolman asked her what she was doing. He told her she couldn't ride around with a pig in her car. It was against the law. She said she didn't know what to do with it because she'd just found it and the highway patrolman said she ought to take it to a park or a zoo or something and she thanked him and drove off.

"A couple of hours later the same highway patrolman saw them coming back down the road and stopped the woman and wanted to know what she was doing and why she hadn't taken the pig to the zoo or the park like he'd suggested. She told him she had taken him to the zoo and the pig had had so much fun she was on her way to Carowinds."

She stopped then, having finished the joke, and looked at Ted, who put his hand over his face and laughed quietly to himself.

"See. I got you," she said.

"I figured I'd better laugh or you'd keep on going."

"I knew I could get you."

It was wonderful to make a sad man laugh. It was wonderful to give a man something he never thought he'd get, to be the gift in his life, if only for a day, to be so dazzling and to be so warm that hearts as cold and sunken as an iceberg at sea unexpectedly rose again. It made Frannie feel good.

"Yeah, you got me," he said. "You sure did that."

"Good, I'm glad I got you because this beer's about to get me. Look at the dadgummed bottles on the table."

"I just figured you were thirsty."

"I was. It's been a long time."

"For what?"

"I mean, for getting out and cutting up and turning loose. My mom died a few months ago."

"I'm sorry."

"It's okay. You got to get over these things."

"You got to try, anyway."

"Hey, listen, let's not get on that stuff," she said.

"Whatever."

She was silent a moment and she looked at him hard and she grabbed his hand and put her knees against his under the table and heard herself saying, "I like you, old buddy. Let's get out of here soon and go somewhere."

"If you want to," he said.

She looked him in the eye and squeezed his hands hard and the words just came out, as if she were making a promise and a declaration of something when no one had asked her to, when it wasn't necessary, when she'd already done more than anyone would have expected. She went right ahead as if she were living up to some agreement within herself, some promise to herself that she did not clearly remember making but that she had to keep.

"Yeah, I want to. You bet I want to. Absolutely. I do.

And you'll never forget me, old buddy. You'll never forget me, you can just know that right now."

Across town, Reuben Baucom, who had one arm and who lived with his old mother, and who lived in the house that his father had once rented for six dollars a month from the mill where he himself now worked and who had saved Frannie from trouble that noonday when she'd wanted to be alone and eat her lunch and have her thoughts and who had once been deeply in love with a woman who broke it off and never even told him why and later married a man in another town and left to live with him, Reuben, who now sat on the porch of the old house high above the mill building itself, smelled the rain coming from the west and then heard it on the houses across town as it swept in and began to pour around him faster and harder than he had expected so that he had to get his hat and coat and run to his truck to roll up his windows.

Back on the porch he smoked another cigarette and heard his mother walking with her cane. He got up and opened the door for her.

"I didn't know it was a-going to rain," she said.

"I didn't either."

She sat beside him. They watched the rain.

Back at the farm Natalie and Jake were about to go to bed when they heard a sound on the front porch.

"It sounds like somebody walking," Natalie said.

"Maybe it's Frannie."

"She said it would be after midnight."

"Do you think she's gotten drunk and can't find her key?"

"She's knocking on the door," Natalie said. "I better go."

"Let me."

"Don't say anything to her. Just let her in."

"Okay."

"I better go with you."

"It's not Frannie," Jake said.

Natalie looked out.

"Damn. The stupid pigs. They're out again."

"I'm not going out in the rain and run them back. I don't think we should."

"No. I don't either."

"She'll have to handle it when she returns."

"I hope they don't tear up anything," Natalie said. "I wish she'd get rid of them. It's turned into a bad joke."

"She doesn't even talk about them anymore."

"She takes them for walks."

"Let's go to sleep."

"Okay," Jake said. "If you want. But—" he started to say something and then stopped.

"But what?"

"But I don't think you're going to be able to sleep. You're as worried over her as if you were her mother and she was on her first date."

"She breaks my heart sometimes," Natalie said.

"You shouldn't let it happen. You've got your own life to live. You can't let her drag you down."

"It's not dragging me down that she does," Natalie said.

"It's knowing that she breaks her own heart that breaks mine."

Frannie parked in her own driveway above the culvert that went along the ditch beside the road. She walked to Ted's house where he waited.

"You've got a light out on your car. The left one," she said.

"I didn't know that."

"It's out completely. The brake light's out as well as the regular light."

"It must be a fuse."

"No," she said while they stood in the yard and looked toward his old Buick, "it wouldn't be a fuse because both sides would be out if it was and anyway the brake light fuse is not the same as the regular light fuse."

"Is that right, now? How do you know such as that?" he asked.

"I just know it because I've worked on my car enough to know. The brake light fuse is on the same circuit as the turn signals."

"I guess I knew that," he said. "I just wasn't thinking."

Frannie had never been in either of the sides of this duplex. The first thing she noticed was that the ceilings were seven feet high instead of the standard eight. When the house had been built there were no codes to require a minimum height. Conceivably, and probably somewhere, there was a house built by someone who knew that the tallest person in his family was five feet eleven inches and had therefore built all the ceilings six feet in height. It was a way to save money. Shorter lumber cost less than longer lumber.

"Weird house, man," she said.

"I know, but it's cheap rent."

"How much do these go for? I've always wondered."

"Mine's two twenty-five a month. That was the cheapest place I could find anywhere when I got out."

"Got out of what?" she asked.

"Got out of jail."

Now it began to make sense to her. Now more things came clear. There were many questions to ask after this news, but she wasn't sure she wanted to ask them.

"Have you got a problem with that?" he asked.

"Not really. Have you?"

"Not unless you do. I paid the price. At least I did that."

"You're right."

It wasn't the first time she'd been out with a man who'd done time, but she had never been out with a man who'd done anything worse than have drugs in his possession or pass a bad check.

"Don't you want to know what I did?"

"If you want to tell me," she said. She was looking around the house now and saw through the doorway the room with the wall that was out of square and that ended in the middle of a window.

"I robbed a store."

It was so sad for a man to live like this. There was not one thing on the walls, not one break in the monotony of the dingy green paint, not one plant or picture or ornament on any table anywhere. Just a chair in front of the television with a small plastic table beside it with a lamp and an old couch with a blanket over the cushions and a bed through the doorway and a pile of clothes on a straight-backed wooden chair nearby.

"It's not much of a place," he said, seeing her eyes go around the house.

"It'd be hard to do anything with this," she said. "It's not your fault."

The interior depressed Frannie. A bad feeling was coming over her like a dark cloud.

"You're getting quiet again," Ted said.

"I'm sorry."

"Well, let's talk."

"Okay."

"What do we want to talk about?" he asked.

"Ummm, let me think," she said.

In the other room she could see a pair of his underpants on the top of the pile of clothes on the chair. He wore briefs. She looked at them a long time. They looked like a size 36 and they looked like the brand she packed. Probably he got them at the outlet. They must have been seconds.

At least he wears underpants, she thought.

The worst man she'd ever been out with in her life didn't wear underpants. He was so in love with himself no woman could ever be as interested in his genitals as he was and she decided it was a good rule never to fall for a man who wore no underpants.

"We could always talk about the weather. I think it's

going to start raining again," Ted said. "It stopped on the way home, but the wind's picking up again."

It seemed as good a way as any to judge a man you didn't know. Maybe there was even a division along the lines of who wore boxers and who wore briefs. What else could a woman go by? How nice he was? That always changed. How much money he had? It might never be for you. How much he said he loved you?

"Look, I'm trying to be nice about this, but if you're going to sit there like a goddamn zombie . . ."

"I'm sorry."

"You're laughing and making jokes and bragging on yourself in the restaurant and now this."

"I'm sorry."

"There's the door," he said. "Use it."

She found herself in the rain. There was her car. She drove up to her house.

I have changed, she thought. I can't do it anymore.

There was Natalie's car. There was Jake's.

I thought I could do it. I thought I could still do it. It seemed like it would make me feel better. It seemed like it would make him feel better. It seemed like everyone needed to feel better.

For a while everyone did. Then, they didn't. For a while it worked. For most of her life, she'd been able to make people happy. Now it was over. It seemed like it had been the right thing to do, to make people happy. Now that she couldn't do it anymore, what was she supposed to do? It seemed like an easy thing to know. What to do. At first it was. Then, it wasn't.

Chapter 22

THREE WEEKS LATER Frannie received a letter in the mail. Inside the letter was one of the notes she had inserted in the packages at the plant. Along with this card was a handwritten letter, on notebook paper, from a woman who said she thought she knew where Frannie's father was. She said she didn't mean to be ugly about it, but if it was the same man she thought it was, he owed her a thousand dollars and she would tell Frannie what she knew if she would pay off the debt.

"It's not real," Natalie said.

"But how do I know? I have to call her. I at least have to do that."

"It's from Illinois?"

"Yes."

"He wouldn't be there."

"How do you know?"

"He just wouldn't. He didn't like the north."

"That's not the north."

"To him it would have been. Anything north of the Mason-Dixon line was enemy territory."

"He never told me that."

Frannie read through the letter again trying to control a sense of jealousy she was feeling that Natalie knew something about her father she didn't.

"Go ahead and call her. Go on," Natalie said.

"You sound like you're daring me to. Why? Why do you sound like that?"

"Because I want you to think about what it's going to mean if you find him. What he might be like. What you might find out."

"I've already thought about all of that. I guess I've thought of every scenario you could think of."

"Then do it."

"I will."

She got a few sheets of paper and a pen and pulled the phone from the counter to the kitchen table and read the letter one more time and then copied the number onto the paper she was going to use to take notes.

"You're going to pay her?"

"I don't know yet. I'll see what she sounds like."

Frannie started dialing the phone, but Natalie gently put her hand over the buttons and stopped her.

"Don't do it. At least not yet. I'm going to give you

something I'm not supposed to give you, but I'm going to do it."

"What?"

"It's a letter Mom wrote before she died and she gave it to me to hold. It's about our father."

Frannie slowly pushed the phone away from her and felt the tears well up in her eyes and the anger overwhelm her voice.

"You mean to tell me that all along you've known and never told me? You mean to tell me that?"

"She asked me to hold it until you got married."

"And it tells me where Dad is?"

"No. It's Mom's way of telling you why he left. Or, actually, why she sent him away."

"Oh damn. Damnation and hell. It was true. All along I was sure everyone knew everything but me, and now I find out it's true. I am so mad. Give it to me. Give it to me now."

"I didn't always know."

"But you knew before me and never told me. I can't stand this. Just give it to me."

Natalie returned with a sealed envelope. On the front of it was Frannie's name in her mother's old-fashioned, almost ornate handwriting. The sight of her name written by her dying mother nearly broke Frannie into the tears she'd been holding back.

"It doesn't tell you where he is," Natalie said. "She didn't know."

She opened the envelope and read the letter to herself while Natalie stood by the kitchen counter and watched.

Dear Frannie, my darling daughter,

I've tried always to protect you from what I knew about your father and not force on you the feelings I had for him. In doing this I chose to remain silent, and in remaining silent, I am afraid I've made everything worse.

It's time now that I know I am going to die and will not live to see you begin your own family and succeed where I failed.

I want you to know that I now understand that everything your father did was out of the goodness of his heart and it was that goodness of his heart that I fell in love with. When it all happened my anger and sense of betrayal told me it was out of something evil, but I was wrong.

What I found out was that your father had been married once before and the way I found out was when your grandmother died an audit was done of the accounts and holdings of our family and it was discovered that he had been siphoning off money from our accounts and giving it to this woman, his ex-wife.

I thought at the time that he was also seeing her, but I am not sure of that now. I do know that after he left, we had to sell the land across the road to recover some of the cash we needed to live on, and selling the land was something I never wanted to do. At least I have saved this house and some of it for you and your sister.

There are things that I'd like to tell you about your father that would justify my decision to ask him to leave, but you don't need to know them.

What you need to know is that I later found out your

father was supporting his ex-wife because she was a frail and sick woman who could not take care of herself and so you could say that his deceit of me and of our family was for "honorable" purposes. You should say that. I never could. But you should think it, because it's best for you.

I do not know where he is now. I do not know if he went to live with his ex-wife but I doubt it. I think he was a man who did not want the responsibilities of marriage, and although he was wonderful as a father, he was a dreadful and disappointing husband.

I'm sorry to tell you this. You should not think badly of him. I have allowed you to build a myth about him because a daughter should love a father this way. My silence about all of this was meant to be a beacon of the truth, but it became a mute cry of my own bitterness.

For this I am sorry. Now that you are married, which like the death of parents, contributes to the inevitable end of childhood, I know you are ready to understand both your father and me, and to know and accept that we both loved you in our own way as much as any parents could love a child.

I love you now, even more, in these last few days of my life.

Please live a good life, take care of Natalie as I have asked her to care for you, and know that I will always be with you.

I do love you so,
Mom

Frannie was crying so hard by the time she finished the letter she had to hold it away from her face so the tears would not drip onto the pages. Across the room, Natalie was also weeping, but waiting for a sign from her sister that she was ready to forgive her for withholding the letter before she went to console her.

"Now what do I do?" Frannie asked. "Now what am I supposed to think? Did you know all this?"

"Yes."

"When?"

"She told me a few years ago."

"You should have told me. Why has everyone thought I can't handle anything?"

"I had to honor what she wanted."

"I feel very bad now. I feel awful. He took our money—he lied to us."

"But not in a mean way."

"I know. It makes it even worse. It kind of breaks my heart now in a way it wasn't broken before. It makes me feel even sorrier for him than ever."

Side by side they walked outside and leaned on the porch rail and looked out over the land. Frannie was quiet, and Natalie waited for her to speak, giving her time to think.

"Mom really hated him, didn't she."

"Yes. I think she did."

"She never said, but I knew it anyway."

"I did, too."

"She's right when she says her silence said it all. She really hated him."

"I've thought about that a lot," Natalie said. "I think maybe Mom isn't entirely blameless in all of this."

"She's probably not, but what do you mean?"

"You know how she was if you ever made fun of her or laughed at something she'd done wrong and how she'd go stiff and wouldn't talk to you about it and would be all in a huff about it all day."

"Yes."

"You know how even if she cooked something and it didn't turn out right she'd leave the table if anyone said anything about it and pout in her room until the next morning. Well, that's kind of what she did with Dad, only forever. I've thought about this a lot and I think it was that she had so much pride and was so hypersensitive about everything she did, she couldn't laugh at herself, and she couldn't stand to make a mistake."

"Yes, that's true."

"But you know what else?"

"Tell me."

"I think she grew more bitter about him as time went on after he left because she was stuck here with us and all the responsibility while he was out there, for all she knew, wild and free and having a ball. I think it made her hate him even more."

"But maybe he wasn't out there having a ball," Frannie said.

"No, maybe not, but she thought he was, and it made her more bitter."

"It kind of fits she never looked for another man after

that. She didn't ever want to get in that kind of trouble again."

"Isn't it awful?"

"Sure, but I still want to know why he never called us. I still want to know where he is. Knowing all this now doesn't change that, although I am a little mad at him, when I never was before. Not really."

"So you're going to call the woman in Illinois?"

"I think so."

"Now?"

"No. Later."

She couldn't have made the phone call then. There were too many things to think about, too many new things. It seemed to Frannie that her sister might be right when she said it could be best not to know, not to find out, that her sister might be right in this in the way she seemed to be right in so much else where Frannie herself had been wrong. It seemed, as she now thought about it, that it could be true that it would be best not to know any more, though her heart, which remained broken and tender, still told her something different.

Chapter 23

THE NEXT DAY at work Frannie went through the warehouse and up the stairwell and into the cool, deserted room for lunch. The room always reminded her of the barn and loft at home.

She took a bite of her sandwich. She wondered if she should see a lawyer because selling the old place meant breaking a legal deed. It seemed too extreme a thing to do to Natalie. It seemed, really, if they needed the money that badly and Jake was right in that they could never keep it up and pay the taxes now that it was valued as development property instead of a farm, because a farm, he'd told her, had to produce at least twenty thousand dollars each year in sales, then it seemed he was right. Technically. But wrong every other way. And now there was the letter from her mother telling her how important the house and land were.

She slowly took a bite and looked straight ahead hoping that she was either wrong and that no one was there, or, if there was, the person would go away when whoever it was saw that she wasn't going to pay any attention to him.

She chewed slowly. Her heart was racing. She tried to breathe evenly and quietly so she would hear if the person approached. She did not want any trouble. She had so much to think about and not much time left.

Ted was eating lunch at the same hour, not on the floor against some boxes, as Frannie was, but sitting on the weighted counterbalanced rear end of a forklift and talking to Eljert, who sat in the seat.

"Man, I can't believe you didn't get nothing," Eljert said.

"Forget it."

"You're the only man in town who ever went out with her what didn't get what he wanted."

"Just shut up about it."

"She made a fool of you."

"She made a fool of herself."

"I know three or four men who've been out with her. You're pathetic, man. Pathetic."

"Drop it, would you."

"I'm going to have to pay her a visit myself just to show you how to do it."

"It's not like you're thinking," Ted said.

"You want me with you next time?"

"Go to hell."

"I saw you and I said to myself, well, old Ted's finally done it."

"I could've done anything I wanted."

"And you didn't?"

"She's messed up."

"So? She can lay on her back, can't she?"

"Yeah."

"Then, hell, man, what's the difference?"

"Probably none."

"Probably none is right. I'd rather a woman keep her damn mouth shut when I was out with her. Except for certain things."

"Yeah. Like you know all about it, huh? When's the damn last time you got anything? When, huh?"

"I guarantee you it was sooner than you."

"Prove it. Where is she?"

"I can prove it if I want to."

"Sure."

"Like hell I can't. I can damn take you right over there and show you."

"I don't spend my money on that kind of stuff," Ted said.

"She didn't cost me a damn cent."

"Good."

"You're the only damn man in town who ever went out with that little gal and missed."

"Whatever. Man, whatever you say, just keep on going because it doesn't mean shit to me. You got it? It doesn't mean shit to me."

"Maybe she was on the rag."

"Yeah. Maybe."

Eljert unsnapped the loop on the sheath hooked into his belt that held his knife.

"You want to throw the knife some?"

Jake was having lunch with his mother. She had taken a cab to the bank. Jake had arranged it and paid for the cab. He tried to have lunch with her in town once a month, though sometimes two months would go by and he'd suddenly realize he had forgotten. She never said anything to remind him.

"So, you're feeling good?" he asked.

"I'm fine."

"I'm sorry I haven't been home much lately. There's so much to look after at Natalie's."

"You do what you have to do," she said.

"You know you can call anytime if you need me."

"As long as I'm at home I can take care of myself perfectly."

"I know."

"It's only getting out that's hard."

They were walking out of the bank's front door to the interior of a mall where the bank was located and were going to have lunch at the cafeteria favored by many of the retired people in the town.

"You don't get out much. That's true. I thought it was because you liked being at home, but what you just said made me realize it's because it's too hard."

"It's both," she said.

"That's inconsiderate of me. Natalie and I ought to take you with us more. Would you like to see a movie this weekend?"

"Movies have nothing to do with my life. They don't interest me."

They passed the double open doors of a fine northern Italian restaurant that had recently opened for business.

"I've got an idea. Let's skip the cafeteria and go in here."

"We don't need to eat in a place like that for lunch. The cafeteria'll be fine."

"No. I insist. You deserve a little high living in your life like everyone else."

"I didn't know everyone else had it," she said, trying to walk past.

"Let me take you here. You and Dad never ate in a place like this in your life."

"If we didn't, we never missed it."

She studied the menu propped on a tripod at the entrance.

The maître d' was waiting for them to step in from the corridor. Jake's mother smiled politely and turned away toward the cafeteria.

"I know the kind of money you make, son. That's why I'm saying no."

Jake walked on beside her and chuckled and shook his head and patted her on her back.

Just before lunch Natalie had talked to Jake on the phone. He'd told her his mother was coming and she knew that the old lady would find something to criticize and she and Jake had laughed about that and prepared themselves. He had told her he'd call her after lunch to tell her how it had gone.

Jake's mother was seventy-two years old and Jake was thirty. She was a conservative and fretful woman but had a clear mind and a strong will and would live a long time, Natalie thought. Though she didn't feel close to her and she didn't like her the way she had her own mother, it was nice that she was there and that she and Jake had a good relationship.

Natalie was eating at her desk. There was something going on with the top brass in Mr. Bosco's office and there was a lot of coming and going between it and Mr. Osteen's. It seemed serious and she tried to catch someone's eye so she could find out.

While she ate, she turned the pages of several real estate weeklies looking at houses for sale. She wasn't sure how much capital gains she would have to pay on something that had been in the family so long it was worth a thousand times more than had ever been actually paid for it, or put into it, but she was excited about finding a house in a nice tree-lined neighborhood with sidewalks for the children and a school nearby and interesting neighbors she might be friends with as her life moved forward and she shared the future with Jake and they did all the right things together that would build a strong family and a secure future.

Frannie, still leaning against the side of a tall box where she had settled down to eat and take a quick nap and still holding the sandwich in her hand and breathing evenly and quietly, listened for any sounds behind her and when she heard nothing for a few minutes, she turned around.

Gosh, she thought. There's not a soul there.

She stood up. Her legs shook. She had not been sleeping well at night. She looked around the corner, where the boxes were against the wall to one side of the chute into which she'd fallen, and saw nothing.

After she finished eating she put her wrapper and her can back in the bag and lay on the floor to take a quick nap. She kept hearing noises, though, and it scared her to think about sleeping on the floor where someone could sneak up on her.

She looked on top of the cardboard boxes towering above her and stepped on a smaller stack to climb the tallest one, which was about ten feet high and large enough to curl up on top of. It was filthy. She climbed down and got a piece of clean cardboard and took it up with her so she could lay on it.

At twelve-thirty Ethel asked Linda where Frannie was. They wanted to see her up front.

"She'll be back soon. Why?"

"I expect you know."

"I expect I don't."

Ethel opened Frannie's drawer below her work space on the table and began to go through it.

"You can't do that," Linda said.

"I'm sure I can. I don't want to, but I can."

"Come on, Ethel. Whatever it is, you got to be on Frannie's side. She's having a hard time these days."

"We're all having a hard time these days."

"There's nothing in there. She doesn't even use it," Linda said.

"I hope there isn't."

At one o'clock two men in suits walked through the mill looking for Frannie. They went in the warehouse and asked Reuben if he'd seen her.

"Nope. Not today."

They walked into the parking lot and located her car and then reported to Mr. Bosco it was there but they could not locate her. Mr. Bosco asked Natalie if she knew where Frannie was. Natalie was upset when they wouldn't tell her what it was about and went herself to look for her.

"I really don't know where she is, Natalie. I'd tell you if I did. I wouldn't tell those jerks, but I would you," Linda said.

While everyone was looking in the production area of the mill and outside, Reuben quietly went upstairs. He was hoping to find her and get her back down before she got into even more trouble.

At first he didn't see or hear anything or anybody. As he walked from the stairway into the middle of the room his eyes caught movement in the middle of the row of boxes. One of the boxes was bumping around as if it were alive, or as if it were trying to break free from the row of boxes it had been standing with all these years. He stood in front of it and watched it moving as if it was trying to hop.

Inside the box was Frannie. While she slept, the top of the box had caved in. She had fallen inside. She had landed on a pile of loose paper and small packets in the bottom. The sides of the box were so tall she could not pull herself out. She could not reach the top edges even by piling up the loose papers and standing on them.

Because the box was wedged in the line of other boxes and against the wall behind it, she could not tilt the box any direction except forward. It was wedged so tightly, however, it would only move very little in that direction.

She had thrown herself against the side of the box facing forward and had dented it some so that from the outside there was a roughly abstract shape of a body, something like the shape of a body in a cartoon as the character runs through a wall, only not as well defined.

The box had rocked when she had done that, but would not fall. It had seemed to her to be wedged in tighter at the bottom. It simply would not fall over. She couldn't call for help. There was nothing she could do but keep trying to get out one way or the other.

After a while she devised a method. She positioned herself at the rear of the box and jumped forward against the front. She did this over and over, hopping with both feet against the base of the box. Each time it skipped an inch or so out from the line of boxes and into the room.

It was at this point in her efforts to get out that Reuben had arrived. He thought that it had to be Frannie inside the box. What he could not figure out was why she was in the box, and what she was doing.

It seemed to him that she had climbed into this box and was bouncing off the walls, either having gone completely mad or playing a strange and curious game. Because she was not calling for help and because she did not seem to be in trouble, he said nothing. He watched the box walking toward him and wondered what he should do in the same way anyone with dignity would wonder about whether to knock on a door, having come up to a house and witnessed the person inside doing something embarrassing, ridiculous, or unfathomable. If he knocked, the person was caught in the act. If he said anything to Frannie, she was caught.

It was a dilemma because they were looking for her downstairs. It was a dilemma because he wasn't even entirely sure, not 110 percent sure, it was her. It had to be. But he couldn't even be sure of that.

Meanwhile, inside, Frannie was furious at herself and figured everyone wondered why she hadn't come back to work. Besides being furious she felt foolish and stupid and a little scared. Of course she would get out. She knew eventually she could break through the heavy cardboard or get out some way, but what if it took hours and the mill was closed when she finally emerged?

Finally, after walking the box forward until she sensed it was loose from its companions in the row, she took a flying leap at the side of the box as high up as she could. The box slowly tilted over as her weight carried it down to the floor.

She tumbled like a prize dumped out of a box of Crackerjacks, and landed at Reuben's feet.

"Oh, hell," she said when she looked up and saw him. "It *would* be you."

"Are you okay?"

"I guess I am."

"You've got a cut on your elbow."

"I'll live," she said, brushing herself off and finally standing up.

"I suppose it's none of my business what you were doing inside that box."

"Help me push it back up in place," she said, "and I'll tell you. I'll tell you because I don't want you to think I'm any crazier than you already think I am."

"I don't think you're crazy," he said after they got it back so that it looked as if it had been there all along.

"What are you doing up here, anyway?" she asked. "Was that you earlier?"

"Earlier when?"

"When I was eating my lunch. I guess you were spying on me."

"I was not. I didn't even know you were here and wouldn't have come up if they hadn't been looking for you downstairs."

"I bet. They're looking for me?"

"Yes."

"Uh-oh. And you weren't up here earlier?"

"No."

"I bet."

"You can believe me, Frannie Vaughan, when I tell you something. I didn't know you were up here."

They stopped at the green iron stairway railings. Frannie felt the need to apologize for her distrust and not take out on him all the stress she was under.

"Listen, thanks for looking for me. I mean it."

"Do you get inside boxes often?" he asked.

"I went up there to take a nap. The top caved in. That's how it happened. Okay?"

"I believe you."

"You do?"

"Of course."

"I guess I better get back to work. Who's looking for me, by the way. Ethel?"

"Everyone. They want you up front."

The part of the mill where the executive offices were did not resemble the rest of the building. The doors to the work area were wood and metal. The doors to the offices were glass and opened automatically. The air, once inside, was clear and the only sounds Frannie heard as she entered were the dull tapping of keyboards, the muted ring of telephones, and the dampened sound of her shoes on the carpet beneath.

"Where have you been?" Natalie asked.

"It's a long story. I'm here, though. I guess I'm in some kind of trouble."

"You're going to kill me someday with worry."

The secretary had Frannie wait while Mr. Bosco assembled the people involved. Then she was asked to come inside.

"Sit down, please," Mr. Bosco said. "You know Mr. Osteen. And Ethel."

"Yes, I do."

"One of our customers recently sent us something in the mail, and we've puzzled over it, and we've discussed it, and we've looked for answers and struggled for reasons, but in the end, we had no choice but to bring you here and ask you about it."

"All right. You can ask me."

"This was found, according to the customer who sent it in, tucked in the folds of a T-shirt. He said the bag was sealed when he got it, and that he didn't think it had been tampered with at all. He sent the bag, as well."

"Uh-huh," Frannie said.

"We have quality checks on a percentage of what leaves this building, but even further we have each set of bags bar coded so we can know who is packing what. For instance, the bags assigned to you are bar coded with your reference and therefore it appears that you packed these T-shirts."

"I might have," she said.

"You mean you admit putting this inside?" he asked.

He handed her the card. Oh no, she thought. This one. It would be the one she wrote when she'd come back from the date with Ted, feeling bad and stupid and disgusted with herself.

It read:

> I'm lonely and I'm hot
> Rich I'm not
> If you've got money
> Be my honey

I used to be free
But now there's a fee
Giving it away
Just don't make my day
I'm young, stupid, and good looking
Now don't that get you cooking?
Ain't that just what you wunt
Not my brains, just my _____?

She had left the last word out and then added a phony name and phone number and when she had written it she had been mad enough at herself and at the kind of men she seemed to always end up with for it to have made her feel better to have written it and to imagine some jerk reading it and believing it.

Now, though, like many other things she'd done in her life, it didn't seem like it had been such a smart idea, or even funny.

"So did you write this? And put this in the package?"

"It was supposed to be a joke," she said.

"It's not a joke, Frances."

"It was meant to be."

"How many of these are out there?"

"Only that one."

"That's hard to believe, Frances."

"Tell the truth," Mr. Osteen said.

"We'll find out sooner or later," Ethel said.

"We will," Mr. Bosco said.

"It's just that one."

"Do you swear to that?"

"I do swear to it."

"I'm not sure we can trust her," Mr. Bosco said to the others in the room as if she were not there. "She has a reputation."

"What do you mean, *she* has a reputation?" Frannie asked.

"Tell us how many you sent out."

"One."

"This pack of T-shirts was bought by a famous man, Frannie. It might not be so bad if this man were not so well-known."

"Who?"

"It was bought by a man who is a well-known Fundamentalist preacher and television evangelist, the Reverend John Will Sukit."

"Oh."

He can make trouble for us. This will likely cost us some money. Are you prepared to pay what it may cost to satisfy Reverend Sukit?"

"Probably not," she said. "And you shouldn't either."

"This could be a scandal. A reputation, a bad one, that is, can follow you forever, but I presume you know that, don't you, Frances?"

"What do you mean by that?"

"Whatever I mean, you know what it is. The point is, someone has to pay."

"Well I can't and I won't, so just fire me."

"No. I don't want to do that. Out of loyalty to your sister, at least not now, I don't."

"Get hold of some money and pay it," Ethel said. "If you can, it'll be the best way out."

"I'm sorry. It was a joke. It backfired. I didn't mean it to cause trouble for you. I'm sorry."

"It's too late for sorry."

She returned to work. She did so in the way she had been taught to get back on her friend's horse when she fell off. Get right back on. Then you won't be scared. Jump right back up. Jump right back into whatever it was that threw you to the ground. It worked with horses. Often it did not with people.

"Yep. They found one," Frannie said.

"Are you fired?" Linda asked.

"Nope."

"Are they docking your pay?"

"Nope."

"Do you want to talk about it?"

"Nope."

At the end of the day she walked out of the mill with a clenched mouth. She hadn't spoken all afternoon, even to Linda, who tried off and on to cheer her up and to find out more about it. Reuben was waiting at her car.

"I heard about it," he said. "It's not good."

"Nope. It's not good."

"I'll see what I can do."

"You don't have to do anything for me."

"What if I want to?"

"Why? Why would you want to?"

"Because I do."

"Because why?"

They sat on the tailgate of his truck. Other people leaving work waved to them or stared and it made Frannie uncomfortable.

"Let's sit in my car or in your cab if we're going to talk about it."

They walked to her car. She still didn't understand or trust him or his motives.

"I can't talk long," she said when they got in. "I've got to get home. I need to make a phone call."

"I'm just offering my help. That's all."

"I guess I need all the help I can get. I guess I do."

"You can trust me, Frannie."

"Maybe. Maybe I can."

"I wish I could tell you something that'd at least make you understand that I don't mean you any harm."

"What is it, Reuben? What is it you want to tell me?"

"Well, I could tell you a lot of things. I could tell you about myself. I could tell you that I sort of knew your family, years ago, before you were born. I could tell you I've even been to your farm."

"You have?"

"Yes, I have."

"I don't remember you, or ever hearing about you."

"It was a long time ago."

Frannie was quiet. She wanted to like this man. She

wanted to believe he was sincere. While she was being quiet, she also fought the feeling she often had when she was close to a man, the feeling of flowing toward him, fought the tantalizing warmth she could feel at her fingertips and at the back of her neck. She fought it while at the same time wanting to believe in what she felt and in what he was saying.

"What do you remember?" she asked.

"I remember buying eggs from your grandfather. I remember going out to your farm with my father on many occasions, on a Saturday or a Sunday afternoon and buying chickens sometimes, and a fresh turkey at Thanksgiving."

"What did my grandfather look like?" she asked, pressing to see if he was telling the truth.

"He was about my size in height, but leaner, maybe even thin, and he had a weathered face that seemed to be tanned even in cold weather, is how I remember him. And his hands were big, or it seemed that way to me."

"What color were his eyes?" she heard herself asking, even though she didn't know the answer herself.

"I couldn't say. But it seemed to me he wore glasses."

"Yes, he did."

"I think I even met your mother a few times. I'm sorry about her passing, by the way."

"Thanks."

"I'd like to see the old place again. Do you still own it?"

"We do."

"I sure did love it out there."

"Well, maybe you'll get a chance to see it someday."

"I hope so. I could tell you more about your grandfather if you want. I remember lots of stories about us being out there."

"Maybe some other time."

They were both silent then until she felt Reuben had been looking at her so long she had to say something.

"Listen, if you want to help me, okay. And to be honest with you, I'd love to hear about my granddad and what it was like out there back then. I really would."

"You just say when."

"Sometime. Not today, but sometime."

"Frannie, you interest me. I can't help telling you. You do."

"I wonder why," she said as he got out of the car and thought about it seriously as he walked around to her side. "I guess you feel sorry for me. That's got to be it. If you knew me, really, you'd run like hell. I'm no good."

"That's not true."

She began to feel sad and began to feel sorry for herself and for what she saw as the mess she'd made of her life.

"Haven't you heard about me? How come you haven't? Everybody else has."

"You're fine, Frannie. And you're a good person. Too good, I would guess."

"I ain't no good at all," she said, and with the engine running and Reuben standing beside her, she let what he'd said about her being too good sink in. As it did tears began to roll down her cheeks and she drove off before he could see them. Unexpected kindness had a way, lately, of moving her to tears.

Back home, Frannie continued to feel sorry for herself, though her sorrow was mixed with anger and fatigue. She was tired of being branded and of making mistakes, and she was tired of not knowing how to proceed in her life, or which way to go, and as she thought about this, she remembered the snide allusions to her "reputation" that Mr. Bosco had made.

Because she had now begun to see herself in a different way, she also began to be aware of what other women long before her had learned. She began to understand the duplicity of not only seeking pleasure and happiness, but of giving it, as well.

It was true, in the past, and even now, that pleasure and the idea of it, was disturbing to many people. Even though there were now the pictures of blissful women and indulgent men everywhere people looked, somehow even today the idea of pleasure remained confused.

In the nineteenth century there was nearly universal agreement that there was to be very little pleasure, very little fun. What there was of pleasure was not that good, not in the new way, not for most people. Laughter and happiness were considered frivolous and simpleminded.

You did not smile. If you did you were to cover your mouth. You were to smile behind the cover of your hand and hold it in as best you could. It was confusing to know that there was supposed to be little pleasure in life and to know that it was a lesser virtue and at the same time, by accident and without warning, to feel it so strongly.

One would think that in modern times when pleasure was the imperative and when the wildly happy face of bliss and sensuality and abandon was the standard by which we all were judged, it would not be so confusing, and that one would not go mad from it and be put away as before.

"I'm just so upset," Frannie said when her sister came home and they talked. "I'm going to scream and not stop screaming."

"You made a mistake. That's all. It'll pass."

"It won't pass. It'll never pass. It seems like I'm always in trouble. Then, there you are, just steady-on Natalie, like a rock, like this house, like this land, whatever, I don't know, but always there, always the same, steady and constant and smart and sensible and then, over here in the loony bin, is me."

"I've made my mistakes."

"I don't even hate you for being like you are. I love you for it."

"You're having a hard time lately."

"Oh, you know that's not it. I'm always going to be this way."

"Maybe it was Mom's death. They say if people die before you've made peace with them, it messes you up."

"But we weren't enemies. I loved her so much and she loved me."

"But she was hurt at the way you were living and you knew that."

"I know she was. I'm sorry about that. But we were still friends. Weren't we?"

"Of course you were. I don't know what it is. I'm just thinking out loud."

"I think thinking is what the problem is. I wasn't having nearly this much trouble before I started thinking so much. Hit me in the head real hard. Go ahead."

"I will not."

"Go on. Hit me real hard and knock me out."

"You really want me to?"

"Yeah."

"I'd like to. You do kind of deserve it."

"I know I do," Frannie said. "Go ahead."

"I couldn't. It's tempting, though."

"I'll hit myself, then."

"I do wonder," Natalie said, "what it is."

"Oh crap, it's everything. It's just everything. And I'm so mad that people don't think I can change. I have changed."

"You really are in trouble at the mill, though. We do need to talk about that."

"Now that's something I don't want to talk about. It's so stupid to make such a big deal out of it."

"It was not smart. I'm sorry, and I love you and I always will, sis, but it wasn't smart."

"Did you see it?"

"Yes. Mr. Osteen showed it to me. That kind of thing isn't funny to most people, and not at all to people who have the legal liability for what you do."

"I give a shit about legal liability. Especially from men like that. I hated that meeting. Do you know what they said to me? Do you?"

"What?"

"They said, we know all about you."

"What did they mean?"

"Maybe I ought to quit. Do you think I should?"

"What will you do for a living? Spend down all Mom left you?"

"I better not."

"Don't."

"I won't."

"And here I was ready to call that mystery woman and find out if she's telling the truth about Dad or not, and now this. How much more of a mess can I get into? I'm going to call her anyway," she said and opened up the refrigerator to see what there was to eat. "By the way, Reuben used to come out here when he was a boy and buy eggs from Granddaddy. Isn't that something?"

Later that evening Frannie came downstairs and plopped down on the couch beside Natalie.

"The woman was a kook. It's not him. The guy's like thirty-five years old she's looking for. It was a really depressing conversation. She was nuts. For a minute when I was talking to her I felt like maybe I sound like her sometimes, and that I must come across like a wacko like her."

"You never do, Frannie. Don't put that on yourself. But she was out of it, huh?"

"Like from Neptune. I mean, nothing. Nothing there at all."

"Well, let it go."

"Let what go?"

"Her."

"Oh. Yeah. I will. Other things I won't. Like this house."

"Don't oppose this house sale. You're not still holding on to that?"

"Oh yes, I am."

"I've tried not to talk about it because I don't want us to fall out over it."

"Okay. When the time comes to talk, you'll know where I stand because it's the same as now. No."

Frannie sat in an empty window opening of her barn. Below her the pigs were waking up. It was early morning.

From the pond she heard the blackbirds. She walked across the wet field to the narrow road that led down to the pond. Every few feet, from tree to tree, a spiderweb had been strung. In the slanting rays of the sun the strands and patterns sparkled with drops of dew hanging like glass jewels from a chandelier. She ducked beneath the webs and emerged above the pond. She looked at the island to her right, which seemed mysterious in the mist that clung to the willows and mimosas her grandfather had planted when the pond had been built.

A white-and-gray feathered crane floated at the far side. It gazed at her with noble head and regal bearing and without visible effort moved into the mist behind the island. A grass-hopper suddenly jumped off the bank into the air and when it did, a fish larger than she knew lived in that pond leaped up and caught it. The fish looked like it weighed fifteen pounds.

She leaned against a tree. Life went on down here as it always had. Morning came. A regal bird calmly made note of the activity and then retired. Somewhere, though she could not see it, a deer probably stood at the edge of the woods and watched her, as well, so much a part of the forest she would never know it was there until it moved.

A few minutes later a fat muskrat nearly the size of a raccoon crawled out of the water and began to amble toward her, sniffing the air and the ground and plodding along as if it were looking for something to do.

It walked past her and only when it had gone a few feet beyond did it see her. Its heart must have pounded the same way hers did as they looked at one another, each afraid to move. The animal was big enough to take a mean bite out of her ankle. After a few seconds of looking into each other's eyes, it slid over the bank and disappeared into the water.

Then everything was still again as Frannie gazed across the surface to the island while the mist cleared and the sun rose higher and it was time to leave for work.

Chapter 24

WHEN NATALIE TOLD Jake how Frannie had acted about the sale of the farm and how she still clung to her refusal to agree to it, he decided it was time to talk about it with her once again.

"So how much are we going to get?" Frannie asked.

"I'll get as much as the market will bear," Jake said.

"But how much will the whole place bring?"

"It could be as much as six hundred thousand if we're lucky."

"How could it be worth that much?"

"Because it's zoned for development. You can even have mixed-use development out here," Jake said.

"Mixed-use," Frannie said sullenly. "What in the hell is that?"

"You can have light manufacturing or high-density housing or a restaurant, things like that," Jake said.

"How disgusting. How boring. I can hardly stay awake."

"It's to your advantage that the zoning allows that. It means more money."

"Right. Like I care."

"You will care. Later in life."

"How much is the house itself worth?" Frannie asked.

"They won't pay anything for the house," Jake said.

"But it's a wonderful house."

"To you. To a developer it's a piece of junk in the way."

"Couldn't we move the house? Couldn't I move it to a new lot?"

"You can't move a house this big. You can't even get it down the road. They'd have to cut it up in little pieces and cut the top half off and then cut the high peaked roof off of it. It'd be impossible out here on these narrow roads, and you sure couldn't get it into town."

"But they move big houses."

"Not this big. They take them apart."

"I don't want to do it anyway," she said, looking down and pouting. "It's the land that makes it what it is. It's the trees and the pond and the barn and the fields and the yard and all that, that make it what it is. That's why I don't want to move it. That's why I'd rather buy the whole place off you guys."

"How are you going to do that?" Natalie asked. "You have six hundred thousand?"

"Technically, all she'd need would be three hundred. Our half," Jake said.

"Oh yes, right."

"No, I don't have it, but you can get me a loan for it."

"I could not."

"You could if you wanted to."

"I could not. You couldn't qualify for a loan that size unless you made ninety or a hundred thousand a year."

"I make three hundred a week," Frannie said.

"That's about fifteen thousand a year."

"So?"

"So?" Jake asked, too dumbfounded by her naiveté to explain it any further.

"Come on, Frannie. I wish there were some way," Natalie said. "But that money is what we have to have to buy our house."

"You need that much?"

"For a nice house we do."

"We might not get that. We can't count on it. I've been advised it could be as much as that."

"Why do you need a house like that? I don't. Why do you two suddenly have to have a mansion?"

"It won't be a mansion. And besides, there'll be taxes and capital gains to work out, and I don't know how that will be. I don't know how the government figures a piece of land that's been in a family for a hundred and fifty years. There must be some cap, some formula that is equitable."

"We're not going to sell it."

"We have no choice. We can't keep it up. It's gotten too

expensive. We're being encroached on. Soon it won't even be a nice area to live."

"It will. It always will."

"We'll help you, Frannie. The adjustment will be hard but both Natalie and I will be here for you. And you can stay with us if you don't want to live alone. I want you to know that."

"I need some air," she said. "There's no air in here."

She started for the door and then looked at Jake.

"Somebody's breathed up all the air in here. There's none left for me."

"There she goes," Eljert said.

It was Saturday. He and Ted were trying to think of something to do.

"Let's follow her and see where she's going," Eljert said.

Ted hadn't talked to Frannie since their date. He had waved to her from his front yard twice. The first time she was with her sister and she didn't wave back.

"I bet she's going out to have a little fun," Eljert said.

He'd noticed they had been talking so maybe it was she hadn't seen him. The second time he waved, she'd been alone and looking straight ahead and she failed to acknowledge him that time, as well.

"I guarantee you she's on her way to meet some fellow."

Of course Frannie was so spaced-out most of the time, at least she had been when she was with him, maybe she didn't see him either time. She was almost not worth the trouble, he had begun to think.

"I know a dozen men who've been with her," Eljert said. "More maybe."

"I don't believe it," Ted said.

"I bet you she'd do it for money."

"No way."

"I bet you ten dollars I could offer her money and she'd do it."

"You're wrong."

"Bet me, then."

"I ain't going to bet you shit. You're just wrong."

"You don't know women like I do, is all there is to it," Eljert said. "You've been away too long. Women has changed over the years."

"They have? How's that?"

"They all do it now. All of them."

The old man next door came out. Ted rarely saw him except when he got his mail. He heard his television blaring day and night, but rarely saw him.

"He's got a goddamn shotgun with him," Eljert said.

They watched the old man sneak around the side of the house. At the same time, they heard the woodpecker that had been knocking on the house and gutters all morning start again. Then they heard the shotgun blast and then saw the old man walk back inside.

They went around the back. Besides the bird splattered all over the edge of the roof and gutter, parts of the gutter itself had been blasted away and the shingles above it were peppered with holes. The bird's head hung from the sharp edge of the torn aluminum gutter along with feathers and blood.

"I guess he don't like birds," Eljert said.

Frannie went to the barn. She opened the gate to the pigs' pen. She let them go. Then she went into the loft and looked out from the high window across her land and the fields and trees beyond, and even to the power poles and high mounted lights of the shopping center farther on.

She closed her eyes and took a deep breath. She let it out, slowly, and then opened her eyes.

Daddy, she said, I need you now. Of all the times in my life, this is it. I haven't asked much of you. Ever. But I'm asking now. Come home. I need you. I really, really do.

Chapter 25

FRANNIE RETURNED TO work Monday. She tried to appear more pleasant than she actually felt. She ate lunch with Linda and Belle and Grace, and she behaved and worked hard and did her worrying and her dreaming in private.

No one from the front office called her in. Natalie could not tell if Frannie's troubles were over, but she, herself, heard no more about it. Belle talked about her new baby and how much better she felt after six months off, and because she was back, Linda talked with her when she might have been talking to Frannie, which freed Frannie to think.

She met with Reuben on Thursday.

"I talked with someone I know in management," he said. "It seems they're waiting to see if the letter of apology they wrote works."

"Good."

"If it did, it's over."

"Thanks."

"That's about all I can do now."

"It's enough. It's going to come down to me in the end. I know that."

He nodded. Then he said nothing. Because he said nothing but waited for something, Frannie became uncomfortable and began to try to fill the empty space of whatever it was he was waiting for with talk.

"So you live with your mom?"

"Yes. How'd you know that?"

"Someone told me. I don't remember who. How old is she?"

"She's seventy-three."

"My mom was sixty-two when she died."

He nodded again, and then she felt him trying to ask her something but unable to do so, so she asked it for him.

"Would you like to come to the farm on Saturday?"

"I would."

"Okay. I want you to try to remember what things were like then, you know, the buildings and the house and where the animals were, and all that. I'm curious about it."

On Saturday morning only Alice, the big sow, who had become the pet, was still around. The other two were gone and Frannie had not seen them in a day or maybe two, she could not remember.

"We're going to be in trouble if those pigs end up on someone's lawn over there in Montvale or whatever it's called," Natalie said.

"They won't go there. They're out in the woods eating acorns or digging up roots."

"Why don't you sell them and get it over with? You admit your mistake, so why not get your money back?"

"I can't kill them. Selling them would be killing them, so I have to leave it in the hands of fate."

"Okay. I'm not going to argue. And thanks for helping clean up everything. The house looks great."

"I wanted it to. I wanted it to look as good as it used to when Granny kept it up."

"For Reuben's visit?"

"Yeah. Why not? He doesn't know I'm a slob. I might as well fake it until he finds out."

"Why do you talk like that?" Natalie asked.

"Habit."

While waiting on the porch and talking to Alice who sniffed around under the shade trees nearby, Frannie was overcome with a feeling that Reuben would not show up. She began to go over all the conversations she'd had with him and all the foolish things she'd done in his presence and it occurred to her that it only made sense that he would not show because she had not explained to him how important this was to her and because he seemed to have said something like, I'll try to be there around noon. If I can't make it I'll call. That's what she remembered, which, now that she thought about it, was a way of giving himself an out.

At noon, however, at exactly noon, his late model pickup turned off the paved road and she watched it slowly coming up the gravel drive and she looked at her watch and shook her head and went out to greet him.

"I didn't think you'd come," she said.

"I told you I would."

"People say things all the time and don't do them."

"I wouldn't have missed coming out here for anything. I've thought about this old place many times in my life."

"Well is it the same?"

He looked around. Frannie noticed he wore leather hunting boots and gray cotton pants and a blue-and-red checked shirt and that he had a cap in his hand that she hadn't remembered ever seeing him wear.

"In a way. It seems to me it was more cleared out, that you could see farther, but maybe that was because I was little."

Natalie came out.

"How are you, Reuben?"

"I'm doing fine. It's nice of you to let me come out here and relive old memories."

"They're our memories, too, even though Frannie says you were out here before we were born."

"I was. It might have even been before your mom was married. Did they live on here after they married?"

"Yes."

"Then maybe it wasn't."

"I hope Jake will be here before you leave," Natalie said. "I'm expecting him."

"Where is he, anyway?" Frannie asked. "He's always here on Saturday," she said to Reuben.

"He's working on an investment plan for our money, for what's left after we buy the house."

"Oh."

"Jake thinks a good financial plan is the best thing a couple starting out can have," she explained to Reuben. "Most people's troubles are because of money."

"I'm sure he's right."

"He's smart," Natalie said and Frannie made a face, which Natalie missed but Reuben saw out of the corner of his eye. "We're trying to plan for all the mistakes other people make so we won't make them. I'm that way, anyway."

"People at work say you're the most organized person they ever met," Reuben said.

"It's my nature to be that way."

"It ain't mine," Frannie said. "I can't walk and chew gum at the same time."

Reuben laughed.

"She can do anything she wants," Natalie said. "Anything."

"No, I can't."

"I bet you can," Reuben said.

"You'd lose that bet," she said. "I want you to meet my pet hog."

"So you still have livestock here," he said.

"Nope. Just Alice. And her two siblings, but they've run off to see the world. They're out there somewhere," she said and pointed toward the woods.

"Your grandfather had a big boar at one time," he said. "I used to have nightmares about that boar. I only saw him a few times, but he was the stuff a kid's nightmares were made of."

"Well the only big bore we got out here now is," Frannie started to say Jake, but then looked at Natalie and stopped herself. "Oh, well, forget it."

While Frannie showed Reuben around the house, Natalie put on pork chops and prepared the potatoes that had already boiled for potato salad and took out the coconut cream pie she and Frannie had made the night before so it would be room temperature by dessert.

"I think he expects I'm still a farm girl," Frannie had said. "That's why I want to put on a big farm lunch when he comes. I've talked it up a little too much to throw a frozen pizza on his plate. He thinks we live old-fashioned," she had said to Natalie. "I guess maybe I kind of exaggerated a little."

"A little," Natalie had said, even though she was happy to go along with it. "We don't even know how to plant a garden."

After lunch, while Reuben waited on the porch and after she and Natalie had washed the dishes and put everything away, Frannie came out and sat with him.

"Here," she said, giving him a toothpick. "I know men like to clean their teeth after they eat."

"Thank you," he said.

"You didn't know my daddy?"

"I never met him. I don't think he was here when we came out."

"How old was my mom?"

"It seemed she was grown. In her twenties. When did they marry?"

"She was about twenty-eight when they married. She didn't have me until she was forty-two. I guess that's why I'm weird. Don't ask me why she waited so long. I don't know."

They walked to the barn. After their eyes got used to the dim light, Reuben went to an area the size of a stall but floored and with a window and a crudely built shelf at desk height.

"Your grandfather used to have a chair in this space. He had some kind of book he kept in a box and he'd sit in that chair and write what we'd bought and figure up the price."

"I didn't know that. It makes sense, but I didn't ever imagine it."

"Did you know he went barefoot in the summer?"

"He went barefoot?"

"He was always barefoot when we came out in the summer. He had his overalls rolled up above his ankles and he was barefoot."

Frannie stared at him with her eyes squinted as if she were trying to decide if he was telling the truth.

"I don't know what to make of that," she said and ran her hand across a smooth stanchion frame. "It makes me sad, for some reason, to hear that."

"I didn't mean to make you sad."

"It makes me sad because it's sweet. There's something sweet and innocent about that old man going around barefoot all day long. But it makes me kind of sad."

"Well, then I don't know whether to tell you the rest of it."

"Go on."

"Your grandmother did, too, and the reason I remember it so well is that the mill families were doing all they could to wear shoes. They'd spent their whole lives making sure they had money enough for shoes for everyone in the family and here were your grandparents walking around barefoot and rich enough to buy the whole shoe store if they'd wanted."

"I don't think of them as being rich. And it seems impossible that the old lady I remember would go around barefoot. I think you must be wrong about that."

"I may be, but I don't think so."

"Are you telling me the truth about all this? I'm going to be real upset if you aren't."

"Of course I am. What reason would I have for making it up?"

"It sounds too odd, too wonderful to be true, that's why. You don't know why I say that, but that's the way I feel."

"I think I do know why."

"Then tell me."

"Because it's the way you want to live. It's the way you'd like to be."

She was having trouble believing this man was real. No man, except her father, had ever seen into her heart before.

"What else do you want to know?" he said.

"I was wondering," she said and thought of something that would draw her back into herself to stop her from flowing toward him once again, "what you meant by rich."

"I meant, compared to us, the people whose parents worked at the mill, your grandparents would have been considered very wealthy people. And they probably were at the least very well-off, if not wealthy."

"I see."

"They were wealthy, relative to their times."

"I guess they were."

"Is there a pond down there?"

"Yes."

"With an island?"

"Yes."

"Now that is something I wasn't sure about. I only saw it once and then I couldn't remember whether I made it up or it was real."

"It's real."

"Can we see it? Do you still own it?"

"I sure do."

They walked to the pond. A boy was fishing on the far side. When they entered the clearing he began to reel in his line.

"Who's that?"

"I don't know. He probably sneaked in from the houses over there. It's only a few thousand feet through the woods."

"Do you let people fish here?"

"We decided not to. We decided to post it because we'd have hundreds of people here if we didn't."

The boy picked up his bait box and two small bream on a line stuck on a stake and trailing in the water and began to run.

"I don't care if he fishes," Frannie said. "It's okay with me. I just don't want a lot of people down here. It's where I get away from things."

"I can believe it."

"We're the last place left, you know. Except for the old Calhoun place next door."

"I've never been there that I recall."

They sat on the bank. Five or six crows were in a tree across the pond. They were all talking at once. Some of them were talking loudly and some others were talking softly, as if they were apologizing for something or trying to calm the louder ones down. While Frannie watched, one of the crows left the tree and flew toward her. When it was above where she and Reuben sat, it dropped something out of its mouth.

"Did you see that?" she said and picked it up.

"What is it?"

"An acorn."

"I wonder why it dropped it?"

She rolled it between her fingers. The cap popped off. What remained was smooth and she put it to her lips.

"It's so smooth," she said.

She handed it to Reuben. He held it in his open palm. She closed his hand around it.

"Keep it."

He put it in his pocket. She looked at his hand. It was rough looking, not calloused, but weathered and tough.

"I guess if you only have one arm you use your one hand twice as much," she said.

"In a way."

"How'd you lose your arm, if you don't mind my asking?"

"I'll tell you someday."

After a few more minutes they went back up the hill and through the woods along the path to the house and barn and across the field to the old wagon road that had connected her farm to the one now abandoned. She explained about the road to Reuben, and why it was lower than the woods around it, from the erosion and the rutting of the traffic, and how it was such a mystery that nothing seemed to grow in it after all these years of disuse, how it was the same now as when she'd first discovered it. As she talked, Alice trotted behind them, stopping now and then to dig something up or push some leaves aside looking for things to eat.

"This is nice. Standing right here and looking around, you wouldn't know about the rest of the world if you didn't already know it."

"That's right."

"Except we do know it, so it's not the same."

"You're worried about something, aren't you?" he said.

"Yep."

"Is it the trouble at the mill?"

"No. More than that."

"Whatever it is seems to be a big worry."

"Yeah, it's a big worry all right."

"Do you know the whole time I've known you, you've only smiled a few times?"

"I'm sorry."

"It's all right. But you look good when you smile. Entirely different."

"Crap, I don't look good anytime. I know myself. You don't have to say that just to make me feel better."

"I was saying it because it's true."

"I think I look like hell. Anyway, if you smiled a lot in the olden days people thought you were crazy."

The road stopped at the field that surrounded the bad-luck Calhoun place. Reuben looked at the burned-out house and the buildings and the chest-high weeds and the vines climbing up the walls of what remained standing. A loose sheet of tin roofing flapped as the wind blew.

"Who owns this? You?"

"No. I wish I did. Except it's a bad-luck farm. But I wish I did, anyway. It'd make things easier. It's owned by some out-of-town investors who started to build something on it years ago and then stopped. I mean, they never even cut a tree down. They just bought it and then ran out of money. That's what Jake found out."

"It's a strange place."

"Do you want to poke around?"

The chimney was standing where the house had burned and in the pile of debris only portions of the largest timbers remained along with the iron counterweights from the windows. There were cut nails in the ashes and pieces of twisted door latches and window locks. In one part of the site Reuben found a warped cast-iron frying pan.

"Maybe the kitchen was here."

"I don't know. It's been vacant so long I wouldn't have thought there would have been anything inside."

"What happened to the family? Were there no heirs?"

She told him about the old man's experience in the town when he was mistakenly locked up, and how he went down and down from then on as he refused to leave the farm, and how so many other unfortunate things occurred that finally ended the family line.

"I can understand it," he said while they walked back. "It makes perfect sense. People who lived like this, in a life like this, weren't prepared for that. For a man to imagine that something like that could happen to him after he'd led a life of virtue and hard work, if that's what he'd lived, would be so difficult to accept he would naturally never be the same again. I completely understand it. The whole story. A whole life destroyed, a whole family, an entire complete life, destroyed by one incident. Like losing an arm. But worse. Similar, though. That fast. And then, nothing is ever the same again."

"You're really into this," she said, watching his face as they walked along back home.

"I understand it, that's all," he said, suddenly shutting down as if he'd not been aware how impassioned he'd seemed until she pointed it out. "I understand betrayal. It's something I've thought about. Let's just leave it at that. I read a lot, Frannie. And when you read a lot, you think a lot. And this man had everything he'd ever believed in cut out from under him. For a man from those times to have his dignity and all he'd believed in suddenly taken away from him would be something he'd never get over."

"You're right. Some things you never get over."

As they walked ahead not talking, Alice lay in the road and waited for them. She had found a bed of pine needles and had taken a nap. Even though it was said that pigs were the smartest of animals, smarter than a dog, and even though it was said they got ulcers, certainly they never had the misfortune to worry about things such as virtue and honor and right and wrong. That was left to men and women, and to children, even, to figure out. For a while it seemed there were ways to know what was right and wrong; mostly everyone believed the same thing. Then it changed.

"You know, thinking about the old man made me remember something else about your grandfather," Reuben said.

"What was that?"

"That he talked quietly. That he seemed shy."

"He was quiet?" Frannie asked. "You mean he didn't laugh or carry on? Or didn't talk much? What do you mean?"

"I mean his manner was different."

"From who?" she asked, looking at him so seriously and intently he had to say something about it.

"Talk about being into something," he said.

"Just tell me what you mean. Different from who? Me, you, who?"

"I mean everybody. When I think about standing in the

barn and listening to him talk to my father I realize that no one else ever talked to him that way. To my father. Or to me. He was the most polite man I'd ever met."

"That's one of the best things you told me all day. I love it."

"It seems you do."

"I like that my grandfather was that way," she said. She put her hand on Reuben's shoulder and made him stop walking. "You've said something real important to me. A whole lot of things. I want you to know it means more to me than I could tell you."

"It's meant a lot to me, too."

"What?"

"To come out here. So I thank you, too."

For the rest of the way neither talked. Frannie looked straight ahead while she walked, but she was aware of Reuben beside her and she felt unusually warm being this close to him and this time she did not mind feeling that warm, and did not fight against it. Thinking about what he'd said and what he remembered and how he seemed to be so sincere about it all, and how he seemed to understand what it meant to her, made her want to put her arm around him while they walked, to be even closer, to thank him, to let him know how she felt about him.

She walked on, though, without touching him, and her eyes sparkled and she looked dreamy and she felt that something she'd been waiting for was nearby, like a piece missing from a puzzle, like words she'd been waiting to hear, like something she'd been trying to see at a distance, coming clear.

Chapter 26

"SHE DOESN'T PLAN," Jake said. "She doesn't understand the concept of planning."

They were eating breakfast. Frannie had already left for work. They were close to the sale of the farm. The only thing left loose and problematic, as Jake called it, was Frannie.

"She's trying," Natalie said.

"Look at the pig fiasco. It's typical."

"You're right. Somehow, though, everything is working out. She lets them run loose and for whatever reason they stay around and cause no trouble."

"She's lucky. She does have that going for her."

"It will be over soon. When we sell."

"I think we need to be sure to choose a house with a wing for her, or a built-in apartment."

"You really don't think she'll ever make it on her own?"

"Not in a normal way. Not with consistency. Not without a lot of trouble, and when the trouble's there, she'll want to move back."

"I hope you're wrong."

"I'm afraid I'm not."

"You're sweet to put up with her. I know she's been mean to you so many times that you have a right to shut her out. You've got so much patience and common sense."

"I try to do what's right."

"You were really mad when she took her money out of your bank. I could see it all over you. But you didn't say a word."

"It's hers. It's not for me, since I'm not her father, to tell her she's made a big mistake."

"She said she put it somewhere else safe. She wouldn't tell me where."

"She probably gave it to the first man who took her home with him."

"God, I hope not. She seems to be over all that."

They finished eating. Jake walked her to her car and kissed her good-bye. He went back inside and read the paper and then went to work himself. By the time he got there, Frannie had already been at the mill an hour and a half. Her day began at seven, and his began at eight-thirty. By the time he got to work, Frannie had already folded and stuffed more T-shirts and briefs into plastic bags than he'd wear in his lifetime. She was good at it now, and she enjoyed the way she didn't have to think about what she was doing, which let her think about everything else.

"I could do this for a few more years, I guess," she said to Linda and Belle. "But there's got to be life after this. Don't you want to move on someday?"

"I don't," Linda said. "I already had too many bad jobs to be stupid enough to try again."

"Me, too," said Belle. "When things are going okay, you know, good enough, then you know that's about as good as they'll ever get. You learn that eventually."

"Maybe so," Frannie said.

"Here comes Ethel," Linda said. "Cover up that Hershey Bar."

Frannie slipped a T-shirt over it and continued working. Out of the corner of her eye she saw Ethel stop and talk to two of the men who were pulling the dollies with the bins on them and give one of them a piece of paper, and then come toward her.

"Take a break, Frannie," she said. "They want to see you again up front."

"Sure. I hope everything's okay?"

"Don't ask me. Just pray."

Linda and Belle shook their heads as she followed Ethel down the long aisle, past the screeching conveyor belt, out from under the buzzing fluorescent fixtures, through the door, and into the carpeted hall leading to the offices.

"Am I fired?" Frannie said, smiling apologetically as she walked in. "Ethel wouldn't tell me."

"You're not fired," Mr. Bosco said. "But you're in deeper trouble. We all are."

"I'm sorry."

"You may recall that the Reverend John Will Sukit was, by misfortune, the recipient of your poetic license."

"I don't like that man," she said.

"It's not important whether you like him or not."

"I saw him on TV. He's not a good person. I don't think he has a sense of humor."

"It was not funny to him."

"Nor to us," Mr. Osteen said.

"I know I ought to be repentant for what I did, and I am in that I didn't want to cause you folks any trouble, but I don't feel sorry for him."

"Your attitude needs to change, Frances, because he's here, right now, and has been discussing legal action against you and against us and we've asked him to talk with you first."

"We thought that if he saw you were just a young woman who meant no harm it might all be forgiven."

"I didn't mean any harm. I never mean anyone any harm."

"Would you talk with him?"

"If I have to. If you want me to. It makes my skin crawl, though, to think about it."

"He's in my office," Mr. Osteen said. "We'd like you to go there now and talk with him."

"Be nice to him."

"I'll try."

"Apologize, would you? Even if you don't mean it."

"All right."

"It wouldn't hurt if he felt sorry for you," Mr. Bosco

said. "If there was a way for you to make that appeal, it wouldn't hurt. Be pitiful and repentant."

"I'll try."

"We want you to stay with us, Frances. You're doing good work. Your sister is invaluable. She's an organizational wonder. Let's put all this behind us."

"Don't worry. I'll do what you want. I don't think he's worth it. But I'll do it."

Reverend Sukit did not get up when Frannie walked in. He remained in the chair behind Mr. Osteen's desk with his hands folded and his chin resting lightly on them and with his elbows on the desk. Because he said nothing and because he stared at Frannie so intently and intimidatingly, she began to talk right away to try to break the ice.

"Hi. I guess you know why I'm here. My name's Frances Vaughan. I've always called myself Frannie. I feel real nervous talking to you since I've seen you on TV and all, but they told me you wanted to talk to me about that little poem I wrote and so here I am. I'm sorry if you got upset by that. I didn't mean it in a bad way. It was a joke. I'm really sorry. I am."

She hated him worse in person than she had watching his show. His face was bony and angular, and his hair was long and full and combed back from his forehead and down his neck like a mane. His nose was tilted up toward the heavens and he looked as if he were braced against a strong wind, stoically, quietly, powerfully, and with the knowledge of his righteousness flowing through his veins. He looked at her as if from on high and said nothing.

"Well, I am sorry. Even if you don't believe me. I'm not a bad person. I swear I'm not. I wish you'd say something."

She liked him less and less the longer he studied her with his unctuous gaze, and the longer he sat there, the closer she felt herself to saying something ugly to shake him up.

"They told me you were so mad about finding that little poem in your T-shirt pack that you might sue them but I can tell you they didn't know anything about it and I don't have much you could sue me for so I hope you don't."

"Continue," he said.

"See," she said and began to think fast as the words spilled out and she sensed her own delight approaching, "this is going to be hard on me. I'm not really like I seem. I've had a lot of problems in my life and I've been in therapy with . . . well, let me back up. You probably think I'm wild and loose and immoral because of what I wrote, but I'm not really. Not at all. It's more of an act. It's a kind of compensating thing is what they call it, that I do because I'm really afraid of things and when the things I'm afraid of happen I try to act through it. See, I learned in my therapy that I'm afraid of sex," she said and watched to see how he'd react. He blinked.

"I'm really messed up about it. I can't have sex. I can't do it. I can't have sex with anyone, not anyone at all. I mean, when I say with anyone, I mean men, of course. I wouldn't have sex with a woman. I don't think I would. Maybe if I had to, like if I was forced to and then I might be able to but I wouldn't want to.

"I've been to a doctor about it and he examined my, well,

you know, my place where the man would put his you know what I mean if things were like they were supposed to be and . . ." She looked up then, having downcast her eyes as she told the story, and saw him clenching his jaw muscles and beginning to get red faced. "And anyway, I can't say the words I'm leaving out because that's one of my problems. I just don't like to say them. But they want me to. They always want me to. They always try to make me say the words. All the doctors and all the men want me to say the words but I don't want to say the words but they want me to and the doctors have helped me learn how to say them by facing the wall, like this, one of them taught me to, and scream real loud," she said and went over to the wall and put her face against it and screamed, "PENIS! VAGINA! PENIS! VAGINA!" and then she returned to her seat and put her face in her hands and acted embarrassed and frail.

"And so, things are not easy for me. I'm really messed up about a lot of things and I hope you'll understand me and forgive and see that when I wrote that poem it was part of my therapy to try to come to terms with my hang-ups. Things get in my mind and, for instance, if you were sitting there listening to me and you had an"—she went back to the wall and put her face against it—"ERECTION!" she screamed and then returned, calm and composed, to her chair. "Excuse me, but then I might be thinking about that. Right?" she asked.

She said nothing then and held his gaze, looking him right in the eye, and he sneered at her and tried to stare her down but in the end, he did have to look away to compose himself, preparing, she thought, some really soft-voiced self-righteous ugly thing to say to her, which she did not want to hear.

"So, like I said," she told him while standing up and heading for the door, "I sure am sorry about writing that poem. Please accept my apologies."

"You come back here," she heard him say as she closed the door and flew past everyone on her way to the warehouse.

Because she did not want to go through the production area she ran out the side door and around the building and entered the warehouse from the door with the sign on it saying No Entry.

She stopped running when she got inside. Far ahead, down the long aisle canyoned in by tall boxes for hundreds of feet, she saw Reuben talking to a woman. She could not tell who it was from where she stood so she cut over one aisle and continued toward them, out of sight.

They were still talking when she was close enough to realize that she had seen this woman before but did not know her name, and that she worked somewhere in the production room, sewing labels. As she watched and waited for her turn, the excitement and crazy feeling she'd built up talking to Reverend Sukit began to subside and the expectation and delight of wanting to rush in to Reuben and tell him what she'd done deflated as well, as the other woman talked on and on, poking Reuben and grabbing his arm when she wanted to make a funny point in whatever it was she was telling him. The longer Frannie watched, the lower she felt, until finally the woman left, and Reuben turned around to his chest-high desk, at which he stood to write the orders, and went back to work.

She tapped him on the shoulder.

"Hi."

"Uh-oh," he said, looking at her face. "What happened?"

"I made a mess of it."

"You look really sad."

"Oh. Well, I'm not. But I guess while I was coming to tell you about it, I realized I'd blown it. I guess that's what you see on my face. But I'm not sad."

"What did you say to him?"

She told him about it. When she was finished, he said, "You know, I understand why you did it, but it may pay to be serious now and then."

"Naw. It don't pay," she said, talking redneck like she did when she wanted to sound stupid. "It don't never pay. It jist makes things worst."

He looked at her, wondering why she was acting like that.

"As long as you can keep on dancing, you're okay," she said.

"You don't believe that."

"Yeah, I do."

"Frannie, of all the people in this world, you don't have to act with me. I understand you."

"You think you do, huh?"

"We're a lot alike."

"Shucks, I ain't like nobody."

"I don't know why you say that."

"Who was that you were talking to, by the way?"

"When? Just now?"

"Yeah."

"Gloria. You know her, don't you?"

"No, and I don't care to."

"She goes to church where me and my mom do."

"Oh, you go to church, huh?"

"Sometimes."

"Well, the world's full of bullshit, isn't it?"

"Frannie," he said and took her by the arm and led her out of sight and hearing from everyone else in the warehouse. "What is this all about?"

"Nothing. I just feel blue, I guess. And stupid. And I'm tired of it. I'm sorry."

"We need to talk later today."

"I'll be fine. I will," she said and thought a few seconds and then said, "Hey, did you hear the one about the lady reading the book?"

"Don't tell it now, Frannie. Wait until later."

"I got to tell it so I won't feel bad. There was this lady on a train and she was sitting beside this man and it was dark and the lights were off and she picked up a book and opened it up and the man beside her said, How can you read in the dark? I went to night school, the lady said."

Back at her table she told Linda and Belle what she'd done, leaving out some details and giving them the general idea of it. Telling it this time, it seemed even less funny and less smart than when she'd told Reuben, and she was embarrassed, almost, by it. It seemed something like daring herself to shoot herself in the foot, just to see if she would, and then actually doing it.

She was pretty sure now she would lose her job, and she did not want that, and she felt she would be sued and lose the money she did have, and then she'd have to go along with the sale of the farm and lose that, too, and she thought she'd made a fool of herself in front of Reuben and she began to hate herself and want to run away. She began to understand how it was and why it was a person might run away, wanting, always wanting, a chance to start over, to try again, to be better, to be someone other than who you were.

Frannie did not come home after work. Natalie and Jake held supper for an hour.

"Ethel was really apologetic to me about it," Natalie said. "She even apologized to Frannie."

"She did what she had to do," Jake said. "Sad as it is, it had to be done."

"I feel so sorry for her."

"You've said that a lot lately."

"I know. For some reason, when she was wild I didn't feel sorry for her. I was mad at her. I was annoyed with her. But lately I feel sorry for her."

"We'll do what we can. The important thing, according to what you read these days about situations like this, is not to make her feel worse than she already does. Not to shut her out."

"They gave her a month's notice. They have to do that

by regulation. I'm sure they wish she were out of there now."

"I expect they think she won't come back. Tomorrow, even. That's usually what happens."

"That phony reverend's going to sue the company. I don't even know on what grounds. And they're going to pass it along to Frannie. I hate that."

"He's trying to get attention for himself."

"But the company's dumping it on her."

"She did do it. They didn't."

While they ate supper and talked, Frannie waited in the loft. Her car was farther down the road. She had seen Jake's car in the driveway and decided to wait until he left. She walked past the ghost farm to her barn and she sat in the loft while Alice settled onto a mat of straw she had thrown down for her. The other two pigs were still missing.

From the dark loft door Frannie could see her sister and Jake in the light of the kitchen. They looked like any couple, at any time in the history of the modern world, sitting together and talking and walking to different parts of the room, their lips moving and their hands and gestures casually accompanying the unheard words. They looked like two people at night should look, the way a man and a woman were supposed to look in a house, in the shelter and the privacy it provided, discussing life.

She did not have this. She did not understand it. She did not believe it would be real because things were mostly too funny, or too sad, but rarely anywhere in between. It was in between where it worked. She only knew that territory in passing, the way a traveler knew a point between two towns as she sped back and forth from one to the other, each day on the same road, looking for something, but unable to stop.

A half hour later Frannie saw someone coming up the driveway on foot. It was Ted. He knocked on the door. Jake answered. Then Natalie came. They talked. Ted walked back down the driveway. Jake appeared at a window. Natalie appeared at his side. Soon Jake left and Frannie went in the house.

Chapter 27

FRANNIE AND REUBEN went up the stairs to where she'd fallen into the box. The wooden floor was dark and dusty and hadn't been oiled in years. Except for a few pieces of paper that had spilled when Frannie fell over, the floor was free of debris.

Across from where they sat, at the base of the box that had caved in but was now back in line with the others and looked the same, were the brick walls of the building itself, and the supporting pillars, and the exposed ductwork of the heating and cooling system and the black iron pipes from the plumbing and the silver conduit of the electrical system leading to the gray boxes with red-tipped handles that had once started and stopped the machines that were no longer there.

"I love it up here," she said.

"It's a nice getaway."

"My pigs are gone. Two of them."

"How'd they get loose?"

"I let them loose, but I thought they'd hang around. They're gone. Only Alice is there."

"They must be somewhere."

"I should never have brought them home. It was a fantasy for me, another stupid dare I took on myself."

"What do you mean?"

"Jake and Natalie are trying to make me sell the farm. We don't have enough money to keep it. In the years to come, we won't, they say."

"I'm sorry to hear that."

"I bought the pigs to pretend I was a farmer."

"Maybe you'll get another chance someday."

"Nope. I don't think so."

She began to eat her lunch. Reuben ate slowly. He watched her eating. She noticed him watching her.

"I'm eating slowly on purpose. The other day I was eating with Belle and Linda and Belle said, you eat like you were mad at your food. Then she imitated me eating, chomping down real hard on the sandwich like I was attacking it. She was right. I was eating like I was mad at my food. That's why I'm doing this."

"Okay."

"I'm sorry I'm such poor company today. The lawsuit thing's really got to me."

"I hope it won't come to much."

"Sometimes I don't care. It feels better not to care sometimes."

"You don't mean that."

"I don't?"

She put her sandwich down on the floor on top of the paper bag and picked up one of the pieces of paper that had fallen from the box.

"Look at this," she said.

"It looks like an old advertising slogan."

"I wondered what that was I fell on," she said. "It was a lot of boxes and papers and some old cotton briefs."

"Is that why you've been feeling bad lately? The sale of your farm?"

"Yep."

"I'm glad you told me. That is something to grieve."

"You don't know the half of it. And I can't tell you now. It's more than just what it looks like. It's the end of something from long ago that shouldn't end. I can't talk about it. I get mad when I do and I'm trying to be calm."

"That's not an easy thing to do when things are going bad."

"I'm trying."

"I wish I knew a joke to tell you. It seems like a good time for one."

"I've got a farm joke I can tell you. It's kind of nasty."

"Tell it."

"This fellow at the feed store told it to a group of guys standing around and I heard it. He said one time this man and this woman went in the barn to do it. The guy put on a rubber and they lay in the straw and when he was finished the rubber came off inside her.

"He took a piece of straw and tried to fish it out but part of the straw got lost up in there and so he gave up. Nine months later a baby was born wearing a rubber raincoat and a straw hat."

"Good Lord, Frannie. That's awful."

She took another bite of her sandwich. The windows in front of her had not been washed in years. The glass had wire embedded in it. None of the panes were broken. The mill had night watchmen who lived in mill-owned houses on the grounds. They were there to prevent people from doing wrong.

"Yeah, it is awful. It is. I shouldn't have repeated it."

Frannie was eating a ham sandwich with mayonnaise and yellow mustard. She had made this sandwich while Natalie was talking to Jake on the phone about wedding plans. While making her sandwich she had caught her sister's eye and asked, by gesture, if she wanted one. She made another one, then, just like hers.

"Give me a few minutes and I'll come up with a good one," she said. "I got a million."

She now noticed she had four slices of ham. That meant she had put Natalie's on hers, as well, and that Natalie had none. It was easier now to make a mistake with ham than it used to be. Slices were thin and they clung together like damp tissue dripping with a slime that resembled the shiny ooze from a slug.

"Things'll work out. You don't have to put on a show for me."

"You can't blame a gal for trying, though. Especially with you."

"Why's that?" he asked.

"Because you never smile."

"I never smile? But that's what I told you the other day, about yourself."

"Yeah, I know. A long time ago, nobody smiled. Nobody at all."

That night Frannie walked to Ted's, looking for company. She had phoned Reuben, but no one answered.

"I saw your car," she said when he answered the door. "I was hoping you were home."

It used to be that without chastity a woman was lost. It was same as a man existing without virtue. Chastity had once been the female component of virtue, so it made sense that to fail either way meant a life on a weary road.

"I feel like getting drunk," Frannie said.

Once a woman married, her chastity and therefore her virtue became the property of the husband. In times past a spirited woman without a husband had little chance to claim the rights of dignity, honor, and virtue.

"Sounds good to me," Ted told her.

Of course it was no longer true. Chastity, as a part of virtue, was of no importance and virtue itself had been replaced by greed and desperation and power.

"Being good gets old," Frannie said. "I'm tired of it."

Because virtue had failed, sadness remained. This sadness was a problem.

"You got to cut loose now and then," Ted replied. "You just got to."

People did not understand why they were sad. Because they did not understand, they tried many things. Most of what they tried involved greed and desperation. This left them even more confused. The sadness endured.

"I tried to tell a joke the other day," Frannie said. "It fell flat. I guess there's nothing to laugh at anymore."

Once, sometime ago, a woman became too happy. Her family took her to a physician. It was thought, at first, she had hydrophobia, but as learned men studied her, they realized it was a case of hysteria. She made the mistake of telling about a blissful experience.

"Do you want to go out or just drink here?" Ted asked.

In the past it was understood that it was not wise to tell the truth. It was also common knowledge that it was unwise to know it or see it or think about it. Then it became important to tell the truth about anything and everything and now it was almost too late to go back.

"I don't know. You decide," Frannie said.

A woman who rarely left home once went to the store in a small town many years ago. Upon leaving the store she was chased by a group of boys and those boys were joined by others. She was only saved when a stranger opened the front door of her house and let her in. This woman was known as Simple Sara and she did not understand how to be in this world. She later killed herself by eating matches.

"Let's just stay here. I got a whole damn refrigerator full of beer."

"Good. I like a man who's prepared."

"How come you never stopped by again until now?"

"I've been busy being good. That takes a lot of time. How come you never asked me again?"

"I didn't think you wanted to see me. I came by the other night. You weren't there."

"Yeah," she said, drinking about half the can in one swallow. "Even if I had been there, I wouldn't have been there."

"Huh?"

"Let's just drink. I wonder what's on TV? I haven't sat around and drank and watched TV in a long time."

"That old set doesn't work too good."

"I don't care."

"The color goes in and out."

"Turn it on anyway. I feel like laughing. Find me something funny."

"Like what?" he said, finishing his beer and turning from channel to channel. "I don't have cable. I can't get but about three channels."

"Anything. Find anything."

A car drove up. It was Eljert. He was introduced to Frannie. She sat between the two men and they drank and they laughed and threw their empty beer cans across the room.

"I'm glad to meet you," Eljert said. "You and me know a lot of the same people."

Frannie was watching the TV. There was a family crisis. Somebody got angry. Then somebody said something funny.

All the actors laughed but one. The one who didn't laugh was the one who'd done something wrong. Now another person said something. The camera was close to his face. Then the camera showed the person who had done the wrong thing who was being laughed at.

"Yeah. You both know me," Ted said.

The actor who was being laughed at turned toward the camera. His face filled the screen. He said something but with the laughter and the applause it was hard to understand it.

"Yeah, I know you. You know me. You know her. She knows me. Yeah, man. We got it."

The actor seemed sad. It looked like he was saying her name. It looked like he was staring at her and saying, Frannie. Then he would pause while everyone laughed and then he would say it again.

"Huh? What? Are you talking to me?" she asked.

Over time, many people have tried to invent the perpetual-motion machine. It seemed like a good idea. Take, for instance, a track. It curves upward, as if it would loop overhead but stops short. It's like two steep hills connected by a valley. Start the marble on one hill. It rolls down and across to the other side. It climbs up and then begins to roll back toward where it started. Just below where it began is a trip device. As the marble hits this, a spring-loaded paddle thumps it back toward the other side again. This should go on forever and ever.

"No, Frannie. We're talking to each other. Have a beer."

It does not. The perpetual-motion machine is just another

one of those things that seems like a good idea at first and later fails.

Natalie was reading a paperback novel. On the floor beside her chair were lists for the wedding, china and silverware catalogs, and three printouts, with pictures, of houses for sale. Jake was at his mother's and they had talked three times already that night by the time Frannie rushed in.

"Are the doors locked?" she asked, wild-eyed.

"I think so. If you locked that one."

"Good," she said, looking out the window and breathing hard.

"Why?"

"Those two guys are mad as hell at me."

She ran up the stairs and looked out all the windows from darkened rooms so she would not be seen. Then she ran down and checked the doors one more time.

"What two guys? What have you done? I don't know what you're talking about."

"The guys across the street."

"What have you done? I thought we were finished with all this."

"I did too. I pulled out of it just in time."

She ran to her room and returned with a pistol. It was a forty-five caliber officer's pistol from World War II that had been a relative's.

"You're not serious?" Natalie asked.

"I'm packing iron the rest of the night. Those guys are

really mad. I kind of left them with their pants down. So to speak."

"What?"

"More or less."

As Natalie walked from her chair, she slipped on the glossy magazines on the rug beneath her bedroom shoes. One leg went in front of her and the other stayed where it was and she fell against the chair.

"I'm calling Jake."

"No. Don't. They might not come. Then he'd be mad at me for nothing."

"I can't believe this. We can't stay here like sitting ducks. Are they drunk?"

"Yep. Pretty bad, too. Worse than me. I outran them without even trying."

Natalie looked out one of the windows toward Ted's house. She saw nothing.

"Doesn't this remind you of something?"

"What? Which thing?"

"Running out a door. Being chased. The way you're talking. Mom's death?"

"Oh, yeah. Well, I didn't plan it this way."

"Is that thing loaded?"

"It's always loaded. I keep it in the space between the mattress and the side rail."

"You said two guys? Who?"

"Ted and Eljert."

"Eljert?"

"Definitely bad news."

"You're not going to shoot anybody. Put it away."

"I would if I had to."

She turned the porch light off and the one in the kitchen and went into the yard. Natalie locked the door and stood at the window waiting for her to return.

"I think it's all clear. Damn, my heart's racing like crazy. They might wait for me to go to sleep and come back then."

"Look, Frannie, if you're serious about this, then let's either call Jake and get him over here or call the sheriff or get in the car and spend the night at Jake's."

"You can if you want, but I'm not. If they see us drive out they might do something to the house. They might break in."

"Something tells me you're exaggerating this. Tell me if you are, because you're scaring me badly."

"I thought they were right behind me. I guess they turned around."

"I think you're making it up. You almost seem like you're enjoying it."

"I'm not."

"Who is Eljert? Whoever heard of such a name?"

"He's some friend of Ted's. I guess he thought he was a friend of mine. He was wrong."

"Would you put the gun down. Please."

"I got the safety on."

She went down the drive. From the dark shadows under the trees in the front yard she saw they were still inside, sitting on the couch.

"They look half asleep. I think everything's okay. I'm sorry I busted in like that."

"Will you put the gun up now. You don't even know how to shoot the thing."

"I do so. I've shot this gun a dozen times before. It kicks like a mule."

Frannie held on to the gun and walked around the room pointing it at various things and acting like she was shooting them.

"Bam. That vase is gone. I never did like it anyway."

She began to use the gun as an extension of her hand, touching things with it and walking with an exaggerated swagger.

"What's this crap?" she asked, pushing a few papers around on the counter with the barrel.

"It's the real-estate contract."

"Bam," Frannie said. "It's not anymore."

"It's what you have to sign."

"It's what I don't have to sign."

"Listen to me, Frannie. We've listed the house. And the land. It had to be done. You said you would do it."

"I did?"

"Yes."

"You must have caught me at a weak moment."

"Read it. Don't be stupid all the way to the end. Show some sense at least in this one thing."

Frannie read through the papers. She held the forty-five in one hand and the papers in the other.

"I can't read them. I can't read this kind of bullshit. I'd

like to blast the brains out of whoever invented this kind of crap."

"Put the gun up. Sit down. Relax. I'll help you with it. Then sign it. Please don't make trouble about it. We've gone over this. You agreed. Let's not fall out over it."

"If I fell out any more over it than I already am, I'd be at the bottom of the Grand Canyon. Dead."

"Jake wants the papers signed by morning."

"I bet he does."

"You're not going to?"

"I didn't say I wasn't going to, I just didn't say I was."

"Do you need him to explain everything again? We can't keep it, we don't have the money to maintain it, the taxes are outrageous, and I don't want it. Okay. I don't want to live here. I want to live in town. This place depresses me. There's too much here that was never right. I want a house in town. I want a life with Jake."

"I know all that."

"Well?"

"Well?"

"Frannie, you can't manage your life. You're not good at making decisions. You can't even go on a date and have it come out right."

"Look, this thing tonight wasn't a date. I did what I wanted to do. I felt like going crazy. That's what I wanted to do. Sometimes it feels good. So don't talk about tonight. You might be right about the house. Financially. But you're not right about a lot of other things."

"Talk to somebody about this other than me. Would you

do that? Other than me and Jake. Anybody's going to tell you the same thing."

"Give me the damn papers. Just give them to me. I don't care what I sign. I don't care, okay? Take them and do what you want. Sell the damn place. Then give me my money when you get it and I'm out of here. You might never see me again. How about that? I might take that money and disappear off the face of this earth. I might just do that."

Chapter 28

FRANNIE MADE UP with Natalie the next morning. She'd slept horribly. She had gone to the bathroom three times in the middle of the night and the last time she went she realized her period had begun. Then, before work, she noticed signs that Natalie's had begun, also. They had always started together. At least, she thought, we're still in harmony that way.

"I feel much better about everything this morning," she said.

"I'm glad."

"I'm going to see a lawyer about the lawsuit. I think I better."

"That's smart."

"Ask Jake who I ought to see."

There was an envelope on her table at work. It was sealed. Inside was a photograph. Frannie could tell it was a photograph without opening it because of how it felt through the paper. The envelope had her name on it, but nothing else on the outside. She opened it and found that the picture was of Reuben, as a child, with her grandfather and her grandmother at the entrance to the dairy barn. There was a note. The note said:

> I found this. There are two more. Meet me upstairs for lunch and I'll show them to you. Hang in there. I think you're going to be okay. Reuben.

All morning she thought about how Reuben looked on the farm with her grandparents with their arms on his shoulders and she thought about the face of this child she'd never seen and how like it was the face of this man, and how it seemed the face of the child in the picture was still there, just under the skin, of the face of grown-up, serious, helpful Reuben. She wasn't seeing it the way people always did when they said you look just like you did when you were younger, you haven't changed a bit. She was seeing it as a part of Reuben she'd never seen before, didn't know about, hadn't thought about, as a laughing happy child with two arms and bright eyes and the look of wonder and expectation and trust, and yet, the grown-up Reuben, the one-armed Reuben, the solemn and dutiful Reuben was there in the child, as well, all of it, suddenly, together, the man as child, the child as man, all still there.

She tried to see Ted's face and Jake's and Eljert's and other men she had known, Mr. Osteen's, Mr. Bosco's, and as she saw them in her mind, it did not seem to her that what she saw in Reuben—now having seen him as child—was there. It seemed with each of them that what remained today was only the man and not the child, not that she'd missed it before this moment, but that it simply had never been there.

"You sure are quiet this morning," Linda said.

"She's got a right to be," Belle said. "Look what's on the poor thing."

Frannie left for lunch five minutes early. Once upstairs she felt in her pocket to be sure she'd brought her box cutter knife with her and then she climbed on top of the cardboard crates and lowered herself into the one she'd fallen into.

Once inside she cut a small window, leaving one side uncut as a flap she could close, which she did while waiting. She had thought of a story she wanted to tell him, as a way of confession, as a way of telling him something about her as a child, because she had seen so much in him as child, and it dawned on her that she could make the box like a confessional, with her, the confessor, inside, and Reuben, the one to hear it, outside.

"I see you," she said, peering through the window without opening the flap.

"Now what is this all about?"

"I've got some things to tell you."

"From in there?"

"Do you want to hear them?"

"Of course I do."

"It's okay with you?"

"I've learned to expect the unexpected with you, Frannie. In fact, I depend on it."

"You do, huh?"

"Yes, I do."

"I had a bad night last night," she said. "I want to confess something to you. I told you I couldn't go out with you because I wasn't going out with anyone. But I lied. I did go out. Not with anyone I'm seeing or anything like that, but I did go out and drink beer with this guy who I don't even care about, but I did it. Went out, I mean."

Reuben leaned against the box and began to eat his lunch. They only had a half hour for break.

"And that's why you're in the box?"

"Sort of."

"Well, I forgive you," he said and turned his head upward and reached his hand toward the window and she held it a few seconds. "Not that it was up to me to forgive you, but it seems that was the line you wanted me to say. Right?"

"Yeah. I didn't do anything with him. I didn't. I swear I didn't. I know you've heard things about me. Everybody seems to. They might even be true. I don't know what all they are, but they might even be true."

"You don't have to talk about that with me, Frannie. I don't know a thing about you except what I see when I'm with you."

"I know I don't. But I've been thinking about childhood

a lot and I want to tell you something I've never told anyone. Some people know parts of it, but no one knows why it happened, or what it meant, and I want to tell you."

"Wouldn't it be more comfortable if you were out here?"

"I need to be in here. The mood's right. I want to tell it to you like this. I want to tell you because when I saw that picture of you with my grandparents it made me think about it. It's so strange that you chose that one to show me because there's one of me just like it, not with my grandparents, but with my dad's great-aunt and uncle, who are dead now.

"I was visiting them in town along with Natalie and we took the trash out after supper and Natalie stepped on this little lever, and a lid opened and there was a metal tube buried in the ground like a space capsule, which is what it made me think of when I saw it. She dropped the trash in there."

"It sounds like it was a buried trash can."

"Yeah, well, it was, but I didn't know it so I said, what's that? And she said, it's where they throw their trash. I looked down in it and it was dark and I couldn't see the bottom. It reminded me of working up the nerve to look into an outhouse hole at one of my relatives' farms up in the mountains. I looked in it with a flashlight and it scared me so bad I dropped the flashlight in the damn thing.

"What happened was something crawled up toward me and I jerked my hand back and the light hit the side of the seat and fell in. They never found out what happened to their flashlight, but when I looked in the hole in the ground at my great-uncle's house in town and saw Natalie drop the bag in

I thought it was the same kind of thing and I asked her where it went.

"She told me the hole went down all the way to hell. She said the fires of hell burned up all the trash and that's what the people in hell did all day, haul the trash to the fire. I was scared to go near it the rest of the night, but the next night I was there I sneaked out and opened the lid and climbed down into the tube because I wanted to go to hell.

"That's the part I've never told anybody before. I wanted to die and go to hell because everything in my life had changed so much and had gotten so awful. I imagined after she showed me that it would be like a long, long sliding board and you would go around in a spiral fast and fall and fall and fall like in a dream and you wouldn't be able to stop until you popped out into the big, hot room where the devil would be in a chair and little people like trolls would take me to fires and burn me up and I would be dead."

Reuben had stopped eating and when she paused he turned around and got on his knees and looked in the window at her face.

"Come on out, Frannie. You need to come out now."

Together they tilted the box over and she tossed out a bundle of packages she'd been sitting on and then climbed out.

"You're really upset?" he said.

"I'm fine. I got a little choked up there, but I'm fine. I want to finish the story. Let's sit down. See, what nobody knows is that I wanted to die because of the hell that was a part of my life then, things I hardly remember, and things

I'm just now starting to remember, between my mother and father, and all of us, but it's odd how upset all of that got me because no one ever knew it. All that time I wanted to die and no one ever knew it. After my father left, I still felt bad, like everything was still going on. And so when Natalie told me the tube went straight to hell, I knew it was meant for me. I knew I would have to use it to kill myself because I wanted to kill myself, I guess, to stop from feeling so bad.

"I never told anyone before. I never even told Nat. But when I lowered myself into that tube, I remember doing it calmly, like it was something I had to do. I think I thought it might hurt, but I had to anyway. Of course I didn't go anywhere. The only thing that happened is when I dropped in, the lid slammed shut and the thing was so narrow I was jammed in so that I couldn't open it. Then I did get scared. I realized I was standing on top of garbage and I began to think about rats and I called out for help and my aunt and uncle got me out. And no one, no one anywhere, until now, knew why I'd lowered myself in there."

She picked up her bag lunch. She unrolled the top and found her sandwich. She set it down on her leg. She removed the bottle of fruit juice she had half frozen earlier in the morning and drank from it. Part of it was still ice. Her hand was trembling and she thought that Reuben had noticed and she was embarrassed.

"Aren't I a mess? Just look at me. I can't even hold a sandwich."

He put his fingers to her lips, as if to stop her from talking. Then he took the sandwich from her lap and put it in her hand and held it to her mouth. She took a bite and her jaw trembled and her throat felt tight and she did not think she would be able to swallow.

It was quiet where they were and for the first time Frannie realized she could feel the floor on which she sat vibrating from the power of the machinery operating below. She felt it rise up through her and she closed her eyes and took a deep breath and shivered.

Two cars traveled down the paved road toward Frannie's farm. One car turned into her driveway. The other continued on. The first car contained agents from the real-estate firm. The second car was occupied by three people from out of town and one agent. The agents from the first car parked in Frannie's spot. They did not know it was her spot. It was chance symbolism that they displaced her. They didn't mean any harm. They saw Alice, the now four-hundred-pound sow, resting in the shade.

The people in the other car turned onto a dirt drive below her land. They sprayed their shoes and pants with insect repellent although it was months past tick season.

The agents looked at Frannie's house. They had seen many houses as large and as once grand as this leveled when the land was sold for development. No one liked it, but economically it was the right thing to do. To move a house like this down the road and under wires and between signs and trees and beneath limbs meant cutting it into two pieces and then taking the roof off each of those pieces. The cost was prohibitive.

The people at the other site represented the new owners of the abandoned farm. The company had finally acquired title to the land from the heirs of the failed developer who had bought it years earlier. It had thirty-seven acres and had cost $1.4 million.

The agents looked into the barn on Frannie's land. Though they were sensitive and decent people and though they had respect for the past, they did not know what this barn had meant beyond its utilitarian purpose as a shelter for animals and hay and grain.

The company that had paid $1.4 million for what remained of the farm where the old man wasted away from despair and the loss of his dignity had paid that much because it intended to put up the seventh in a chain of small amusement parks for children. They were high-class parks, and this was a perfect site.

Frannie reflected on the story she'd told Reuben. They had been eating their lunches and not saying anything.

"That's not much of a story," she said.

"It was fine."

"It was stupid. I didn't tell it well."

"It wasn't stupid," he said.

"Well, what was it, then? Smart? No. It wasn't smart. I wish I remembered it better."

"It's the kind of thing children do. It's the way kids think."

"I've been so nostalgic lately."

"You know, Frannie, in one way it is a sad story, but in another way, it's funny."

"Yeah, everything's funny in some way."

"You're sad because you're having to move. You're losing your home."

"I feel like changing the subject."

"I don't mind talking about it."

"I'm tired of it. I'm bored of it. I'm everything of it."

"If you say so."

"Let's talk about something else. The mill. The lawsuit. This stuff here on the floor. Anything. What are these, anyway?"

She took one of the packets that had fallen from the larger box she had used for her confessional. It was rectangular and cardboard and had a paper band around it. It was the size of one volume of an encyclopedia.

"It looks like the old-style packaging they used here. Before my time," Reuben said.

On the paper band that wrapped around the box and held it closed was printed the price, $1.00, and the slogan, A BUCK WELL SPENT, after it. The words and the price were printed at regular intervals on the paper band all the way around the box.

"This is what we do in plastic now," he said as she tore the band and opened the box.

"A whole cardboard box just for each set," she said. "And look at the briefs. They look the same."

"Only a dollar for three pair. I wonder when it was."

"I don't know."

She was going through the box when she found a card with a picture and paragraph of advertising copy on it. She smiled for the first time that afternoon.

"I'll be damned," she said. "I will be damned."

She handed it to Reuben.

"Well, how about that?" he said. "Are there more?"

The card Frannie had discovered had a picture of a young Indian woman. She was dressed in shapely buckskins. She had a single feather in her headband. The Indian woman looked relaxed and happy but most of all she looked satisfied.

Behind her, dressed only in a pair of briefs but with a headband and a single feather like hers, was a young Indian man leaning against a tree. He had a dazed look on his face as he watched the young woman walk away.

Below the picture was the slogan, A BUCK WELL SPENT, and then a short paragraph of copy that read: "You'll always look your best in Bosco Briefs, at work, at play, you can't do better today than this buck, well spent." After that there was the price, $1.00.

Chapter 29

ELJERT WALKED AROUND the back of the duplex and around the edge of the yard and then down the road and then back to the house where he perched on the stoop. Ted's door was locked.

He looked across the road at Frannie's farm and at the old buildings.

It would be perfect to have a place like that out in the middle of nowhere, he thought. It'd be great to have a building like the potato barn and keep a woman in it and have women in all the other buildings, just keeping them there for when you wanted them.

The idea of simply opening the door and taking out a woman and doing what you wanted was a nice idea to Eljert. It made him think of movies where a woman was kidnapped and hidden away until the man was ready for her.

You could clean up the stalls and work on them and have a whole bunch of women in each stall. If you kept them locked up long enough they'd be happy to see you when you came for them. They'd be grateful to you and would treat you right and would give you no trouble. You could keep a woman in every building. You could bring one inside now and again and be nice to her.

It'd be nice to find a nice one and have a nice time with her and treat her real nice and show her how nice a nice man could be to a nice woman.

Ted drove up. Eljert gave him the finger. He was only kidding.

A half hour after Ted returned home, Frannie and Natalie were waiting for Reuben and Jake, but Jake was late. Natalie went inside to call his house.

"His mom said he never came home and she thought he was over here."

"He's tied up at work. Or maybe he's looking into the real estate crap."

"He usually calls."

"He will."

"Where are you guys going?" Natalie asked.

"We're going to hang here. Reuben loves it out here. Like me."

"Come on, Frannie. You were never that way until recently."

"I was too. I was always like that when I was younger."

"I guess you were."

"Where are you going?"

"To Greensboro, to the new French restaurant that got a review in the Sunday paper."

"Sounds nice."

"Why don't you come?"

"I don't think so. I don't think he would want to. I can ask him."

"Do. I really wish we'd go out together more. I want us to be closer, Frannie, now that the trouble with selling the place is all behind us."

"It's all behind you, maybe."

"Everything you read says families have got to stick together no matter what. I wish Jake would call."

"Reuben said he wanted to look at how the barn was built because it's still so plumb after all these years."

"Maybe I can try him at work."

"Reuben's the first man I've ever been out with who hasn't had his hands all over me right off."

"I'm going to wait a few more minutes," Natalie said, distracted and looking at her watch.

"We've been to the movies twice and once out to eat and he hasn't even tried. It makes me feel odd, if you want to know the truth."

"I thought you were just friends."

"We are. It's still odd, though."

"When are you going to talk to Mr. Bosco? You ought to do it soon. I wish you'd tell me what you found."

"Reuben said to keep it a secret until we were ready."

"I guess it's better if I don't know. I'm about to worry

myself to death over waiting for a buyer for this place and thinking about the wedding and your trouble and everything else."

"Don't worry about me."

"I'm curious about something," Natalie said.

"What?"

"You don't mention looking for our father anymore. What happened?"

"Nothing happened. I'm still going to do it. Everything else just got too much to handle and do that also."

"What time did Reuben say he'd come?"

"Seven."

"It's seven now."

"Here he comes."

"I'm going to call the bank."

There was a half hour of light remaining when Frannie and Reuben rowed out to the island. They sat on the bench she had built. A flock of geese came honking from the northwest heading southeast and flew over them in a ragged V with stragglers calling ahead to the lead group.

"What animal would you be if you had to be an animal?" Frannie asked.

"I've never thought about it."

"I'd be a bird. Some kind of bird."

"I wouldn't even know where to start."

"What's your favorite color?"

"Frannie, I'm sorry, but in my life no one ever asked me

that, either. I guess red or blue or green. I actually don't know."

"Mine's the color of the sky at sunset, just above the horizon."

"I hear a car engine."

"That's probably Jake. I don't like him, you know."

"You can't choose your relatives."

"I like most people. At least, I try to. Listen. You can almost make out what they're saying. You can hear people talking down here on really quiet evenings. Voices carry a long way. It's strange. It makes me feel funny when I'm down here at night and I hear people talking I've never seen and don't know where the voices are coming from. It's scary in a strange way. It makes my heart beat fast. It makes me feel lonely, too. I don't know why."

Natalie was quiet in Jake's new car. He hadn't told her he was buying a new car. The car was quiet, too.

"Really, you should have called."

"I see that now. I didn't see it before."

"I was worried."

"It won't happen again. Now that I know."

"I called your mother. I even called the bank."

"This is the first fight we've had in a long time."

"This is not a fight, Jake. And we don't ever fight so I don't know what you mean."

"It seems like we've had some. Maybe I'm wrong."

"It's not worth ruining the night over. Just call me the

next time you're going to be late. Okay? Can you do that?"

"Absolutely."

"All right. It's over then, okay. Give me a kiss at the next stoplight and let's forget about it."

It began to drizzle. The roads became shiny and the lights glared and Natalie checked her seat belt.

"There are two air bags in this car. It's one of the safest cars on the road."

"I love it, by the way. I'm sorry I was sour. It's really so beautiful. I'm crazy about it."

"I thought it was time for a new one. For us."

"I know it cost a lot. Don't tell me how much."

"We're fine. I'm doing great. You know what I was thinking?"

"Tell me, darling."

"If we live with Mother after we get our three hundred thousand, if that's what we get, but if we live with her for six months, and I invest it right and get lucky on the return, we could make fifteen to thirty thousand dollars extra on top of it all by not spending it right away."

"That'd be great, I guess. But why do we need it?"

"It was just a thought. It's rare when you have a lump sum that large you can work with."

"What about Frannie?"

"She can come along if she needs to. I've always said so."

"Would you do it for Frannie, too?"

"If she wants. I don't know yet if what I'm thinking will come about. But it's a possibility."

"It sounds good, but I want to choose a house and move

in soon. I don't want to wait long. It's all I think about."

"We're going to be in great shape. We'll get Mom's place when she passes on and the little bit she's got put away. We're going to have a great life, Nat. It's all going to work out. It really is. It's amazing. Our life, since we've been together, has been like us looking at something far away and working toward it, just like walking steady and slowly toward it, and now we're there. It's amazing."

"We can thank my ancestors for a lot of it, for settling on land that became so valuable. And Mom for holding on to it, for us. I'm not ungrateful for all of that, regardless of what Frannie thinks."

"I'm starved. I've heard this place is great. We'll be there soon. It's going to be a good night."

Frannie and Reuben had rowed back from the island when it began to rain. It was lovely as the drops began to fall and the water shimmered as the boat neatly cut across the surface. When they got to the bank and it began to rain harder, they did not run for the house. They enjoyed the change in the sound around them, the change in the color of the sky and the air and the fresh smell of the wet pines and the grass underfoot.

"Rain makes me sleepy," Frannie said.

She had made toasted cheese sandwiches while Reuben made the iced tea. Frannie noticed he knew to keep it strong so that when it was poured hot over the ice it wouldn't dilute badly. This impressed her.

"I love the sound of it," she said.

They had eaten on the porch in the dark. She had led Alice to her pen and locked her in for the first time in weeks. The sound of the rain against the porch's tin roof gave her the chills, pleasantly, as if warm fingers were running up and down her back, across her shoulders and down her arms.

"It's a cozy feeling," she said.

She had made the sandwiches out of two kinds of cheese. Then she'd put thick patties of butter on the bread and grilled them, one side at a time, in an iron skillet. The skillet had been her grandmother's. It was she who taught Frannie how to make grilled cheese sandwiches.

"It's like there's no one in the world but me when it rains. Or us. That's the way it makes me feel."

As Reuben had stood by the teapot after he'd poured in the water to wait for it to brew, Frannie had put in two sprigs of mint. The mint was from what remained of the herb garden that had been behind the house for generations. Not much remained, but the mint returned each year and flourished.

"I always did love the rain. And the wind. And storms. Anything like that."

Frannie knew how to make bread, rolls, biscuits, corn bread because as a child she'd hung out in the kitchen with her granny and her mom, before her mother became ill. Then, for a while, she and Natalie took turns cooking and then it seemed it wasn't worth the trouble and they ate anything they could whip up or thaw out or microwave in a hurry. If she had thought about it and planned better and realized how she would feel she could have had homemade bread with real butter for supper.

"Sometimes, in the summer, I think about going out in the field and laying on my back and letting it rain all over me. With no clothes on."

The ends of the porch flooring began to darken as the rain splashed from the puddles where the overhang dripped onto the ground. A breeze from the west blew the mist onto the porch. It was cool and made her shiver.

"When I was a little girl I was in the attic once when a big storm came. There wasn't anything between me and the rain and hail but the tin roofing."

The windows around the house were closed. The house was safe and dry and its protection over time remained unabated. Beneath the shut windows, on the outside, were the sills. Sills were always beveled with a slant away from the house so that the water dripping down the panes and from the siding above, and collecting on the only horizontal surface on the face of the house, would shed quickly. Often there is a piece set in above the window itself called a drip cap. This prevented water from the siding above from weeping into the interior cavity of the walls. When all of these parts of the window were properly done, when the right thing had been done, the house, and therefore the life within, endured.

"It started pounding on the roof so hard I got down on the attic floor and closed my eyes and covered my ears and didn't move until it was over. It was wonderful."

Sometimes a person, a young woman, sees something in passing. At a glance, something wonderful is learned. Words arrive unexpectedly. Lips open and close in a new way while the fine ends of primly falling hair rise off the shoulders in electrified suspension.

"I think I love you," she said.

There. She'd said it. She'd said it to a man for the first time in her life. She'd said it because he was quiet and thoughtful and he made her feel safe, and sitting beside him, in the rain, in her house, on her land, with her ancestors all around her, he made her feel different than she'd ever felt in her life, like a child, and like a woman, at the same time, free now to be both for the first time in her life, free to be herself, the child who believed she could fly and the woman who had tried.

Chapter 30

THREE DAYS LATER an offer of $400,000 was made for the land. This was $200,000 below what they were asking. Natalie and Jake decided they would counteroffer $550,000 and see what happened. Frannie wouldn't talk about it.

The next day, as prearranged, Natalie waited for Frannie and Reuben to meet her for a meeting with Mr. Bosco, Osteen, a secretary, and Ethel. Jake took off two hours for the meeting, as well.

"Mr. Bosco," Jake said, "I'm here, not as a lawyer, which I'm not, but as a friend of the family and as a witness to these proceedings."

"That's why I'm here, too," Reuben said.

Frannie sat beside Reuben with a smile on her face that made no sense to the management officers across from her. She was dressed in a skirt and blouse, which they'd never seen her in before, and she rested one hand on Reuben's arm. In her lap were three of the boxes from upstairs.

"Natalie has asked me to speak for Frannie and to help present new evidence we're sure will change your mind as regards the lawsuit you have passed on to Frannie when the one from Reverend Sukit was presented to you."

Jake sat on Reuben's left, on the side where his arm was missing, and then, on Jake's left, sat Natalie. The men were in the middle two chairs, and their women were in the outer two. Natalie had a pad in her lap and now and then wrote.

"As we all know, Frannie admitted to creating what she considered at the time a harmless poem and putting it into one of the packets she handled. You stated in the suit that Frannie's poem was an unheard-of attack on the reputation of your company and that never in the history of your company had anything obscene, as you called it, been disseminated with your product."

Mr. Bosco listened while Osteen leaned forward and Ethel cocked her head to one side trying to figure out where Jake was heading.

"Well, Frannie, who has luck on her side as well as her determination, has discovered that your company actually did engage in this kind of humor to promote your product long before her time, and that precedent is therefore established for what she did."

Reuben took one of the boxes from her lap and handed it to Jake who then passed it to Mr. Bosco. He frowned as he studied it, but he did not open it.

"There are more where that came from. Lots more," Reuben said.

"That's an unopened and untampered with package in your hands just as Frannie found it and just as your company packed it when they used that slogan."

Mr. Bosco handed the package to Ethel, who looked at it. She gave it to Osteen. He read the band around the package and then returned it to Mr. Bosco.

"You'll have to open it to see what we're talking about. I only gave it to you sealed to let you know it's as it was when it was produced."

Mr. Bosco carefully cut the band. On the top of the first brief was the card with the spent Indian buck and the very satisfied Indian woman along with the copy explaining the picture and furthering the double meaning.

"How will it be possible for you to say that Frannie has done anything you haven't already done?" Jake asked.

Bosco handed the open box with the card to Ethel, who read it, it seemed, three or four times, and then she handed it to Osteen, who took the card out and went through the box after reading it and then returned it to Bosco.

"You say there are more of these?" he asked.

"Many," Reuben said.

"Where did you find them?" he asked Frannie.

"We've decided not to answer that at this time. We figured you'd want to know, but we want to keep the whereabouts secret until you make your decision in Frannie's favor."

"We will need to see the original source before we can decide anything. If it's as you say, then we'll get back to you about a decision."

The defendant and her entourage left the room. Mr. Bosco and Osteen and Ethel sat silent for a minute more, as if their jaws were clamped.

"If she made this up," Osteen said, "she certainly did a good job."

"I don't think she did," Ethel said. "But where did it come from?"

"Something in the back of my mind, from my father's day, tells me this is true. I had forgotten all about it."

"It doesn't seem like the kind of thing your father would have done."

"My recollection is that he was persuaded it would get attention for the product. It seems to me there was trouble over the campaign, and that the company had to pull it."

"Then the stock is stored somewhere here and they found it. That has to be it."

"I don't know. I don't know why the product wasn't repackaged and sent back out. Maybe it was. Maybe there's only a few left. But she's right."

"What are we going to do?" Ethel asked. "Do we drop the suit? Does she get her job back?"

"I think it's time for me to contact the attorneys and have them call the Reverend and make a cash offer. It looks as if we cannot shunt the blame onto Frannie. It looks as if this will cost us something, and if that's true, then so be it."

"Jake was great," Frannie said to Reuben as they walked in the parking lot. "He was just great."

"He did well."

"I guess it pays sometimes to have a straight arrow like him in the family. He sure was good to do it for me. After the way I've treated him."

"It's not over yet."

"They won't dare do anything now."

"No. They won't. But on the outside chance of one in a million that they try to pretend it away, let's not celebrate yet."

"You're right. But we won. I'm so happy I could float," she said and then looked worried a moment before she spoke again. "You got no way of knowing how different I feel since I met you, and dumb me, it took me forever to see it."

"There's still the sale of the land."

"I know, but it's like people say, do something about the things you can do something about, and quit worrying about the rest."

"Maybe."

"Maybe what?"

"Maybe there's something that can be done about anything, if you think hard enough and get lucky."

"Well, you know I'm lucky."

She returned to work still dressed in her skirt and blouse. The mill was noisy and it hummed, as usual, from the worn conveyor, the lights, and the effort to talk above the din by four hundred people. It was a pretty good job, as jobs went. There were good people there. It felt good to be with good people doing something you were good at, which was, it seemed to Frannie, what everybody else had known all along.

That night Frannie called Millie and they talked for more than an hour. It was the first time in months they'd talked that long. Millie wanted to have Frannie and Reuben over for supper with her and her mother, and they made a date for it.

"You know, I used to have dreams. When I was little," Frannie said. "Then I didn't for a long time."

"You mean you didn't have dreams at night?" Millie asked.

"I mean dreams of a life. I got mad at Natalie once and I yelled at her, you don't understand dreams, and she said, oh yes, I understand dreams, but I understand waking up, too."

While Frannie talked to Millie, Eljert and Ted were having an argument across the road.

"I'm leaving this man's town and I don't give a damn what I do," Eljert said.

He had been fired from his job for taking merchandise concealed in supposedly empty boxes that he would later take out of the Dumpster and transfer to his car.

"I got me a score to settle first."

"Forget it," Ted said. "Just forget it."

"Ain't no prick-teasing bitch ever took me that far and then walked out on me."

"I'm not going to let you go over there. I got to live here, buddy. I got to live here after you leave."

"You going to stop me?" Eljert asked. "You and who else?"

Eljert was throwing his knife against Ted's bedroom door. It hit the rippled veneer again and again and bounced off as many times as he threw it.

"Give me the goddamn knife and go get yourself drunk somewhere else. I got to stay clean, and you know it."

"I won't hurt her bad. All I'm asking is you call her and get her over here. I just want to scare her."

"I won't do it."

"Call her, man. I want to give her something to remember me by."

"Look, I don't like what she did any more than you, but I can let it go. Some things are worth getting in trouble over and some aren't."

"You don't get it, man. This girl is trash. She hadn't never think she ain't."

"She's not trash, Eljert."

"Shit, we're the only two men in town what hadn't been with her."

"I don't even care, man. I don't give a damn."

"Call her up. She'll come over for you."

"She won't do anything for me. Forget it."

"Listen, Ted. You get her over here so I can tell her what I think of her, or I'm going over there."

At eight-thirty, Natalie knocked on Frannie's door. Frannie had heard the shower running and heard Natalie's creaky sliding closet doors banging one way and then the other as she looked from one side of the closet to the other for something to wear.

"I see you found something."

"I've got next to nothing in there that looks right on me anymore," Natalie said. "Everything's stretched out or has got little pin-size holes in it or missing buttons or I don't know what."

"I heard you bamming around."

"I'm going to buy some clothes when the money comes in. I hope those people let us know something about the counteroffer soon."

"Where are you going?"

"I told you last night I was going to stay with Jake tonight because his mother hurt her ankle and he's got work he's been bringing home from the bank to do."

"Oh, right."

"Are you going to be okay? You looked funny when I said I was leaving."

"Oh, sure. I'm so happy these days that if you're not here for me to talk to I'll end up walking around the house talking to myself."

"It makes me happy to see you so happy."

"Oh, I'm happy, except for one thing. And you know what it is."

After Natalie left she called Reuben.

"Natalie's gone," she said. "I found these letters from camp when I was eleven I want you to read. I forgot what I was like until I read them. I wrote Nat and Mom each a letter a day the whole time I was there. I even wrote them one on the day they were coming to pick me up and got home before it got here. I must have been homesick but I don't remember. I went there because Mom wouldn't buy me a horse and they had horseback riding at the camp.

"Do you think I ought to buy a little farm somewhere way out with the money I'm being forced to take? It wouldn't be the same but it'd be something. But it's this place that should never be let go. This place is what's kept us all alive. I might blunder into some bad-luck farm like the one up the road and end up hanging from the rafters," Frannie said and finally paused long enough for him to answer.

Eljert didn't care how happy Frannie was. He wouldn't have cared that she was about to break the curse of what happened in her family when the women got too happy. If he'd have known, it'd have made him all the madder. He did know he'd drunk too much. He knew that because he always found out later that he'd gotten a little too rough when he drank that much and he hoped he hadn't hurt Ted badly when he'd knocked him out.

Ted had fallen hard and lay still afterwards, but sometimes, in Eljert's experience, when they fell hard they were better off than when they hit the ground trembling and convulsing and bubbling out the mouth.

It was nearly midnight. Eljert and Ted had continued to argue about Frannie and everything else and by the time Eljert struck him, she had already gone to bed, Eljert figured, because as he waited in the woods the lights in the room he guessed was hers finally went out. That left only a light in the front of the house, which was dim and Eljert thought it most likely a night-light in the hall or bathroom.

The grass in the field was dry. Small pines were beginning to sprout and if they were left unmowed or neglected a few more years, all the work that Frannie's ancestors' had done to clear this field would be lost. Wrapped around the young pines and in among the weeds and grass were vines and briars, all of it below knee level.

The cuffs and pant legs of his trousers were covered with seeds and beggar's-lice and sharp pods designed by God to stick to anything that brushed against them so as to be carried to a new home and a new life. One of his ankles was bleeding from a thornbush. Blood had discolored his sock all the way into his shoe. He never felt the puncture and wouldn't know his sock was bloody until morning when he would try to peel it from where it would have formed a scab, which he would have to tear loose. It might hurt then. Sometimes being hurt felt good, especially when you'd done something wrong.

As Eljert crept around the corner of the house and approached the porch he realized that someone was out there with him. In the dim light he could see that Frannie was asleep on the porch on a blanket. He couldn't believe his luck. He didn't know exactly what it was he wanted to do with her, but he knew he had her and could, at the very least, scare the living hell out of her, and, if he wanted, make her do what she'd promised before she said no.

Sometimes, when people are just learning how to say no and aren't used to it, they say yes first, like they always had, because they thought it was the right thing to do, and then, having learned they could say no, say it too late. It was a dilemma, but when people are just learning to use the word no, and especially women who think that the word yes is a brave and kind word, and the yes is supposed to make up for all the wrong that had been done in the history of mankind, then, when they realize they shouldn't have said yes, it's too late, and the first person they end up telling no, turns out to be a man with a knife who doesn't like to be told no.

Eljert stepped carefully onto the porch and walked toward her shape in the far corner. It looked to him like she had a large down comforter over her and a couple of pillows under her head and one she seemed to be hugging as if she were sleeping with someone. He tried to figure out her posture so he could better know how to approach her and how she would be once he woke her up or jerked the covers off.

He was ten feet from her when he realized it wasn't Frannie and he was trying to figure out who it was when Alice rose up and squealed and snorted and tried to run past him.

When she did, she knocked him off his feet, and he fell onto her, and in trying to get him away from her and get past him, she clamped down on what had been, until that second, Eljert's pride and joy, and she shook him like a rag and flipped him into the air as effortlessly as someone who had eaten an apple would toss the core behind her.

About thirty seconds later Eljert's breath finally returned and he cried out and Frannie stumbled out of bed and began to run toward the sound.

At the same time Ted cleared the cobwebs from his head,

heard the noise, and realized that Eljert had actually gone over there and that Frannie was in trouble. He picked up the iron bar he kept behind the couch and ran across the road.

Frannie switched on the outside light and ran onto the porch. She saw Eljert staggering toward her and out of the corner of her eye she saw Alice running off. She tore back up the stairs and got her forty-five.

By that time Eljert had begun to hop like a kangaroo toward Ted's house. As he hopped he held what remained of his pride and joy with both hands.

Ted saw him coming across the dark lawn and swung the iron bar and knocked him onto his back in the grass, rendering him as motionless as he, himself, had been a few minutes earlier.

Still concerned about Frannie and not seeing her anywhere outside the house, Ted entered through the kitchen and began turning on the lights as he called her name.

He still had the bar in his hand when he flipped the lights on in the den.

"Just stop right there," Frannie said.

He looked down the barrel of the forty-five. It looked like it was the size of a howitzer.

"Frannie. You're all right?"

"Put the bar down."

"I didn't come over here to hurt you. I knocked Eljert out in your front yard."

"Drop it."

"Sure. But put the gun down. I'm on your side. I was afraid Eljert had hurt you."

"Sit down on the floor and don't move."

"Don't shoot me, Frannie.

"I better call the cops."

"Please don't do that. I'll get sent back. I swear—I swear to God—I was trying to stop him and he knocked me out and came over, and when I woke up, I ran over here to stop him. I swear."

"Where is he?"

"I told you I hit him in the front yard. He's laying out there now."

"I'm going to take a look," she said. "If you move from where you are, I'll shoot you. And I mean it. I'll blow you in half. Give me that crowbar."

"I won't move, Frannie. I won't. Here, take it."

With the flashlight she went into the yard and found Eljert in the grass. He was moaning and trying to get up. She stood beside him until he had gotten onto all fours. Then she kicked him as hard as she could and he fell over again.

"Jerk," she said and stayed above him awhile longer making sure he wasn't going to get up again.

While she was out there, Ted was looking around the room. On a table at his eye level as he sat on the floor were pictures of Frannie's family, including the last picture she had of her father. There were also pictures of Frannie as a little girl, and one of her with her father, as well.

A minute later Frannie returned and sat in a chair across the room with the forty-five still pointed at Ted.

"He's out there."

"Put the gun down, girl. It might go off."

"I might put it down, but first I'm going to call my boyfriend and see if he wants to come over here and bust you up a little bit."

"Look, I'm telling you the truth. Just quit pointing it at me."

"Why should I?"

"Because I'm not going to hurt you and I've got something to tell you."

She considered his position beneath her and across the room on the floor and decided she was safe enough to move the barrel away from him but she kept her finger on the trigger.

"What is it?"

"I've seen this picture of you before."

"Yeah?"

"It's just dawned on me who you are," he said and held up the photo of Frannie and her father.

"Put that back."

"I knew this man. He's your father, right?"

"That's not hard to guess," she said.

"I met him one time when I was in jail and he was put in with me for a day while he was waiting to get bail for writing a bad check."

"You're full of shit."

"I'm telling you the truth. I'd never forget this picture. He talked about you all the time."

Frannie swung the forty-five back toward him and said,

"If you're making this up to try to get on my good side, I'm going to shoot you right now."

"I'm not making it up. It's all coming back to me now. He used to call you Frankie, didn't he? Am I right?"

She wasn't going to reveal a thing in front of this man and certainly wasn't going to cry even though what he'd said had gone deep.

"Maybe. Maybe he did and maybe he didn't."

"It's got to be the same man. He said he hadn't seen you in years."

"What else did he say?"

"Well, I can't remember all that much, but it seemed like when we got to talking about women and children, because I've been in the same situation myself, he said he couldn't go back because he'd made such a mess of his life, which was kind of the way I felt myself. He was a good man. What little I knew of him."

"Uh-huh. And what else?" she said, trying to restrain herself from not only bursting apart with curiosity, but from actually believing it at all.

"I don't know what else. He just showed me that picture a bunch of times and talked about this or that."

"What did he look like?"

"You don't believe me. Well, I guess I can understand why. I wish I could remember something that would make you believe me. I mean, he looked kind of like he does there, but older. He was about my height. I can't remember much because I didn't think I'd ever have to remember it. It was just one of those things."

"Try to remember something else."

"Well, ask him yourself. Don't you know where he is?"

"What I know and what I don't know is none of your business right now."

"You sure do run hot and cold, Frannie."

"Where'd all this take place?"

"In Asheville. I believe he lived there. I'm not sure, but it seemed like he did. I believe it was some woman who finally got him the money for the bail."

"Who? Who was it?"

"I just don't know. You mean all this time since then you haven't seen him? You mean he ain't never been back at all?"

"I'm asking the questions, Ted."

"Well, I don't believe you believe me so I'm getting tired of answering them. What gives you the right to ask all the questions, anyway?"

"This here," she said and leveled the forty-five at him again.

"Hell," he said. "I don't believe you'd shoot me now. I just kind of don't believe you would at all," he said and rose off the floor and slowly began to walk past her, keeping his eye on the gun in case he was wrong. "Nope. I don't believe you will. You ain't that stupid," he said and walked out of the room with Frannie following.

"Go to hell," she said, unable to stop him and tell him how much she needed him to tell her more because she didn't want him to see how much it meant to her. It seemed, now that she was very close to the truth about her father, that it was more of a private matter, more intimate than she had guessed it would be, and sharing it with Ted seemed wrong, as if she would be giving something away to the wrong person.

"I tell you what, though, Frannie," Ted said as he stepped off the porch, "he was a nice man. I liked him. What little I knew of him, I have to say he was a good man."

She watched him leave her yard. She could see that Eljert's car was already gone. Only after Ted was inside his own house did she begin to shake like she'd been afraid she was going to do in front of him, and she went back to the den and picked up the picture Ted had talked about and sat in a chair with it.

Of course he was a good man, she thought. Of course he was. She wondered what the bad check was all about and considered that it might have been something to do with helping that woman, or helping someone, or being too nice, probably, like her.

She was on to something in her thoughts, but she didn't know what. She was close to understanding how it was that good people can sometimes become victims of their own goodness, how trying to do right can sometimes make you weak and how it was that you could lose your virtue while trying to be virtuous.

It seemed it was possible to be both good and bad at the same time, and this was something new for Frannie to understand, to reflect upon, to consider in the light of what she now knew about her father and what she knew about herself, as well.

Later she called Reuben and asked him to drive over, and well into the morning she talked with him about her father. By four in the morning she was asleep on the bed. Reuben watched her from the chair he had pulled up to be close while she had talked until she fell asleep.

After a while he began to walk around the house and think about all she'd said and about himself and his life and about their life, now, together. While he walked through the rooms he looked at the objects from this family from times past until now. He trailed his fingers down the smoothly painted wood walls in the hallway as he felt, like a blind man, the sense of the house, and he touched the tops of the chairs as he passed them, the turned posts of the old beds, the shaped and rounded edges of the tables and dressers, and the finish of the wood like the skin of Frannie's face, like the resilience of her cheeks.

All of this that he touched and sensed began to feel the same as he checked on her one more time and walked through the house until he began to know it and love it in much the same way he did Frannie.

Chapter 31

IN THE MORNING she called Natalie and told her what had happened and told her what Ted had claimed to know about their father. Reuben kept his hand on her shoulders as she talked, encouraging her and keeping her calm.

"Well," Natalie said, "the more you're finding out, the worse it's getting."

"In a way."

"That's why I never wanted to as much as you."

"But I still want to find him. I have to. And at least now there's something to go on."

"You feel sorry for him," Natalie said. "I guess I do, too."

They talked awhile longer and then Reuben drove Frannie to work and they made it through a day that seemed unfit and awkward for how they felt and what they'd been through, and after they finished their shift, Reuben drove her to his house so she could meet his mother.

"She's so sweet," she said as he drove her back to her house an hour later. "Her voice is so sweet. It's almost like she's singing when she talked. I mean, it makes me feel that way, like I'm being sung to."

"She's special, all right."

"I don't know how she worked in the mill. It seems like she would have just faded away in all the noise and dirt and loudness of the place. I don't know how she made it."

"She wasn't meant to be a part of that. She was always grateful to Dad for getting her free of it. She used to say he'd saved her life."

"Yeah," Frannie said. "I know what she means."

Once at home, she prevailed upon him to prevail upon Natalie not to call the police about the night before and not to even tell Jake, for fear he might do it anyway.

"It's a sign, anyway," Natalie said. "You're a big one for signs, Frannie. It ought to be clear that this house is no longer the good-luck house it used to be and that its time is over."

"No way. If it's a sign, it's a sign that the house saved my life."

"Well, it's a moot point. The last offer fell through when they wouldn't come up even halfway to our counteroffer."

"If you don't mind my asking," Reuben said, "how much did they offer for it?"

"Four hundred thousand, which isn't enough and even the agents, who want their commission, said not to take it. Not yet, anyway."

"So if you sold it for five hundred thousand, then each of you would get two hundred and fifty, or about? You're going to split it like that, right?"

"Half of all of it is Frannie's, so of course we'll split it down the middle."

"I see."

"You see what?" Frannie asked.

"I'm thinking, is all."

"I can't buy it," Frannie said. "All I've got is my twenty-five thousand I told you about sitting in some stupid bank I shouldn't have put it in and earning me about four or five percent interest."

"She took it from Jake, who's invested mine, and she's losing about ten percent in earnings she could be racking up if she hadn't."

"I was mad then, okay?"

"It's a sad thing to lose a house like this on land like this. The days when places like this will be left in this world are few in number."

"I see you got him convinced," Natalie said.

"We think alike," she said.

The next night as Reuben took Frannie to have dinner with his mother, Ted watched out the window as they drove away. She saw him and she looked into his eyes to see if she could tell what he was thinking. When she arrived, she began helping Mrs. Baucom with the food while Reuben started to set the table.

"Let me do that," Frannie said.

"No, I always set the table," Reuben answered.

"Oh. Okay."

They had biscuits and fried chicken and snap beans from the garden and corn and a peach pie for dessert. It reminded Frannie of the meals her granny had fixed, where there was always so much more food on the table than anyone would ever eat, but all of it was so good you wanted to eat it all.

"She's so soft," Frannie said. "She reminds me of my granny in so many ways."

They were on the porch while the old lady cleaned up and did the dishes. She had refused their offer of help.

"Granny worked the farm with Granddaddy, as you know since you saw them together and I never did, but still she was soft and quiet and patient and kind of dizzy, in a harmless way."

"Maybe that's just the way she was when she got old."

"That could be. People change so much. I wonder what I'll be like when I'm old. You'll be the same, I can tell. I know that, but there's no guessing what'll happen to me."

Across the street and down into the grassy valley the long brick mill building was empty and still. From the watchman's house they saw the old man who had looked after the property for so many years begin his rounds. Because they were above the building they could see some children riding bicycles up and down a bank behind the mill. First they would ride the long way around to get to the top, and then zoom down the grassy hill out from the dark and under the lamp high on the pole, and then skid to a stop.

"They don't know he's coming," Frannie said.

"Yeah."

"I wonder what he'll do."

"I don't know."

"They're not hurting anything. Not really."

"Nope."

"You're warm. My hands feel cold, but yours is warm. Why'd you lose your arm?"

"Well, I certainly didn't mean to."

"I mean, how?"

"In an accident in the mill. In the belt."

"Was it your fault?"

"I guess you could say so."

"I'm sorry I said that. Why the hell does it matter whose fault it was? That was stupid for me to ask."

"I was a fixer, loom mechanic and the like back then. That's when we had looms, the last few years they were here. Something jammed in the belt and I was freeing it and I'd forgotten to release the slip clutch and when it freed I was holding on to what had jammed and it pulled me through the sprockets. I don't remember anything after that until I was in the hospital."

"That hurts me, baby. That hurts me to think about."

"That's why I got put into the supervisor track. They paid me five thousand dollars and promised me a job for life. That's what I got out of it."

"I'm sorry. I had to know. Because you wouldn't ever tell me what happened, I thought something bad had happened, like it had been cut off in a fight over a woman or something. That's kind of the way my mind works when it gets the best of me. How come you wouldn't tell me until now?"

"I don't know. I didn't want to talk about it. I thought it'd be asking for pity."

"I don't pity you. You seem sad, though. What is it? You've been this way all night."

"I apologize."

"Is it me? Did I say something wrong?"

"No."

"Do you still love me?"

"Of course."

"Did that mess last night make you feel funny about me? I never did anything with those two men. Never. Not once."

"I never thought you did."

"I love you. If it means anything to say it."

"Don't worry about me being quiet. I'm trying to figure out something."

"Maybe I can help?"

"You might."

"I'm pretty good sometimes at figuring things out. I think about them until I beat them to death and then I get the answer."

"There's a whole lot of things happening at once," he said, "and I'm trying to figure out how to make it all work."

"Oh."

He took her hand and they looked at the drama below as the watchman came down the side of the building where, when he turned the corner, he would see the children racing up and down the bank. A dog was with the children and it barked when it sensed the watchman's presence. The children then stopped their bikes. When they saw who it was, they rode up to him. Frannie and Reuben watched him take something out of his pocket and give one to each of the children and then one to the dog. They talked for a minute or so and then the children rode off eating whatever it was he'd given them and the dog, after finishing his, ran to catch up with them.

"They're friends," Frannie said.

"Yeah. He's a nice man. He always has been."

She kissed him on his hand and then on his arm and then all over his face.

"You look so worried. I wish you'd tell me what it is."

"I will. I think I will. I've been trying to think of how to say it, and I thought I'd tell you a joke first."

"You're going to tell a joke? You?"

"Strange?"

"I've never heard you tell one."

"I never have."

"You really never have?"

"No. I never got into jokes. Most of them didn't seem to be funny. Until you came along."

"You mean I make you laugh? I always was something of a clown."

"I made this up. It's a knock-knock."

"I can always guess those," she said.

"Guess it, then, if you can. Knock-knock."

"Who's there?"

"Dewey."

"Hmmmmm," she said as she thought about it. "I can't guess it. Dewey who?"

"Dewey think we'll ever get married?"

She looked at him a long time. He didn't laugh and she wasn't laughing either.

"It's a joke, right?"

"No."

"I'm afraid I might have missed it. Because it sounded kind of like you were asking me something."

"I was."

"You don't want to marry me."

"Yes, I do."

"You feel sorry for me. Right?"

"No."

"Then why?"

"I've asked too soon," he said. "I talked it over with Mom and she said it was too soon. You looked at me like I was nuts."

"You mean you don't want to marry me now?"

"I mean I do, but I can't expect you to say yes. You could say you'd think about it."

"I'll think about it."

"Thanks."

"Okay. I've thought about it. Yes."

"Really?"

"Yes."

"You really want to?"

"Yes," she said. "Damn, I never thought a few months

ago I'd ever be falling in love and getting married. I never thought it."

It was past midnight when he drove her back to her house. Ted's lights were out and the rest of the road was dark. Natalie had left their lights on.

"You can stay here tonight," she said as they drove in. "Nat won't mind."

"I'd kind of like to."

"Do it. I don't want you to go back now."

"But I better not. It would seem wrong with her here."

"Then let's not go to sleep. Tomorrow's Saturday. Let's stay up all night and never go to sleep. Can we do that? Can we just talk all night? Everything's going so fast I can't even keep up with it."

Reuben returned home in the morning. He told his mother. Natalie and Frannie talked all morning. Frannie took a nap until one. Reuben was due back at one-thirty to have lunch with everyone including Jake.

Soon after he arrived, he and Frannie went to the barn. They looked out from the high door down the fall of the land and over the tops of the trees toward the pond and island and the swooping birds skimming above the water.

"I'm not very good at taking my time once I get an idea," he said.

"You did just right. Everything seems right about everything we've done. It's like it's meant to be when nothing else was."

"Well, then, there're two more things I need to tell you."

"Okay."

"The first is, I got an Asheville phone book at the library and looked up your dad's name, but I couldn't find it."

"Oh."

"That doesn't mean he's not in the area. It might mean he has no phone or he's in another district."

"I see."

"But I did locate an agency that specializes in finding missing persons, and we can call them if you want."

"Okay."

"Okay what?"

"I mean, I'm glad you found it."

"You don't want to go through with it now?"

"I don't know. I mean, I do, but when you started telling me about the Asheville phone book, my heart started racing and I got scared—like really scared."

"I'm sorry if I moved too fast."

"You did the right thing. It's just that the closer it gets, the more it scares me."

"Maybe you should talk to Natalie more about it."

"I will."

A chain saw cranked up in the distance. Both of them listened as its sound rose and fell as it ate through a tree, and then heard, in the quiet of the finished cut, the crack of the wood as the tree fell.

"What was the other thing you wanted to tell me?" she asked.

"It's something I've been thinking about a long time, and

working out, but it had to wait until you agreed to marry me, so it would be a pure answer you gave me."

"What?"

"Can we walk to the pond?"

"Sure."

"What about lunch?"

"We ate late this morning. It'll be okay to wait."

As they made the turn from the road to the grassy apron around the pond, a half a dozen frogs leaped into the water and the buzz of insects paused.

"Can we go out to the island?" he asked.

"It's my favorite place."

They flipped the boat over. The oars and old piece of iron used as an anchor were under it. Frannie crawled in first and held the boat steady as Reuben came aboard. They sat side by side on the middle bench and rowed together to the island. The sound of the oars lapping through the water, slowly but with force, made her want to kiss Reuben as she watched his strong arm pull with as much power as she was able to do with two. The thirsty pulling sound of the oars and the boat bumping and nudging against its own wake made her wish that Reuben would lay her down on the island and make love to her.

"This is nice," she said.

"It's more than nice."

They pulled the boat halfway up the bank and walked the narrow shore once around the island and then sat on the bench Frannie had built. "I've got some money," Reuben said. "It's really money my dad saved. He saved every penny he ever made we didn't need to live on and never bought a thing for himself. He had the first car he ever bought when he died."

"What kind was it?"

"A fifty-three Ford. It was a beautiful car, a kind of gold and cream-colored two tone. I wish I still had it."

"I do, too."

"But the money I've got is money he left to me and Mom. She hasn't spent a penny of it because we live on my wages and the mill owns the house and the rent's almost nothing."

"Yeah?" she asked, wondering where he was going.

"So this is what I want to ask you. I fell in love with your house the other night, just like I fell in love with you, and just like I think I've always been in love with this land. So, here's the deal. If you could save your house and move it anywhere you wanted, where would it be?"

"But you can't move it. It's too big."

"But if you could, where would it be?"

She thought, and then her face lit up as she realized the answer.

"Here? To the island? Is that what you mean?"

"Yes, it is."

"But how? I mean, we're selling the place. Do you have that much money? That much?"

"I don't have that much, but I have a plan." He told her and they talked for another half hour before deciding they should return and eat lunch and then discuss it with Natalie and Jake.

Let my newfound good luck hold, Frannie prayed as she walked back to the house. Let it hold awhile longer.

"Here they come," Jake said. "They're just leaving the woods road."

"Doesn't she look happy? Have you ever seen her look so good?"

"She looks wonderful. I just question whether this man knows what he's getting into."

"I think he does. I think he likes who she is."

"He may like who she is, but I hope he never finds out who she was."

"I don't think he'd care."

"He'd care. You bet he would."

"Frannie's really okay. She's better than me or you or anyone else in some ways. Granny used to say she took after her grandmother. She used to call Frannie a flibbertygibbet. When she was little everybody loved her so much. She was everybody's favorite."

"They're talking to Alice now. What did she say when you told her the real-estate company wanted her to keep the pig put up?"

"She didn't mind. I'm sure she wishes she'd never gotten those pigs. Although, I must say, lately she's been pampering Alice and making over her in a mighty big way."

After lunch Frannie made the announcement that they wanted to talk to them about something important.

"Reuben's got a plan. I want you to listen to what he says, Natalie, and you too, Jake, because, don't forget, I didn't have to go along with selling the farm. I could have balked worse than I did. Just remember that."

"And still could," Reuben said.

Jake and Natalie looked at each other and then back to Reuben.

"Here's what I'm going to propose, and, Jake, since you're a man who's good with money, you check me out on my figures. I've already gone over this myself, but I might be wrong. I'm just an old mill worker when it comes to finance and that's why I want you to check me out.

"I've got a little money saved up. We want to buy the house and a couple of acres down at the pond and move the house to the island."

"That's ridiculous," Jake said. "It's impossible."

"Well, hear me out. I've already done some checking with the building department and code compliance and they tell me we can't put in a septic tank and drain field on an island that small or even drill a well, but we can pay to have city water and sewer run to the house.

"Second, I've asked a house mover if he could move a house this size across a field and down through the woods road if we cut the trees back, and he says yes, no problem. He said the total cost would be around fifteen thousand dollars."

"Right. No problem. What about the pond?"

"He says it's never been done before around here, but he heard of a mover one time who hired two eighty-ton cranes to swing a house to an island and he thinks we could do it, too. If we could afford it."

"This is madness," Jake said.

"Actually, it's not. Madness is destroying this house and this beautiful sanctuary out here. Your ancestors knew that. That's what madness would be, if you'll excuse my saying so."

"Damn right," Frannie said.

"I think, if you'll go along with it, and you can sell what remains, you'll come out better than before," Reuben said. "Suppose you can sell the remaining eight or nine acres for three hundred thousand. Well, you would get to keep it all. On top of that, we can pay you fifty thousand for the house and three to four acres that would make up the pond and island and a little land around it, and you would give us a deeded right-of-way to it. You'll come out with three hundred and fifty thousand against what Frannie says would be less, split in half, since the highest offer you've gotten so far is four hundred thousand for the entire place. I'm offering more for what remains because it may be harder to sell without the pond."

"Please, Nat. It's so fabulous. It's a miracle."

"Well, personally speaking, if it wouldn't make any difference in what we got for the place, I'd say, why not?"

"Why not is because the land is worth less without the pond," Jake said.

"But you'll be asking less for the acreage remaining and you can get three hundred thousand for the eight or nine acres easier than six hundred thousand for the twelve, which you've already seen you can't get."

"You have that much money?" Jake asked. "Fifty thousand dollars? And then the money to move it and set it up?"

"I think we can come up with it. Frannie has some."

"I suppose this is something for the sisters to decide," Jake said. "We're not married, and neither are you, so we're out of this, legally."

"You're in it, and you know you are," Natalie said.

"He's right. I thought we would let the sisters decide," Reuben said.

"It is our decision," Frannie said. "What do you say, Nat?"

"I'd say if it will work out, and if, that is, if, we can get more money or the same than we'd have had without doing all this, ending up with our half, I mean, with more or the same, at least, then why not? It'd be lovely for Frannie to have this house forever and preserve it and carry on like it's always been. It's not as if I hate this place, you know. It's just not for me."

"It'll always be your place, too, Nat. That's what it's supposed to be."

"No. It'll be yours. I'll be fine, but I think you belong here. It's always meant more to you than me."

Jake called the real-estate agent and they agreed to meet Sunday afternoon at the office to change the contract.

Frannie returned to the pond for the rest of the afternoon. She went out in the boat and fished. She fished along the edges and under the overhanging limbs of trees that had not been there when she'd fished with her father. She cast the way he'd taught her and floated in the boat with the current.

She rowed between the bank nearest her house and the

island and imagined the footbridge they would build to get from where they parked their cars to their house. It will have to be an arch, she thought, a lovely graceful arch above the water. It will have pickets on either side and handrails as smooth to the touch as the rubbed and polished wood of the barn.

Children would love this bridge and would run back and forth between the two sides, between the two worlds, while Frannie imagined herself looking out the window watching life begin again, free and pure and safe as she'd once been in her home, on her land, in Silk Hope.

Chapter 32

A MONTH AFTER an offer had been accepted for the eight acres, more or less, that would remain when the plan for life as Frannie and Reuben saw it would begin, and the money had changed hands and the time allotted for all the moves to be made had been agreed upon, at the abandoned farm down the road where the old man had further lost the mind he had lost that fateful day when he went to town, the surveyors began to lay off the sites for the amusements and games.

Where the house itself once sat would be a miniature golf course. People would putt the little balls back and forth that would bounce off the walls and traps and ricochet off the dead-end panels like the old man's demons had bumped around in his head hour after hour, never finding a way out.

The cars would park over the pet cemetery where the

generations of friendly dogs and cats were buried. Paved over, it would be as if nothing had ever been there.

The batting cages and the basketball toss and the pits full of Styrofoam pellets into which children would throw themselves pretending to fly, defying death and living to tell about it, all of this now where the old man had gone silent from thoughts that would not let him rest. Now laughter and joy and bliss for children where he fell mute.

Enter the hall of mirrors on this amusement land and discover what it's like to be lost, finding no way out, finding only another face that seems to be yours, moving toward you.

Dignity becomes the giant plastic dog whose mouth you enter, virtue is the tongue you lay upon and honor the end out which you come.

Jump now into the fun. Life as laughter, demons as friends. Bewilderment and confusion as dare.

Enter soon abandon and delight as the commerce of childhood, and witness the thrill of action and adventure paving over the memory of the past.

Chapter 33

IN ANOTHER MONTH the bridge with the graceful arch had been built. The footings had been dug by hand on the island and the concrete pumper had lumbered down the temporary road, wide enough to drive a house, and pumped the trenches full.

"I'm worried," Frannie said.

The bridge was five feet wide, wide enough for two children to run full speed across side by side, or wide enough for masons to wheel barrows full of block and mortar mix and sand across. The bridge had been floored with old boards. Later, when all the work was done, it would be floored with the red cedar of the trees that had been cut to make room for the house.

"Natalie seems like she's mad about something," Frannie said.

While the house had been jacked up and was undergoing preparation to be hauled, Jake and Natalie moved in with his mother. They slept in separate bedrooms. Their wedding was a month away.

"It's probably me. I probably did something," Frannie said.

Frannie had beat her to it. Not that it was a competition, but she had. She and Reuben had quietly married with Natalie and Jake and his mother and Reuben's mother in attendance. Then the newlyweds had moved into Reuben's house while waiting on their island home.

"I don't know what. Maybe I said something I shouldn't have. I probably insulted Jake. I still don't like him."

She was given an informal party at the mill during lunch one day. Belle and Linda and a few of the other women who worked nearby bought them an under-the-cabinet-type microwave oven. It was the space-saver model and they knew Frannie would need it now that she had begun her life as a wife, and soon, they imagined, as a mother. There was never enough space or shelves or closets or hooks or corner cubbies for everything that could fill up a house once you started.

"I wish Granddaddy and Granny could see this. They'd laugh. I know they'd laugh, in a happy way."

The old house sat in the center of the island on the natural knoll of the land. It faced east. The trees had been cleared twenty feet back from the house on three sides. Toward the east, where the bridge connected with the mainland, the land was cleared all the way to the water.

"I hate there's no way to save the barn. Do you think we

could get some of the wood from the loft and build a little shed or playhouse out back and make it look on the inside the way it used to?"

A backhoe had dug out a number of trees after the house was resettled and planted them in a double line across the wide cut through which the house had been moved. This would help begin the screen between the paradise and whatever there would be beyond.

"I think Nat's blue and got claustrophobia from living in Jake's dinky little matchbox house. I mean, not that she doesn't love him and won't do anything for him, the same way I would for you, but she really had her heart set on buying her city slicker mansion right away."

Alice was gone. Frannie had found her a place on a farm by advertising her free to a good home where she would be kept for breeding and not slaughtered. She was the right age and had been so well fed and exercised, the farm couple couldn't believe their luck in getting a sow of her quality free.

"You know, I miss Alice, but it just wasn't going to work," she said to Reuben. "Some things you can give up in life, and some things you can't. I think I know that now."

They were sitting on the porch. They'd been living in the house for two weeks. It had been decided that Reuben's mother should live with them. It seemed the right thing to do.

"It's so quiet here. I guess it'll change when they start building up the hill. It'll be okay. I wonder if we'll have to put a fence around the whole pond. I bet we will."

"You might be right," Reuben said.

"I love you."

"I love you, too."

"You know, I've been thinking. When you lose something it makes you different. You lost your arm and I lost my father and it made us different," she said. "I don't know why I brought that up. I talk too much."

"Don't change, Frannie. Don't change a thing."

"I saw Ted the other day. He was walking down our drive when I came home."

"Ted?"

"The guy across the street."

"Oh."

"He said he was moving away. He said he thought the old man next door had shot the other two pigs. He said he was sorry about everything and wished he could figure out how to quit getting in trouble. I wonder why people have to do ugly, mean things."

"I don't know. They're always there. You just have to stay away from them."

"I wish you had been here to beat the tar out of Eljert. Of course, Alice did a pretty good job."

There were new sounds at night. Frannie had grown up with some of these sounds from the pond, but at a distance. Now, when they slept, they heard all manner of new sounds that they began to identify. A muskrat slipping into the water made far less splash and commotion than a stray dog bounding in for a drink or to cool off. The frogs and the crickets wound up and down much of the night like raspy divas competing for attention. The lap of the water against the shore felt like the pat of a parent's hand across the back of a sleeping child, comforting and serene.

"Are you ready for bed?" Reuben asked. "I'm beat."

They were back on the porch after eating a late supper and then watching a little television. It was the third day of balmy weather in what was predicted to be at least a week of Indian summer in this the second week of November.

"You bet. Did you call your mom?"

"Yes. She sends her love. She's fine and says she's not ready to leave yet and for me to quit asking her."

"She's a card. A sweet old card."

A few minutes later they heard a car on the paved road and then heard the same car turning in to their driveway, and they listened and saw the lights in and out of the trees and off into the sky as the car went up a hill and slowly came toward them.

"It's Natalie," Frannie said.

"Yeah. Maybe she tried to call when I was talking to Mom. I was on for twenty minutes."

"I bet she wants something from the house. It's going to feel creepy when she takes her half of the furniture. I'm not going to fight with her about it. She can have whatever she wants."

"That's the right way to go about it. You two getting along forever is more important than furniture."

"Of course, she will want all the really good stuff. He will, too. She'll want the dining-room table, I know. And the rolltop desk for Jake. He's always talking about it."

Natalie parked behind Reuben's truck. She opened the

door and the dome light shone on her. She started to the bridge and then went back to the car. She got her purse and then came over. Frannie's heart began to race as she saw that her sister did not look like she'd ever seen her look, that she appeared haggard and puffy and lost, and lost was something Natalie had never been in her life. She almost looked like a picture of someone from an institution who stares straight ahead seeing nothing, day in and day out.

"Nat, what's wrong?" Frannie ran down the steps and met her as she came off the bridge onto the island.

Reuben joined her. They led her into the house. She wouldn't look at either of them and when she sat in the chair in the kitchen she kept her head down.

"Talk to us. Please. Has something happened to Jake? Has he been hurt?"

She shook her head no but wouldn't look up. Frannie exchanged glances with Reuben, and they both shrugged. She began to stroke Natalie's hair as if she were combing it with her hand. When she did Natalie closed her eyes and seemed to be holding her breath and then a few seconds later as Frannie stroked her and looked at her face, she broke down. She wept like Frannie had never seen her weep, sobbing and gasping for breath so hard it scared her.

"I'll leave the room," Reuben said.

"Don't," Frannie said. "Make us some hot tea. Put the water on."

"Is Jake dead? Was he in a wreck?"

After a minute more of sobbing, Natalie shook her head no.

"Did he do something to you? Did he call off the wedding? I mean, tell me something, Nat. I don't know what's going on."

Finally she began to talk. While she talked she kept her hands over her face as if she could neither look at her sister and Reuben, nor wanted them to see her.

"He's lost all my money. It's all gone. He's lost it all."

"Oh, hell," Frannie said. "I knew it. I knew he was up to something. I knew it all along."

Reuben put his hand on Frannie to stop her from going further. He shook his head to indicate that it wouldn't do any good to say I told you so.

"Damn him," Frannie said. "What happened? There's nothing left? Nothing?"

"He put it all in this company that went suddenly broke or something. I can't even talk about it. It's gone. It's all gone."

"There may be some way to get it back," Reuben offered. "There often is some way to get at least part of it back."

Natalie wiped her face with her hands and then Frannie handed her a dishcloth and she wiped her eyes and nose on it.

"It's gone. It's something to do with buying on margin and things I don't understand. The stock fell and I'm wiped out. That's all I know."

"I'll kill him," Frannie said. "I'll kill him dead."

"Is there any way you can check on this to be sure it's gone for good?" Reuben asked.

"It's gone. He said he bought some of it outright at four

dollars a share and then bought short or something—I don't know what it's called—the rest of it and then it all crashed and everything he bought outright is worth less than a dollar a share now, something like 3/8 of a dollar, whatever the hell that is, and the rest of it he owes to make up for gambling on it going up. I want to die, Frannie. I just want to die."

"Where is he?" Frannie asked. "I'm going to beat the living hell out of him. Where is he?"

"He's home. I think he's going to come over here though. I told him not to, but he said he wanted to explain it to you. I told him not to. I don't want to see him. Even the twenty-five thousand dollars Mother left me is gone. He even lost that."

"I'm going to hit him so hard, I'll kick him back to the stone age," Frannie said. "I knew not to trust him. I knew it."

"Leave her alone, Frannie. It doesn't sound like he meant to do it."

"You know what he said? He told me he thought he could get it back. He thought he could recover what we'd lost given enough time and if he had a little more money to work with."

"He'll never recover from me if I get ahold of him," Frannie said.

"Maybe the stock'll go back up," Reuben said.

"No. He admitted that company was finished. The money's gone."

Natalie began to cry again, but this time she talked as she cried as she tried to drink the hot tea Reuben had made.

She had to hold the cup with two hands to guide it to her lips.

"I'm not going back to him. It's all come apart in the past few days. We've been talking and talking all night long about everything. I'm so tired I don't know how I've been going to work. He lost the money Mother left me months ago and never said anything about it. And then, over the past few weeks he's been trying to put off the wedding, but never telling me why. Now I know. I can't trust him anymore. I can never trust anybody again. If Jake could do this to me, as much as I loved him and as much as I've given him, then there's no hope in this world. There's no one you can trust. No one."

"You can trust me. And Reuben," Frannie said. "Always."

"No I can't. I can't trust anyone. He's kept all this from me. He's kept other things as well. It's over. For the past few days I've been feeling like it was over, that something was wrong, and now I know I was right."

"I hate his guts."

"It's gone, Frannie. All gone."

They heard another car coming and this time it was Jake. He had a flashlight with him, which he shone on the ground until he got to the bridge.

"I don't want to see him. I don't. Please tell him to go away."

"I'll tell him," Reuben said, "if you mean it. I'll tell him you'll call him tomorrow. How about that?"

"Don't say that. Just tell him to go away."

While Reuben talked to Jake at the end of the bridge, Frannie and Natalie watched out of a window from a darkened room.

"I hurt so bad, Frannie. My stomach hurts from crying. My life is over. It's over."

"No way. His life is over, but not yours. He's a dead man as far as I'm concerned. Dead. I hope he tries something with Reuben. Reuben'll kill him. He'll squash him like an ant."

"I don't want him to get hurt. I just want to go back to the way it was. I just want everything to be right again."

"We'll sue him. We'll sue the hell out of him."

"He doesn't have anything. He's lost it all, too."

"His mother's money, too?"

"No. She never would give it to him."

Reuben came back inside and told them Jake said for Natalie to call him any time day or night and please come back to him.

"I have nowhere to go," she said. "I have no money and nowhere to go. My life is over. I ought to kill myself. I'm so ashamed. How can I face anyone again? How?"

"You've got somewhere to go," Frannie said. "Here. You can always stay here, forever, for as long as you want. And you know that, so don't say you have nowhere to go. This is your home forever, too, isn't it, Reuben?"

"Of course it is."

Their kindness was then, after all she'd been through, too much for Natalie, and she began to sob again and waved them off as she went through the old house to her old room.

She knew the way. She could have been blind and found her way. She knew where it was better than she knew anything else in her life at that moment, knew it by heart, by touch, by feel, knew it to be real, at least, when nothing else seemed to be.

The next day all three of them phoned in sick. They were sick. They were sick of trouble and meanness and heartbreak and sorrow. They were sick from Natalie's sickness, which was as bad, if not worse, that day than the night before.

Natalie began to fail as the day progressed. She talked about quitting her job. She talked about never leaving the house again. She talked about Jake and how it could have happened.

"Maybe it was just the money he was after all along," she said.

"Could be," Frannie said. "You never know with a guy like him."

"But he didn't mean to lose it. So it's not his fault, not really."

"He lost it. It's his fault."

"He did change after Mom died, and he began to talk me into selling the place. Maybe it was the money."

"Well, like you told me, call a lawyer."

"I should. I guess I should."

"Reuben will if you want. He'll do anything."

"I really don't want to go back to work, Frannie. I don't."

"You might feel better in a few weeks."

"I doubt it."

"I feel bad feeling so happy with you so blue," Frannie said.

"You be happy. I never will be again."

"Do you think you'll be okay if we go to work tomorrow, if you're not going? Will you be okay alone?"

"I guess."

"You can get a job somewhere else. As a secretary anywhere, you're so good."

Natalie didn't answer. Frannie watched her pulling on her hair. She was in a trance of rumination and distraction the whole time Frannie watched her and she never blinked or took her eyes off whatever it was she was seeing in her mind.

"I bet I can make you laugh."

Natalie didn't answer this time, either.

"What's a secretary called who works for a health insurance company?"

There was no response.

"A sick-retary. Everybody she deals with is sick. Pretty bad, huh?"

It appeared that Natalie did not hear the joke.

"How about a secretary who works at a massage parlor? What's she called?"

Natalie stopped twirling her hair and closed her eyes.

"A suck-retary. Is that bad, or what?" Frannie asked and then began to feel afraid as her sister seemed unable to come out of her distraction.

"I've been talking to you," she said and took her hand and pulled her around so she had to face her.

"What is it? What did you want?"

"Nothing but to make you smile. To get you to talk."

"But don't you see, it's all gone. Everything's gone. All the money and him, too."

"Good riddance."

"I have no one now."

"You have me and Reuben."

"I have nowhere to go."

"We told you, you could stay here forever if you wanted."

"How could this happen? How?"

It was evening. The water birds began to skim the pond and eye the ripples on the surface for a late meal. The old catfish who had lived there longer than anything else came to the shore of the island and looked at the big house and the two women and the man on the steps above him. He pulled himself out of the water and onto the bank, inching forward like a caterpillar.

"I don't feel well," Natalie said.

"You just need to rest."

"I'm a fool. I'm a stupid fool, and all the time I thought I was being so smart."

The catfish crawled forward until it was close enough to hear the conversation. After a minute, it turned around and crawled back. Just before it slipped into the water, it looked at the humans one more time and then quietly, so as not to disturb them, swam away.

"You are smart, and you're good, and I don't want you to be down on yourself. You didn't do anything wrong, okay?

Listen to me," Frannie said. "I love you, Nat, and I always will."

Natalie had not improved much from the day before. She still did not look like the Natalie Frannie had always known. It may have been that she looked, at this time, like her great-great-grandmother Delia when she found out she'd been driven around in circles. She probably looked something like the old farmer next door when he found himself locked away with nothing of what he had believed in still intact. She probably looked a little like Great-Aunt Daphne when she'd been told she was too happy to be sane and had to be taken away.

There was a house. At least, in the end, there was that house. The house that would be a home when nothing else remained. There was the sanctity that a strong and virtuous heart had created out of deceit and despair.

If virtue remained in pieces only, and if the pieces were for you to find in whatever form they took, and if, for someone, virtue was the color of the setting sun, or the tradition of wheat at harvest, if it was the clear eye in a picture from the past, if it lived in the heart of a child, if it was in the manner of certain men or the laughter of women or the spirit of a daughter looking for her father, then it was also in a home.

It was surviving in a home on an island in Silk Hope on ancestral land where the strength of vision from the past remained, for now, at a safe distance from the amusements and predatory warmth that had replaced the lessons of history and of wise thought, where it would continue to survive in the radiance of two sisters looking out for one another.

"We're going to be fine," Frannie said.

If it was to be that virtuous lives would be replaced by greed and power and by the edgy, desperate, restive motion that now resembled life, then sadness would be the lesson.

"I'm going to see to it," Frannie said.

She put her arm around her sister and led her back inside. She sat with her in the seat by the window and hugged her and talked to her and looked at Reuben standing by the smoothly turned post of the graceful bridge.

Yes, she thought. I am going to see to it.

Books in the
Harvest American Writing series

DIANA ABU-JABER
Arabian Jazz

TINA McELROY ANSA
Baby of the Family
Ugly Ways

CAROLYN CHUTE
The Beans of Egypt, Maine
Letourneau's Used Auto Parts
Merry Men

HARRIET DOERR
Consider This, Señora

DONALD HARINGTON
The Choiring of the Trees
Ekaterina

RANDALL KENAN
Let the Dead Bury Their Dead

DAN McCALL
Messenger Bird

LAWRENCE NAUMOFF
Silk Hope, NC
Taller Women: A Cautionary Tale

KAREN OSBORN
Patchwork

JIM SHEPARD
Kiss of the Wolf

BROOKE STEVENS
The Circus of the Earth and the Air

OXFORD STROUD
Marbles

SANDRA TYLER
Blue Glass